CW00751655

THE HOME FRONT NURSES

RACHEL BRIMBLE

Boldwood

First published in Great Britain in 2024 by Boldwood Books Ltd.

Copyright © Rachel Brimble, 2024

Cover Design by Colin Thomas

Cover Photography: Colin Thomas

The moral right of Rachel Brimble to be identified as the author of this work has been asserted in accordance with the Copyright, Designs and Patents Act 1988.

All rights reserved. No part of this book may be reproduced in any form or by any electronic or mechanical means, including information storage and retrieval systems, without written permission from the author, except for the use of brief quotations in a book review.

This book is a work of fiction and, except in the case of historical fact, any resemblance to actual persons, living or dead, is purely coincidental.

Every effort has been made to obtain the necessary permissions with reference to copyright material, both illustrative and quoted. We apologise for any omissions in this respect and will be pleased to make the appropriate acknowledgements in any future edition.

A CIP catalogue record for this book is available from the British Library.

Paperback ISBN 978-1-83561-773-1

Large Print ISBN 978-1-83561-774-8

Hardback ISBN 978-1-83561-772-4

Ebook ISBN 978-1-83561-775-5

Kindle ISBN 978-1-83561-776-2

Audio CD ISBN 978-1-83561-767-0

MP3 CD ISBN 978-1-83561-768-7

Digital audio download ISBN 978-1-83561-770-0

Boldwood Books Ltd
23 Bowerdean Street
London SW6 3TN
www.boldwoodbooks.com

For the one and only Lizzie Lane.
My friend, my cheerleader, and a woman who tells me exactly how it is... always!
Thank you so much for telling me about the Bath raids that inspired this series.
You're the best!

1

SYLVIA

Bath, September 1941

Sylvia Roberts marched with a spring in her step past Queen Square, its emerald-green grass, colourful flower beds and criss-cross of gravelled pathways looking picturesque in the early evening summer sunshine. Humming to herself, she continued along the shallow incline of Barton Street and shamelessly basked in the admiring glances sent her way by the young fire officers and appointed war officials standing in the street.

Smiling, she upped her swagger, her fingers tight on the envelope she held.

She'd done it.

She had completed three years of nursing training, the first year of which passed within the realms of normalcy, then every-thing that followed was made all the more strenuous and tense by the outbreak of war. Having stood firm and determined in her work and mind – not to mention remaining stalwart in the face of the daily physical strain – from today, she was a fully regis-tered nurse. The world was her oyster, with at least the beginnings of some financial independence from her mother imminent. Satisfaction wound tight in Sylvia's stomach. Her mother had told her countless times she would fail to become a nurse, and Sylvia could not wait to tell the old battle-axe she'd succeeded.

Sylvia breathed deep, the sunshine providing momentary and welcome brightness in a time that too often felt full of wartime darkness.

'Well, well, if it ain't the lovely Nurse Roberts...'

Sylvia muttered a curse and slowed her approach along the narrow and shadowed alleyway that housed her mother's place of work, the Garrick's Head pub. She lifted her chin, working hard to assess the mood of the individual who stood less than ten feet away from her. Harry Galloway. A drinker of the highest order who thought himself something of a Lothario but looked like someone – or something – known for loitering on the tower of Notre-Dame cathedral.

'Harry.' She sighed. 'Always a pleasure.'

He grinned, revealing more gum than teeth, and supped his pint of ale, a cigarette smouldering in his other hand. Sylvia shifted her gaze to a couple of blokes around her age standing a few feet away, their conversation halted as they watched her and Harry, smiles pulling at their lips and their eyes alert with interest.

She pinned Harry with an unwavering stare. 'You know, it does little to impress a woman when a man greets her with a shout along the street.'

His balding pate shone beneath a spear of dusty sunlight that streamed into the narrow space and directly onto his head. 'What's a man to do when that woman refuses to give him the time of day?' he asked, taking a long pull on his cigarette before flicking it away.

Sylvia raised her pencilled eyebrows. 'Maybe give up bothering her and accept he's old enough to be her father?'

His smile vanished and the flirtatious glint in his eyes turned notably colder. 'Is that right?'

'Yep. Now if you'll excuse me...' She moved to step past him to the open pub door. 'I'd like a quick chat with my moth—'

His hand came around her forearm and gripped like a vice. 'Who do you think you are, Sylvia Roberts? Swanning around in your nurse's uniform like you're a cut above. You ain't nothing but your mother's daughter. A good-time girl who thinks about nothing else than where her next bloke is coming from.'

Sylvia's heart beat a little faster as a telling pain jabbed at her stomach. One particular man had been all she'd wanted. But what did Harry know of the happy domesticity she'd had planned with the fiancé who'd dumped her? A man she had loved with her entire being, but he'd walked away without as much as a backward glance, leaving her flailing and hurt to her core. But she'd come a long way in the last twelve months, and she would not allow the likes of Harry Galloway to unravel her progress.

'Just get lost, will you, Harry,' she snapped, yanking her arm from his grasp. 'If you knew me at all, you would know I am nothing like my mother. Nothing. Do you hear me?'

'Ha! Hit on a sore subject, have I?'

She threw him a glare before sliding her gaze to the two younger men a second time. Both had now abandoned their pints to the windowsill and stood tall, their eyes narrowed and clearly ready to intervene on her say-so. They'd be waiting a long time. No matter how wrong – how bloody slanderous – Harry's words might be, she could handle the likes of him with her eyes shut.

'What's interesting is the question of how you know what my mother is or isn't,' she said.

He frowned. 'What?'

'Well, she's as likely to give you the time of day as you are to have a wash this week, wouldn't you say? So, when all is said and done, your mistaken opinion of who I might or might not be doesn't really bother me at all. And if you take into account the hardships I've endured and the things I've seen in the hospital since the start of the war, you are dafter than I thought if you think anything you have to say interests me.'

His thread-veined cheeks mottled as he glared. 'You're always carrying on as though you're something special and I'm here to tell you, you ain't.'

'Well, thanks for clearing that up. Now...' She shoved past him. 'Get out of my way before I take the spare syringe I carry around and shove it right up your arse.'

The two men beside them erupted with laughter and Sylvia grinned, tipping them a wink as she pushed open the pub door. 'Have a good evening, gentlemen.'

She stepped inside and was immediately assaulted by a thick blanket of grey-white cigarette and pipe smoke that hovered from the ceiling almost to the floor. Squinting, she shouldered her way to the dark wood bar, nodding acknowledgement to the odd person she had the time of day for and ignoring the rest. Her mother's voice drifted in her direction and Sylvia pulled back her shoulders.

'Oh, get on with you.' Her mother cackled, patting her platinum-blonde hair, her eyes alight with lust on the punter who did not look a day older than Sylvia. 'You wouldn't be able to keep up with me on a bad day, let alone a good night.'

Suppressing a smile, Sylvia planted her bag on the bar. Her and her mother might not get along the majority of the time, but there was no mistaking from whom Sylvia had inherited her quick wit and sass.

She cleared her throat. 'All right, Mum?'

Her mother's peal of laughter stopped short, her smile vanishing as her eyes met Sylvia's across the bar. Sylvia's heart beat out the seconds as her defences rose, knowing how much her mother hated her coming into the pub and reminding her she was old enough to have a twenty-three-year-old daughter.

She muttered something that Sylvia couldn't hear but the three punters hanging on her every word clearly did, considering how their heads snapped Sylvia's way like they were joined on a length of elastic.

Her mother strolled closer, hands on her ample hips, the wide black belt at her waist pulled in tight enough to accentuate a bosom more bounteous than her hips. 'What are you doing here? You should be at the hospital or even the nurses' home,' she said from between clenched teeth, her dark brown eyes the exact same shade as her daughter's, though they held none of Sylvia's renowned warmth. 'It gets busy this time of day. Clear off.'

'I have news,' Sylvia said, holding the envelope confirming her qualification as a registered nurse aloft. 'I did it, I'm a fully-fledged nurse.'

Her mother sniffed. 'And?'

'I'll be moving out of the nurses' home tomorrow.' She smiled even though bitter dread coated her throat. 'So we'll be back living together for a while. Won't that be nice?'

'Nothin' about the two of us in a two-up, two-down is nice, my girl.'

'Yeah, maybe you're right.' Sylvia shrugged. 'But there's no way I'm staying a minute longer in a place where I've got Matron watching my every move, a curfew that should apply to sixteen-year-olds and rules that have no place outside my work life.'

'It might do you some good to behave yourself now and then.'

'A bit pot calling the kettle black, wouldn't you say, Mum?' Sylvia pinned her with a glare, hating that she still wanted her mother to acknowledge her studying and working from time to time. Just the once would be fine. 'Anyway, I'm sure what I'll give you out of my wages will be welcomed, if nothing else.'

Her mother's eyes narrowed.

Sylvia blew out a breath. 'This could be a whole new start for us.' She held her mother's icy gaze and fought to bury the treacherous hope that poked at her heart. 'Why don't we try to make a go of it this time, eh? I'm a nurse now. A proper nurse. We're in the middle of a war and—'

'A proper nurse?' Her mother huffed a laugh. 'What difference does that make to my life? After all is said and done, my girl, you were rejected first by your father, then by a bloke you stupidly set your heart on marrying and now you're back under my bloody roof. A piece of paper saying you're a nurse don't mean nothing other than you'll be clearing up other people's piss and shit for years on end.' Her mother flung her arm out in the direction of the door. 'Go on, I've got work to be getting on with.'

Humiliation burned hot at Sylvia's cheeks, anger building like an inferno in the centre of her chest. Snatching her bag from the bar, she lifted her chin and strode from the pub, ignoring the stares and whistles that surrounded her as she concentrated on the pub door, her vision impeded by the tears she would not allow to fall.

2

FREDA

Freda Parkes surreptitiously studied her father where he sat at the other end of their age-old dining table that was her mother's pride and joy. Just another item amongst the hundred and one other knicks-knacks, china ornaments and seaside souvenirs that filled every shelf and surface in the communal rooms of their small terrace house on the outskirts of the city. Freda turned back to her plate and speared some potato with her fork. Her father appeared too preoccupied to catch as much as a whiff of his elder daughter's discomfort. She put the potato into her mouth and did her utmost to chew and swallow it, but her mouth was so dry it was like trying to digest a piece of coal.

'Freda, darling, your father and I are so very proud of you. A fully registered nurse!' Her mother beamed, her blue eyes alight with happiness.

Her mother preened like a mother hen, her eyes reflecting the fantasised pictures she had for Freda's future. The problem was, Freda wanted a life so much different to the one her mother had planned for her. But how could she let her down? All their lives, Mary Parkes' children had been trained to ensure their mother's happiness. But now one of her sons had been shot dead in France and the other was serving God-only-knew where, his family receiving no word from him in over four months. The last thing her mother deserved was another one of her children adding to her anguish.

'You will not only be helping others,' her mother continued, her eyes wide, 'but you will now be irresistibly attractive to any number of suitable young doctors. Mark my words, you'll be courting by the year's end.'

Freda tightened her fingers around her cutlery. 'I did not become a nurse to attract a husband, Mum. Please, let's not go down this road again tonight. I've only just received my qualification.'

'Which is why I cooked this special meal to celebrate. Isn't that right, Clive?'

Freda's father looked up from his plate and gave her a reassuring wink. 'Indeed it is, dear, but Freda's right. Let her get used to her new job before you start adding more expectations.'

Relief lowered Freda's shoulders. 'Thank you, Da—'

'Oh, Clive! What a thing to say.'

'I mean it. At least give Freda time to settle into the hospital before you start bothering her about finding some young lad, a doctor, no less, to take up with.' Her father blew out a breath, the humour leaving his eyes. 'Believe me, the way Hitler is going on – when the world is in such a state of uncertainty – romance is the last thing our children should be thinking about. The ferocity with which Germany is bombarding Bristol might have lessened, but they've by no means stopped and I seriously doubt they will any time soon.' He shook his head. 'At some point, Bath will be inundated with hundreds of poor buggers from Bristol who've been maimed or injured, lost their homes and families. Mark my words, there is worse to come for Bath.'

'Such talk at the table.' His wife looked first at Freda and then her younger daughter sitting opposite her. 'You'll frighten Dorothy.'

Dorothy smiled and plunged her fork into her pie. 'I'm twenty, Mum, not ten. I'm perfectly all right hearing anything Dad says. After all, this war can't go on forever and as soon as it's over, Robert will be back, and he'll propose. Then all this endless talk of war will be a distant memory.'

'It's not talk, Dorothy,' Freda said quietly.

'No? Then what is it, wise big sister of mine?'

Freda pinned Dorothy with a glare. She loved her dearly, but sometimes her loudly and frequently announced ambition of marrying her beau and having Robert take care of her while she kept home for him made Freda want to strangle her. 'You can say people worrying about the war is just talk because you haven't experienced anything first-hand. If you had seen half of what I—'

'Oh, here we go,' Dorothy sneered. 'I know you're the one with the big responsibilities and I am nothing but a daughter who stays at home with her mother, but to me, I have a good and happy life. You, on the other hand, look far from happy.'

Considering her sister spoke the absolute truth, Freda held her tongue and faced her father. 'Do you think Hitler will eventually bomb Bath, Dad?'

'No, love,' he said, putting down his fork and reaching for his glass of ale. 'He won't bomb us. We ain't got anything here to bother him. I'm just saying it's inevitable that sooner or later the hospitals in Bath will be drawn into the thick of things.'

Freda frowned as she contemplated her father's frightening prediction. 'But none of us can know for certain he won't bomb us.'

He touched her arm, his dark eyes sombre. 'I'm a police officer, love. I know more than most and, for the time being, Hitler doesn't have any interest in Bath. It's the ever-increasing number of injured in Bristol that should concern us. I've heard the hospitals and rest centres are fit to bursting. The authorities will soon look to Bath and surrounding towns to help them out.'

'Please,' her mother sighed. 'Enough talk of war, bombs and goodness knows what else. Freda is now a qualified nurse, and Dorothy' – she smiled at her youngest daughter – 'wants nothing more than to marry the man she loves and become a housewife. There is nothing wrong with that. In fact, I think it's something Freda will want too...' She glanced at Freda. 'In time. After all, the only way to a good life is to be a...?' She looked at her daughters in turn, her eyebrows raised expectantly.

'A good girl,' Dorothy cried, beaming.

'A good girl,' Freda mumbled, her heart sinking.

'Exactly!' Her mother laughed. 'Good girls are the best girls.'

Struggling to not roll her eyes, Freda turned to her father. 'I'd really like to do something more to bolster people's morale now that I'm qualified.'

'Oh? Like what?'

Freda sat forward eagerly, pleased she had her father's attention when he was so rarely home for family meals these days. 'I thought I could write some—'

'Write?' Her dad smiled. 'You're at the hospital to care for people, love. You'll have more than enough to keep you busy. Just concentrate on what you're there for, what you've trained for, and you won't go far wrong.'

'I agree, Freda,' her mother said sharply. 'You keep going back to this writing nonsense and it serves no purpose. You are a nurse and nursing is a wholesome occupation for a woman before she marries. We might not have a lot, but I have raised you girls to be sensible, homely young ladies and it would break my heart for you to be anything else.'

'Hear, hear,' Dorothy said and smirked at Freda.

Freda narrowed her eyes at her sister before her family resumed eating their dinner. Freda watched them, her appetite entirely vanished. If her hunger for becoming so much more than a good girl, in a good marriage, running a good home, dutifully dissipated, she had no doubt she would make her parents happy. Yet, as the war waged on, there was little chance of that happening. Instead, her desire to do more to support the people at home only burned ever more fiercely and she refused to douse it. Sensing her mother's gaze on her, Freda sat straighter and pushed her food this way and that in a show of eating, relieved when the dinner conversation turned to the latest gossip Dorothy had heard about the Jamesons at number twenty-three.

Exhaling a shaky breath, Freda willed for tomorrow to come. Once she was at the hospital, she'd feel better. She was looking forward to seeing which nurses from the training school she would be put with on the ward and hoped a couple of friendly faces were amongst them. If not, then she would do her utmost to start forging friendships because, if nothing else, this war had taught her how important human beings were to one another. How everyone needed someone else to rely on, to trust. Maybe there would come a day she would manage to bury her belief she was in the wrong place, embarking on the wrong profession, and succumb to her mother's philosophy of life. After all, how on earth could she let her mother down and witness heart-breaking disappointment in her eyes after she had scrimped and saved all her married life, taking in extra sewing and mending to supplement the family income so that her children were fed, clothed and cared for? The war had already stolen so much from her when it took Freda's brother's life. Anything less than adhering to her mother's wishes was selfish. Her mother had taught her children that, too.

3

SYLVIA

'Ah, Nurse Roberts. You're early.'

In the hospital staff room, Sylvia jumped and spun away from the window where she'd been assessing other newly qualified nurses as they walked through the hospital's stone-arched entrance – now minus its iron gates – and made their way into the building.

She pulled back her shoulders and met the sister's gaze directly. 'I am, Sister.'

The woman standing in the doorway, a clipboard held to her chest, looked a force to be reckoned with. Her dark blonde hair was swept up beneath a white cap, her blue uniform pressed to within an inch of its life and her steely grey eyes pinning Sylvia where she stood.

'Well, as impressed as I am by your eagerness, you might also ask how I know who you are, Nurse Roberts. You see, your reputation precedes you, and with that reputation and your' – she cast a disapproving glance over Sylvia's hair – 'rather conspicuous hair, it is clear any antics you might get up to on the ward will be difficult to miss.'

'Antics, Sister?' Sylvia fought to keep her temper and not raise her hand to her auburn hair. 'Has someone been telling tales on me? Should I not be innocent until proven guilty before you—'

'Before I what, Nurse? Pass judgement? Mark your card?' The sister slowly smiled, her eyes gleaming with undisguised malice. 'There has been no telling tales, only warnings from the senior nurses who trained you. You might have passed every exam and done all that's been asked of you to a satisfactory degree, but I have also been warned you are not backwards in coming forwards… as you have just given clear credence to.'

Damn my inability to button it…

The sister sniffed and made a show of looking at her clipboard, lifting a page or two before meeting Sylvia's gaze once more. 'Nor, it seems, do you always believe the rules and regulations of the nurses' home apply to you. Now it remains to be seen if you have what it takes to stay the course.'

'I can promise you I will, Sister. Nursing means everything to me.'

'Well, we'll see, won't we? I will be watching you and will not tolerate any insubordination from you or any of my other nurses. Is that clear?'

'Yes, Sister.'

'Very good. I'll be in charge of you and the five other graduating nurses assigned to the ward. I will leave you for the time being…' She lifted the watch attached at her chest. 'But I'm sure you will soon be joined by the others due to start at eight o'clock and we can begin the day.'

The sister gave a curt nod and strode from the staff room, leaving the door ajar.

Sylvia glared at the open doorway, fighting the injustice of the sister's presumptions. She had not just passed her nursing exams, but had come top of the class. She had not only done all that had been asked of her, but she had also received commendations over and over again from her superiors. Well, whoever had said what they'd said about her could only have done so out of spite, which meant it had most likely been Kathy Scott, a fellow nursing student who had taken a dislike to Sylvia the moment they started training together three years before. Turning back to the locker she had commandeered, Sylvia withdrew her hat and a box of pins. Well, she just hoped Kathy wasn't put on the same ward as her because if she was...

The sound of female voices drifted through the doorway and Sylvia turned from the mirror on the back of her locker door.

The first girl who entered was blonde and maybe a year or so younger than Sylvia. The nurse she was talking to had dark hair and gave Sylvia the immediate impression of someone in need of a good night out. Her eyes flitted about, and two spots of colour stained her cheeks, her nerves as obvious as the nose on her face.

Pushing a final pin into her hair, Sylvia planted on a smile, strode forward, her hand outstretched to the dark-haired girl first. 'Hello, I'm Sylvia Roberts.'

She smiled shyly, revealing white teeth, her stunning green eyes showing her caution. 'Veronica Campbell.'

'Nice to meet you, Veronica.' Sylvia beamed and turned to the girl next to her, offering her hand. 'And you are?'

'Freda Parkes.' Her handshake was firm, her blue eyes kind. 'I recognise you from training, but we've never had the chance to speak. It's nice to finally meet you.'

'You too,' Sylvia said, warming to Freda immediately. She faced Veronica. 'Both of you.' She leaned forward and lowered her voice. 'Although I have to warn you the sister in charge of us is not the friendliest person on the planet. We might have our work cut out, I'm afraid.'

Veronica's smile faltered, her concerned gaze darting to the door. 'My mother told me Sister Dyer can be a bit harsh at times, but not to take anything she says too much to heart.'

'Your mother knows her?'

A faint blush darkened Veronica's cheeks as she nodded. 'My mother's a sister on another ward.'

'Ah, I see. Well, I'm sure Sister Dyer will be nothing to worry about,' Sylvia said, gently touching the other girl's arm, hoping to allay her fears having unwittingly roused them. 'It's most likely just me she's taken an instant dislike to.'

'Well, that hardly seems fair.' Freda scowled and narrowed her eyes as she followed Veronica's look to the door. 'I don't like bullies of any sort, sister or no sister, so you can count on me for back-up if needed.'

Sylvia grinned. 'Great. I'll remember that.'

'So, do we just choose any locker?' Freda brushed past Sylvia and approached the row of the lockers on the far wall of the small room. 'Which is yours?'

'This one.' Sylvia gestured with a wave towards her open locker door, before turning to Veronica who stood in the exact same spot, looking uncertain. 'Why don't you two take a locker either side of mine?'

Freda gave a decisive nod. 'Good idea.'

Veronica seemed to hesitate before she flashed Sylvia another shy smile and walked to one of the lockers next to hers. Unlike her and Freda, Veronica had arrived with her hat neatly pinned and, when she removed her jacket, her apron was on and her watch in place. Sylvia bit back a smile. She loved a challenge, and she had a feeling bringing Nurse Campbell out of her shell was going to be one she would thoroughly enjoy. More often than not, the shy ones only needed a nudge now and then to get them moving in the right direction. The girl was beautiful and deserved to bask in it. Freda was pretty too, but in a less obvious way. Or maybe it was the seriousness that hovered around her that made it seem that way.

Sylvia inhaled, happy with two of her fellow ward nurses. Now she just had to wait for the others to arrive…

'Well, well, Sylvia Roberts,' Kathy Scott exclaimed as she entered the room. 'Here we are, back together again.'

Sylvia's happiness popped like a damn balloon as her eyes met Kathy Scott's. 'Oh, deep joy. Who could've guessed?'

The other girl grinned, undisguised delight lighting her hazel eyes. 'It was almost as if I asked for it to happen.' She walked past her. 'I'll take this locker, shall I?'

Sylvia pressed her lips together to stop the curse biting her tongue from escaping. *Give me strength…*

4

VERONICA

Veronica pretended to be busy putting things away in her locker for the third – or maybe it was the fourth – time since she had arrived in the staff room. Her hands slightly trembled as she pulled things from her bag and rearranged them in her locker. The atmosphere between Nurse Scott and Sylvia had been palpable from the minute Nurse Scott had entered the room. It soon became clear the two of them had been up against each other time and again during training.

Closing her eyes, Veronica tried to get a hold of herself. It would do no good worrying about what the women she would be working with were like. She would find out one way or the other soon enough.

'Are you coming, Veronica? It's almost eight.'

She jumped at the sound of Sylvia's voice behind her and turned. 'I'll be right there. I just want to...'

'Powder your nose. I get it.' Sylvia winked. 'We'll see you on the ward. Don't be long or you'll give Sister Long Face reason to start on you.'

'I won't.'

With Kathy Scott leading the pack, the other nurses left the room, including the two others who'd join them on the ward. Nurses Carr and Taylor hadn't really said much at all during their brief time in the staff room, but considering the long hours they would all be working together from now on, there would be plenty of time to get to know each other.

Veronica closed her locker door and took a deep breath, relieved to be supervised by Sister Dyer rather than her mother, who was in charge of another ward further along the corridor. Excitement to start this new adventure away from her increasingly demanding mother unfurled inside Veronica, even if her habitual self-doubt continued to niggle. Was she really up to doing this job? Her mother seemed to think so, but then again, she saw very little of the truth about her daughter and most likely never would. She chose to only see what she wanted to see in Veronica and nothing else.

The voice that had kept her company for the last four years whispered gleefully in her ear.

Your judgement can't be trusted. You make bad decisions. You read people all wrong. You wouldn't know who is good or bad even they wore a placard stating it.

'Go away,' she whispered. 'Please, don't torment me. Not today.'

Veronica pressed her hand to her stomach as sickness rolled through her on a wave. The last time she had trusted her instinct about someone, despite only talking to him a handful of times, her entire life had been turned on an evil axis and stayed there. Until this very day.

'It won't happen again. Not here. Not amongst these women.'

Lifting her chin, Veronica dropped her hand from her stomach and strode from the room into the corridor. Once she reached the ward, she quickly walked past the sister who was scrutinising some paperwork at a wooden desk by the ward entrance. As Veronica approached the semi-circle of nurses waiting for the sister's instructions, Sylvia and Freda opened a space for her in between them.

'Are you alright?' Sylvia asked her, her dark brown eyes concerned.

Veronica stood straighter and pushed as much authority into her voice as possible. The last thing she wanted was to appear weak in front of her new colleagues. 'Of course. You?'

'Oh, yes.' Sylvia grinned. 'I can't wait to get started. Come hell or high water, we've got this, girls. Right?'

Freda smiled. 'Absolutely.'

Veronica nodded, and purposefully embraced the optimism emanating from the two women either side of her. 'Yes.' She smiled. 'Yes, we have.'

'Although...' Freda exhaled a shaky breath. 'If my dad's right, we might be seeing a lot more serious casualties along the way, so it's not going to be fun and games.'

Veronica frowned. 'What do you mean, if your dad's right?'

'He's a police officer and thinks Bristol will soon need us to take up caring for their injured. Bristol's overrun already and it doesn't look as though Germany is likely to let up bombing them any time soon.'

Sylvia slumped her shoulders. 'Unfortunately, I think your dad could be right.'

The sister's shoes sounded on the tiled floor before she came around the back of the semi-circle and stood in front of the assembled nurses.

'Good,' she said, peering at each of them in turn from behind her spectacles. 'We're all here and it is three minutes to eight. Tomorrow, we'll try for five to eight. Now...' Sister Dyer cleared her throat. 'For the last few nights, Bristol city centre has suffered an influx of bombing, meaning many injured people have been brought to hospital, leaving a shortage of beds. Therefore, we will be taking patients from Bristol who are well on their way to being recovered enough to go home. If they still have a home, of course.' She briefly closed her eyes before opening them again. 'So, this morning I would like you to see that the ward is thoroughly cleaned down, all the beds made with fresh linen and basic necessities like water jugs, cups, bandages and dressings are all well stocked and in order.'

'Looks like your dad was right, Freda,' Veronica whispered, looking at the piles of neatly folded sheets and blankets atop the beds waiting to be made up.

'He very often is,' Freda whispered back.

The sister consulted her clipboard. 'Right, I would like Nurses Scott, Carr and Taylor working together along the far side of the ward and Nurses Campbell, Parkes and Roberts working together on the near side. Any problems, I will be at my desk by the ward entrance.'

Veronica glanced at Freda and then Sylvia, who gave her a wink. She smiled and exhaled her held breath, pleased to be working with two women she hoped to get to know better as time went on.

'Roberts!'

Veronica and the others jumped.

Sylvia flinched and met the sister's gaze. 'Yes, Sister?'

'Why on earth are you grinning like that? This is not the nurses' home, and this is not a game. Patients will start arriving at midday and I expect you to be one hundred per cent professional and proficient. One word from me and you'll be transferred elsewhere. Do I make myself clear?'

'Yes, Sister.'

'Good. Now, all of you, get to work. You know where everything is.'

As the others dispersed, Veronica walked alongside Freda and Sylvia across the ward towards a row of unmade beds.

'Are you all right, Sylvia?' she asked, throwing a glare at the sister as she slid into her seat behind her desk. 'The sister singling you out that way was totally uncalled for.'

'I'm fine.' Sylvia shrugged, but the annoyance in her eyes showed differently. 'It is what it is. I'll just have to work harder at behaving myself whenever she's around. It finally feels like I'm on the road to making a life of my own and no one, including Sister Dyer, is going to stop me.' Sylvia's jaw tightened as they walked closer to the beds. 'I might not have been enough for certain people in my life, but I am good enough for Bath hospital and I'm determined to become one of the best nurses this city has ever seen.'

Freda grinned. 'Hear, hear.'

Sylvia laughed and Veronica stared after her and Freda as they each stood beside a bed and began their work. Maybe her work at the hospital would be what changed everything for her, too. God, she hoped so...

5

SYLVIA

Sylvia secured the ties of her headscarf under her chin and gave a satisfied smile as she left the hallway mirror and walked into the kitchen, humming the latest tune by the Andrews Sisters. She grabbed a bucket from by the back door and bobbed back and forth in her mule slippers as she filled it with water at the sink. It was always a good day when her mother decided to take herself out somewhere with her only mate on the street, Glenda, who lived a few doors down.

It was an even better day when it fell on Sylvia's day off.

She had nothing planned other than giving the house a thorough going over while her mother was gone. First on the agenda was attacking the grimy, muddy, entirely embarrassing front step. Then, armed with a scrubbing brush and vinegar, she planned to have a go at the bathroom. In its current state, she wouldn't have let the chimney sweep use it.

The extra money for the overtime she'd worked at the hospital was welcome, but it had also meant leaving the household duties to her mother. Hence nothing had been done for days. She lifted the boiled kettle from the stove and added hot water to the bucket, before heaving it from the sink and grabbing the scrubbing brush she'd left on the drainer.

She paused at the front door and put down the bucket and brush to sneak another quick look in the mirror. She patted her scarf, pouted her red painted lips and smoothed her blue and white flowered apron over her trousers. She had standards; standards she hoped separated her from her mother as much as humanly possible.

She opened the front door, picked up her cleaning bits and bobs and stepped outside. Breathing deep, she looked up and down the street. Apron- or housecoat-clad women, young and old, thin and not so thin, either chatted to one another on their doorsteps, or else were on their hands and knees doing the same as Sylvia was about to do. She glanced at a group of lads kicking a brown leather football back and forth across the road and then at another group of kids, clearly less fortunate, who were making do with kicking an empty tin can up and down the cobbles.

Her heart constricted as she watched the young boys and girls play, the longing she fought so hard to bury stubbornly coming to the surface. Trying not to and failing miserably, her mind wandered to her ex-fiancé, a man she had always known deep down was not right for her, but he had still somehow managed to convince her he could give her the life she'd always dreamed of. A life where she could enjoy sharing time with a man who loved and respected her, whose arms she could step into for comfort and a bit of loving from time to time. A fiancé who had made her imagine herself happy and content as she cooked and cleaned for a family she loved, kiddies held to her tight and safe. But none of those things mattered. Not any more. He'd unceremoniously called everything off, telling her he'd fallen in love with someone else… a girl he'd been carrying on with for weeks behind her back.

Well, she'd learned her lesson and the same thing would never happen to her again.

Swallowing the lump in her throat, Sylvia lowered onto her knees in front of the doorstep. It was time to forget the past and concentrate on creating a different kind of dream. A different kind of future. She shoved her scrubbing brush into the bucket and then slapped it, sodden with soapy water, onto the doorstep. As she cleaned, every now and then she'd look each way along the street, receiving the odd nodded hello from a friendly neighbour or the scowl of a not-so-friendly neighbour. It didn't matter whether she was dressed to the nines or on her knees scrubbing concrete; she was never going to be fully accepted around here as someone to befriend. She was Eileen Roberts' daughter, after all.

A deep cough sounded above her. 'Um, Miss Roberts?'

Sylvia flinched from her thoughts, sat back on her haunches and looked up into the rather handsome, dirt-smeared face of the eldest son of the only black family who lived on Castle Street. A family who kept themselves to themselves… seemingly until now.

Sylvia smiled, determined to be friendly when everyone else was so damn aloof – or more likely ignorant – to him and his family. 'Hello. What can I do for you?'

His shoulders lowered and he returned her smile, unmistakable relief in his eyes. 'I wonder if I might ask you a favour?'

'A favour?' Intrigued, Sylvia dried her hands on the edge of her apron and moved to push to her feet. He held out his hand to help her and she slid her hand into his, caught off-guard by the unexpected warmth in her cheeks. 'Thank you.'

'You're welcome.' He glanced towards his house across the street. 'You're a nurse, right?'

'I am.' She followed his gaze to his blue front door, her study gliding to the doorstep that everyone on the street knew to be so clean you could eat your dinner off it. 'Is everything alright?'

Uncertainty flickered in his dark brown eyes before he closed them, his brow furrowing before he opened them again. 'It's my brother.'

Unease tip-tapped along her spine. 'Your brother?'

'Yeah.' His intense gaze bored into hers. 'Could you come across the road? Have a little look at him?'

She looked at the darkened windows of his house, the door wide open. 'What's the matter with him?'

'He's...'

Worry showed in his eyes, sending a jolt of concern through her heart, and she touched his hand. 'What is it?'

'He's really not well, but Mum refuses to accept anything's wrong with him.'

'What? Why?'

He swiped his hand over his face and scowled. 'Money. Or lack of. You know, if we need the doctor or medicine.'

Annoyance that any mother should have to feel that way when their child was suffering twisted inside her. 'I see.'

'Look, I know it's a lot to ask, but—'

'It's not a lot to ask.' She touched his arm and smiled. 'It will be my pleasure to help, if I can.' He looked so bloody irresistible standing there all vulnerable despite his height and width, his broad shoulders and chest, eyes like melted chocolate. How could she refuse? 'Go on home,' she said. 'I'll put this lot away, clean myself up a bit and make my way over. Alright?'

'Do you think you could come straight over? I haven't told my mum that I was coming to speak to you, and I'd prefer you at least made it through the front door before she realises.'

'Fine.' She raised her hands in surrender. 'After you.'

Relief swept over his face again, making his eyes brighter and his smile wide. 'You're a star, Miss Roberts. Thank you so much.'

'You're welcome.' She looked away from him, not liking the

treacherous knotting in her stomach his expression ignited. 'And it's Sylvia.'

He nodded. 'Jesse. Jesse Howard.'

Leaving her bucket on her front step, she put her front door on the catch and followed Jesse's ridiculous height and even more ridiculous shoulders across the cobbled street.

As soon as she stepped over the threshold and into Jesse's house, she knew all the gossip about the family was true. Jesse's mother really did have the cleanest house known to man and was making a fine job of raising five kids alone. Jesse and his eldest sister were grown and working, but still, what the woman was managing, presumably while her husband was away serving – Sylvia drew in a breath – or possibly passed away considering no one had seen hide nor hair of a man older than Jesse around and about the house, was admirable.

'Lordy, should I take my shoes off?' Sylvia smiled, trying to tease the same from Jesse, whose expression had sobered.

'No, you're fine. Michael's in here.'

Sylvia followed him into the front room where the patient lay on a brown upholstered settee, a cloth across his forehead and his eyes half-closed. Immediately concerned about him, any nervous humour Sylvia had disappeared.

She walked directly to the settee and hunkered down by the side of the little boy of no more than seven or eight. Gently removing the cloth from his forehead, she pressed the back of her hand to his cheeks, then lower to his chest. He was hot to the touch, his body shiny with perspiration anywhere not hidden beneath his damp green-striped pyjamas.

'Have you got a torch or a lamp?' she asked over her shoulder to Jesse who hovered behind her. 'I need to look inside his mouth.'

'Sure.'

He swept from the room.

'Hey, Michael,' Sylvia said softly. 'Can you open your eyes for me, sweetheart?'

The little boy did, his gaze unfocused.

'I'm Sylvia. Jesse has just gone to find some light so I can look inside your mouth. Is that alright?'

He managed a weak nod.

'Good boy. I'm going to—'

'What in God's name are you doing in my house?'

Sylvia sprang to her feet and looked straight into the angry face of Jesse's mother. 'Oh, Mrs Howard. Hello. I'm Sylvia Rob—'

'I couldn't care less if you were Florence Nightingale. Get away from my boy.'

'Mrs Howard—'

'Don't you Mrs Howard me. I know who you are, my girl.'

Sylvia locked eyes with the other woman, retaliation biting at her tongue, but before she could respond – which was probably just as well – Jesse reappeared brandishing an already lit torch and brushed past his mother.

'Sylvia is a nurse, Mum. She's kindly agreed to take a little look at Michael so let's not risk upsetting her, shall we?' He had the torch out to Sylvia. 'Here.'

Dragging her glare from Mrs Howard, Sylvia planted on a smile and bent over Michael. 'Now then, do you think you could be a brave boy and open your mouth for me? I'll be as quick as a flash, promise.'

The boy slowly opened his mouth, his lips dry and slightly cracked at the corners. Sylvia shone the light and immediately winced at the sight of Michael's swollen and pus-spotted tonsils. He must be in agony, the poor baby. She snapped off the torch and re-laid the cloth across his head.

She faced the thankfully silent, but clearly distraught, Mrs

Howard and then Jesse, who stared at her intently. 'Well?' he asked. 'Is it serious?'

Sylvia sighed. 'Serious enough that the poor lad must be in a lot of pain. Has he managed to eat anything over the last couple of days?' She looked between mother and son. 'Anything at all?'

Mrs Howard defensively puffed out her chest, but her eyes glinted with tears. 'I do my best by my children. He's had some soup and water. Even managed some tea this morning. He'll be as right as rain soon enough.'

'I'm inclined to agree with you, but right now, he must be in terrible pain, Mrs Howard,' Sylvia said gently, fighting the urge to take the woman's hand. 'I recommend a fusion of hot water with mustard, cover his head with a towel over the bowl and let him breathe it in, two or three times a day.' She glanced at the little boy, his eyes closed once more. 'And a tiny amount of aspirin mixed with sugar will help him with the pain.'

A soft sob escaped her before she strode past Sylvia and dropped down on the settee beside her son, gently cupping his cheek and whispering in his ear. 'I'm sorry, darling. I'm sorry.'

Sylvia looked at Jesse and he tilted his head towards the door.

She followed him from the room and he walked her outside the house. He turned and his dark gaze fell on hers. 'I've been telling Mum for days to ask for your help, but she wouldn't. She hasn't been the same since Dad was killed, but we were managing well enough until this. Never known her to be so stubborn when one of us was unwell before.'

Sympathy swelled inside her and she shook her head. 'I assumed your father was serving when he was killed?'

'Yeah. He was shot down less than two months after he left.'

'He was a pilot?'

He nodded.

'I'm so sorry.'

His gaze wandered over her face, lingered a moment at her lips, before he blinked and looked away along the street. 'Well, thanks for coming over.' He met her eyes. 'I'd better get back inside before Mum comes out looking for me.'

She forced a smile. 'Good idea. Michael will be back to normal in no time. Trust me.'

'Somehow, I do, Sylvia Roberts. Completely.'

He turned back into the house, closing the door behind him.

Sylvia stared at the closed door and a telling – entirely unwelcome – shiver rippled through her. Willing her feet to move, she hurried across the street to the safety of her house. She was woman enough to admit a slight attraction to Jesse Howard, but she was also woman enough to know it was imperative she steered clear of him. She had more important things to worry about than men. Like her independence, the chance of a future made on her own terms and – most importantly – keeping her heart intact.

6

FREDA

Freda puffed the pillows behind Mrs Marshall, the latest patient to arrive from Bristol, before gently easing her back against them. 'There you go. How's that?'

'Better, thank you.'

'I'm so sorry for everything you've been through. I can't imagine...' Freda bit her bottom lip, her heart breaking for this young mother who had been made so suddenly and cruelly childless and with no idea if her husband was dead or alive. 'You did everything right. This war...' She shook her head and squeezed Mrs Marshall's hand where it lay lifeless on the bedcovers. 'It's taken so much already and there's still no end in sight.'

Tears shone in Mrs Marshall's eyes, the grey smudges under them seeming to darken with each passing second as she stared at Freda, her gaze devoid of anger or sadness, just entirely blank. 'They said the Morrison shelters would protect us, protect our children. I told my babies to climb inside that thing and lie down beneath some blankets, just like they told us, and they did.'

Freda held her hand tighter, willing the other woman to stay strong. But how was she supposed to do that? 'Mrs Marshall, you did the right—'

'Now they're dead and I'm alive.' Her tears broke and ran down her pale cheeks. 'I should have kept taking them to the public shelter. We've survived well enough going there for the last two years. Now I have no children, no home.'

'You did what you thought was best, the same as everyone else living through this stupid war.'

'Why did I leave them to get the dog?' A sob racked her, and she covered her face with her hands. 'Why?'

Freda put her arms around the devastated, heartbroken mother and held her tight, her cheek against Mrs Marshall's hair. 'I'm so sorry.'

Freda rocked her gently, hot tears pricking her eyes as anger and frustration balled in her throat. Newspaper images of the destruction and devastation the war had inflicted on Bristol, along with pictures from her own imagination, ran like a cinefilm through her mind. Such horror and suffering. There was so much being done to help and protect, yet how could it ever be enough? She closed her eyes as her passion to know what it was really like to exist – to survive – in the real thick of war, rather in the so-far un-bombed Bath, burned through her, igniting the words she wanted to scream.

What did the people left at home know about what was really happening at the front? Were they being told the truth of what went on so they could do all they could to protect themselves and their loved ones? Or was the truth of this blasted war really so bad that it was being kept from the people at home and they were left flailing with no real idea of what they should or shouldn't do? Freda's heart beat fast as her determination to be more – do more – rose up inside of her. All she knew was, for the time being at least, it was up to nurses like her, Sylvia, Veronica and the others to do what they could, to pick up the frayed threads of people's previously happy lives and weave them back together as best they could.

Mrs Marshall slowly pulled from Veronica's embrace and wiped her fingers under her eyes. 'I don't know what I'm supposed to do next. They've moved me here from Bristol to recover, but how will I ever recover from losing my children?'

'I honestly don't know.' Freda's frustration that she wasn't closer to the danger was wrong, bad and selfish. Her mother was right. This poor woman was nowhere near the battle lines and look how she suffered. Maybe being good and behaving well was best for everyone. To do anything else was entirely self-serving. Freda forced a smile. 'I'll get you a cup of tea. Maybe I can find a slice of something nice to go with it. Do you think you could eat? Even a little is better than nothing.'

Mrs Marshall looked at the bed opposite her where a woman in her mid-fifties sat, her head bandaged and bloody, her face bruised and cut. 'I'll try some tea.'

Freda's heart ached with her patient's pain. What was Mrs Marshall thinking as she looked at the other woman? From one human experience to another, the war affected people in every imaginable way. In ways that could be seen and ways that could not, and she hated that nursing made her feel that she was not doing enough.

She left Mrs Marshall and walked through the ward, passing Veronica helping a woman from a wheelchair into bed, then Sylvia making another woman with a broken arm and a patch over one eye grin so widely that Freda smiled, too. Then her eyes met Nurse Carr's at a third bed. They smiled at one another, and Freda continued on her way. All the women she began this new part of her life with seemed nice and worth getting to know – well, maybe not all, but she'd give Nurse Scott the benefit of the doubt for the time being. She had to bury her thoughts of being anywhere else and help those who needed her here.

Just as she reached the kitchen, hurried footsteps sounded behind her before Sylvia looped her arm through hers. 'Are you all right?' she asked, her gaze concerned. 'I was watching you with one of your patients. You know you're not supposed to cuddle them like that, right?'

'I know,' Freda said, pleased by Sylvia's gregariousness. She hoped they would grow to become friends before long. Both Sylvia and Veronica. She liked both girls equally, and hoped they felt the same way about her. 'But Sister has pretty much left us to it so I thought I'd comfort Mrs Marshall the best way I can, while I can get away with it.'

Sylvia grinned. 'Well, good on you. We have to do what we feel is right at the time, whatever the situation. And I for one will not hold back from doing what I can to offer any small amount of comfort to anyone suffering.'

'I agree. I'm just going to get Mrs Marshall a cup of tea. I did mention cake, too, but I have no idea if—'

'Then you're in luck, my lovely new friend.'

'I am?'

'I brought some cake in with me this morning.' Sylvia pulled her in the direction of the staff room rather than the kitchen. 'The oldest son of a neighbour I helped by looking over his poorly brother a few days ago gave it to me as a thank you. He's really quite sweet.'

'Who?' Freda smiled. 'The older son or the younger?'

'Are you teasing me, Nurse Parkes?' Sylvia snatched her arm from Freda's and planted her hands on her hips, laughter shining in her brown eyes. 'You really are getting comfortable around here, aren't you?'

Freda arched an eyebrow. 'I'll assume from that subtle diversion to our conversation it's the elder son.'

Sylvia narrowed her eyes at her before promptly lifting her nose in the air and sashaying past her. Freda smiled, enjoying the colour in Sylvia's face and wondering if she was aware how her gaze had softened when she'd called the neighbour's son 'sweet'.

'So,' Freda said, following Sylvia into the staff room. 'All this fancy man needs to do to get your attention is ply you with cake? Although it's not a bad tactic, considering the country's circumstances right now.'

'Correct. And, for the record, Jesse is not my "fancy man". It's just that since I saw to his brother, he's had a knack of obstructing my path to talk to me whenever he sees me arriving or leaving Mum's. Which, if I had my way, I wouldn't have to do at all.'

Freda's smile dissolved. After listening to Sylvia's stories about her mother over the last couple of weeks, it was fair to say that Mrs Roberts did not sound like the best of mothers, and it made Freda realise how she so often needlessly complained about her own.

'Anyway,' Sylvia continued. 'I'll gladly take all the cake going, if I can share it with a patient or two, and with my fellow graduated nurses.'

'Well, there is that, of course.'

Sylvia carried a cardboard box from the top shelf of her locker to the table and opened it. 'Believe me, if he keeps bringing me cakes like this, it's all to our good. Look at that. It's a masterpiece.'

Freda dropped her mouth open as she stared wide-eyed at the precious sponge with fancy cream icing edged in piped pale blue flowers. 'Wow, he must be grateful. I haven't seen anything so fancy since the war started,' she said. 'And Jesse made it? My God.'

Sylvia elbowed her in the ribs. 'Bloody hell, Freda, 'course he didn't! He's a railway worker for crying out loud. I can't imagine a man as big and strong as Jesse Howard with his hands plastered in flour and butter.' She wiggled her eyebrows. 'Other parts of him, maybe.'

Freda laughed. 'You are so bad.'

Sylvia's brow creased as she stared at the cake, her voice taking on a melancholy tone that Freda hadn't heard before. 'I'm just glad little Michael is on his way to making a full recovery. Jesse told me the mustard fusion and aspirin I recommended have worked wonders. I just feel for his mother being put in a position that she was afraid to get him seen to because she had no idea how she'd pay for the medicine if he'd needed it.'

'That's terrible, and so unfair.'

'I get the feeling her pride is such that she doesn't even want to ask her own children for help. This damn war is doing so much to everyone. Mrs Howard's already lost her husband and she has five kids to worry about, too.' Sylvia blinked and her habitual smile leaped back into place. 'So, she really shouldn't have spent her rations on making a cake like this for me, but who am I to complain? Listen to me telling you all about Jesse Howard and his family. The man is becoming nothing more than a thorn in my side, believe me.'

'Well,' Freda said, still looking at the cake and thinking how much she was going to enjoy presenting a slice to Mrs Marshall, 'I wouldn't be too quick to brush him off if I were you. That cake is amazing.'

'It is, isn't it?' Sylvia's eyes lit with happiness. 'And best of all, we get to give a cheeky slice to Mrs Marshall. It might go some way to giving her a moment's respite from her grief. What do you think?'

'I think it's most definitely worth a try.' Freda grinned, the heaviness in her heart lifting. 'I'll go and get a knife from the kitchen.'

7

VERONICA

'I would like to see Nurses Campbell, Parkes and Roberts straight away, please.'

Veronica inwardly groaned as Sister Dyer turned sharply on her heel and headed back to her desk at the ward entrance. Or back to her perch, as Sylvia liked to say.

She finished expertly folding and tucking in the sheet at the corner of the eighth bed she had made up that afternoon and slapped out the top sheet. Straightening, Veronica pressed her hands into the base of her aching back and glanced along the ward. Freda and Sylvia were similarly hurrying to finish their tasks so they could answer the sister's summons.

Veronica joined her friends and they walked towards the sister's desk.

'I am so glad we're almost done for the day.' She sighed. 'I'm ready to collapse into bed and sleep for the entirety of my day off tomorrow.'

Freda smiled. 'I think I'll be doing the same.'

'Whereas I' – Sylvia looked at Veronica, her dark brown eyes glittering with mischief – 'will be finding myself a bit of male company to help me blow away the smell of antiseptic and bleach.'

'And does this male company go by the name of Jesse, by any chance?' Freda asked, wiggling her eyebrows.

'Jesse?' Veronica flicked her gaze between her friends. 'Who's Jesse?'

Sylvia shot Freda a glare. 'No one.'

Veronica bristled. 'It's not fair to leave me out of any excitement, you know. My life is hardly the epitome of romance and rose—'

'If you've quite finished with your chitchat, ladies...'

Veronica stiffened. They were just a few feet from the sister's desk, and judging by her livid expression she had heard their conversation, and the last thing she needed was the sister reporting back to her mother. The tension between them steadily grew as time wore on and Veronica's yearning to move out and live anywhere else but her childhood home gathered strength. As much as she and her mother might care for one another, for Veronica, every week became harder than the one before. She wanted her own space; needed to escape the ghosts that refused to leave her home. Goodness knew when or how she would have the means to get away, or how her mother would feel being left to live alone. Veronica pulled back her shoulders. But she had to do something...

The three of them formed a straight-backed line in front of Sister Dyer.

'Now...' The sister ran her gaze over each of them in turn before drawing in a long breath, her bosom rising. 'In varying ways, each of you has impressed me this week, which is extremely encouraging when I want to ensure the ward is kept to a high operating standard at all times.'

Relief eased some of Veronica's tension. This job meant everything to her, and it was sorely needed to keep her from falling apart again. The busyness of nursing in wartime filled her head with thoughts of the professional rather than the personal, which was a much safer place to be. To lose her position now would mean spiralling into the abyss that she had visited more than once. She had to remain strong against revisiting the past. Nursing was her future.

'...And to that end,' Sister Dyer continued, 'I would like to assign two of you at a time to escorting patients, by ambulance, from here to the rural hospital in Gloucester and possibly another, depending on necessity. We have taken in ten patients from Bristol over the last seven days, but it is likely this will double next week and possibly again the following week. Therefore, we must transfer patients who require minimal tended convalescence to the quieter hospitals, freeing space for more of Bristol's injured incoming.'

Unease rippled through Veronica as she glanced at Freda and then Sylvia, before clearing her throat. 'Will it only be the three of us escorting the transfers, Sister? Or will the other nurses on the ward be assigned at some point, too?'

'That's an interesting question to ask at this early stage, Nurse Campbell,' Sister Dyer said, her grey eyes shadowed with curiosity. 'Does it matter?'

Veronica looked again at her friends and they both stared back at her, frowns creasing their foreheads and questions in their eyes.

She quickly faced the sister, her knees ever-so-slightly trembling as a slowly burning panic swirled deep in the pit of her stomach. The last thing she wanted was to cause the sister to watch her more closely than any of the others, but she did not want to do the transfers with anyone other than Sylvia and Freda. The only two women on the ward she was tentatively beginning to trust.

'It's just that I'd rather carry out the transfers with nurses I'm working more closely with than I am the others. I'm sure' – she swallowed, trying not to squirm under the sister's narrowed gaze – 'in time, I'll get to know the other nurses as well as I do Nurse Roberts and Nurse Parkes, but for now—'

'You are here to work, serve and take orders, Nurse Campbell,' Sister Dyer snapped. 'The hospital is not a social club.'

'Oh, I know. It's just...' Veronica held the sister's stare despite her mouth draining dry. 'I don't like the thought of travelling halfway across the county with a driver I do not know at all and a nurse I have barely shared half a dozen words with.'

'I agree,' Sylvia said firmly.

Veronica felt the gentle pressure of her friend's hand on the small of her back and fought to keep her face impassive. Freda's stare bored into her temple.

'And you, Nurse Parkes. Do you have the same concerns as your colleagues?'

'Um, yes.' Freda stood a little taller. 'I'd prefer to travel with Nurse Campbell or Nurse Roberts.'

Sister Dyer's lips tightened into a thin line, her eyes narrowing as she stared at Veronica. Veronica's heart pulsed in her ears. Now she would have some explaining to do. Freda and Sylvia would almost certainly want to know why she had insisted it was just the three of them who travelled back and forth to the country hospital. How in God's name was she supposed to explain herself?

'Well, then...' Sister Dyer said, firmly. 'That will be the way of it for the time being. Two out of the three of you will escort patients during the final hours of your late shift next week. It will only be twice a week to begin with. I will work out which of you will go together and when. Now...' She looked at her watch. 'There is half an hour left of your shift, so I suggest you finish up the jobs I called you away from and then get yourselves home.

Make the most of your day off. Things are only going to get busier.'

'Yes, Sister,' they chorused.

Veronica quickly turned and attempted a head start along the ward, but Freda and Sylvia were on either side of her before she'd managed seven paces.

Sylvia touched her elbow. 'What was all that about, V?'

Oh, God...

Veronica stopped and plastered on a smile, purposefully facing her friends. 'All what?'

'You know what,' Freda said quietly, her bright blue eyes concerned. 'You were so quick to say you only want to do the hospital transfers with Sylvia and me.'

Veronica fought to keep eye contact with the two women she was coming to like more and more. At least she couldn't feel herself blushing. She tipped them a wink. 'Why wouldn't I? We want to have a little fun while we work. Right?'

'Hmm, well, this is true,' agreed Sylvia.

Freda continued to frown as she studied Veronica. 'And that's it? You want to be with one of us, just for the fun?'

Veronica shrugged. 'Isn't that reason enough?'

''Course it is!' Sylvia grinned. 'It's only right we find some fun where we can right now, Freda. There's a war on, in case you haven't noticed. Come on, girls. I'm not staying here one more minute over my shift.'

As Sylvia sauntered off along the ward, Freda turned her canny gaze on Veronica. 'Are you sure you're alright?'

'I'm fine.'

'Because if you need to talk—'

'I don't.' Veronica laughed, cursing the sting of tears at the back of her eyes as she gave Freda a friendly prod in the back. 'Now come on, let's get back to work.'

8

SYLVIA

As Sylvia rounded the corner into Castle Street, the late afternoon sun hovered above the red-tiled roofs of the terrace houses either side. Tired to the marrow of her bones, she could not wait to fall into bed after another gruelling shift. There was every possibility she would sleep for ten hours straight. But as she took a further few steps along the pavement, she was greeted by a cacophony of screaming and shouting, jeering and name calling – the loudest of the voices belonging to none other than her bloody mother. Unusually grateful she was wearing her sensible black work shoes rather than her preferred high heels, Sylvia muttered a curse and strode forward.

She'd barely covered a dozen paving slabs when she drew to a sharp halt, sickness coating her throat.

A heated fracas was playing out in front of Jesse's house.

He, his four siblings – all younger, two boys, including sweet Michael who looked decidedly healthier than he had a week or so ago, and two girls – and their mother were each giving as good as they got from the mob standing on the pavement outside their house. The slurs and insults about the Howards' African origin and the accusations about whose role it was to do what on the street and in the community had a particularly racist slant that made Sylvia's blood boil. She clenched her fists at her sides and strode forward. A nurse learned only too quickly that the colour of a person's skin made no difference to the injuries and losses they sustained, or how they hurt and scarred a person's heart and memory.

'How I choose to look after my house has sod all to do with you!' shouted Jesse's mother, her eyes bulging with anger, her hands fisted on her hips. 'If you can't look after your own to the standard I look after mine, that's nothing to do with me.'

Sylvia winced and hurried forward. God, there would be hell to pay if Mrs Howard carried on baiting the Castle Street mothers that way.

A roar of female voices resounded around the brick and cobbled space, bouncing from the houses and damn-near shattering the windows, regardless of the criss-cross of tape covering them.

'Who the bloody hell do you think you are? I'll tell you something for nothing, we don't need your sort—'

'Mum!' Sylvia shoved her arm through a gap between the two women in front of her and grasped her mother's elbow. 'Knock it off. For crying out loud.' She turned around and faced the crowd, her fingers tightly gripping her mother even as she fought for release. 'Go on, go home, all of you. I have just returned from a nine-hour shift, stitching up and caring for people who've lost limbs, their homes and loved ones, and you lot are spending your time out here ripping strips off one another!'

The ensuing and immediate silence surprised Sylvia as much as her shouting seemed to have everyone else. With a satisfied nod, she steadfastly avoided looking at Jesse where he stood just a few feet away from her, his dark intense stare boring into her like a revolving hand drill.

'Good. Now...' She spun around and unceremoniously pulled her mother in front of her, prodded a finger in her back and none-too-gently urged her forward. 'Let's leave the Howard family in peace, shall we?'

Feeling a little like the Pied Piper, albeit rather than rats following her, she had disgruntled, scarf-wearing housewives, Sylvia marched her mother across the street and along the pavement towards their house, sending up a silent thank you to God when the other women also dispersed.

She blew out a breath. 'For the love of God, Mum!'

'What?'

Sylvia drew to a stop. 'What has that family ever done to you, eh? The things you lot were saying about them, the colour of their skin and God knows what else...' Sylvia shook her head. 'You should be ashamed of yourself. Mrs Howard has lost her husband, the same as a thousand other women. Just leave her and her family be, will you?'

'It was her that started it.' Her mother glared. 'Anyway, it's nice someone else is on the receiving end of the sharp tongues on this street rather than me for once. I'm hardly going to miss the opportunity to take my place on the winning side when I can, am I?'

Shame enveloped Sylvia and she narrowed her eyes. 'My God, you're happy to join in the harassment of someone else if it keeps the bullies away from you. Is that what you're saying?'

Her mother shrugged.

'That, dearest mother, is not the way it should be. You should have stood beside the Howards and supported them when you know what the women on this street can be like.'

'Oh, that's right, blame me,' her mother said, drawing a packet of cigarettes and matches from her skirt pocket. She stuck a cigarette in her mouth and lit it, took a long drag. 'It's only a bit of carry-on, Sylv. Don't get your knickers in such a twist. It'll blow over.'

Sylvia pinned her with a glare. 'Will it?'

''Course. No doubt I'll do something to upset that lot sooner or later and the attention will be back on yours truly. Well, if not me, maybe you.'

Impervious to the picture most of the women had chosen to paint of her and her mother without making any sort of attempt to get to know them, memories of the cake Mrs Howard had baked for her as a thank you filled Sylvia's mind. 'Well, I for one have been treated nothing but kindly by that family, and by the way her kids were gathered around Mrs Howard just now, it's obvious they love the bones of her and, on top of it all, she keeps a good house. So, when all is said and done—'

'What are you insinuating? That the rest of us are rubbish cooks, despise our kids and live in pigsties? Is that it?'

She held her mother's gaze, crossed her arms. 'I wouldn't say *everyone*, no.'

Her mother narrowed her gaze. 'Just me.'

'If the shoe fits...'

'You cheeky mare!'

Sylvia shrugged and glanced across the road, her heart giving a little stumble. Jesse stood alone watching her from the same spot she'd left him, his hands in his pockets, his face unreadable. The rest of the Howard family were nowhere to be seen and Sylvia assumed he'd ushered them inside, the same as she was trying to with her mother. She quickly turned and dread knotted Sylvia's stomach as she recognised the calculating glint in her mother's eyes as she appraised Jesse Howard through a stream of grey-white smoke.

Curling her fingers around her mother's arm, she eased her to the front door of their house. 'Go on in, Mum. I'll be two minutes and then I'll get some tea on the go. I assume you haven't eaten since breakfast?'

Her mother backed up to the front door, her gaze still fixed on Jesse and a smile twitching her lips. 'Are you going over there to talk to Mr Handsome by any chance?'

Sylvia pointedly raised her eyebrows. 'Oh, so he's handsome now, is he? The colour of his skin doesn't matter?'

Her mother took a puff of her cigarette. 'Handsome enough for a—'

'Just get inside, will you?'

Her mother laughed, took another long drag on her cigarette before exhaling a stream of smoke into Sylvia's face. 'Don't go thinking the likes of him will have any interest in someone like you. You know he'll walk away once he gets to know you. They all do, remember?'

The swipe was quick and sharp.

Sylvia somehow managed not to flinch or falter and instead kept silent, her glare trained on her mother as she cackled her way indoors. Closing her eyes, Sylvia breathed deep before slowly exhaling, her heart treacherously beating just a little too fast. God, sometimes she despised her mother even if her stupid heart often said differently.

'Seems you arrived right on time.'

She snapped her eyes open and spun around.

Jesse smiled, revealing beautiful white teeth as he strode across the remainder of the cobbled road until he stood barely two feet away from her. She met his phenomenal dark brown eyes. She estimated him to be around six foot four and was grateful that he hadn't stepped up onto the pavement. She needed the extra inches of the kerb to aid her feigned nonchalance. If he stood too close, towered over her too much, then her bravado would likely desert her. She could tell herself night and day she didn't fancy him, but with his dark skin and even darker eyes, the man was as handsome as a man could be.

She cleared her throat and tilted her chin. 'That's the story of my life.'

'Arriving right on time?'

'Uh-huh. Whether at work or play, I always seem to be where I am needed most.'

'I'll bear that in mind.'

Sylvia was momentarily caught in the trap of his stare before she quickly looked past him towards his house. 'No shift at the railway today?'

He arched an eyebrow. 'How do you know I work at the station?'

She crossed her arms, ignoring the warmth at her cheeks. 'I might have asked people around here a question or two about you.'

'Is that right?' He continued to stare at her, his gaze amused. 'The same people that just did their best to rip strips off my family?'

'Yeah, well.' Sylvia dropped her arms and sighed. 'Don't paint us all with the same brush. Will your mum be all right?' She glanced at the closed door of his house. 'I hate to think of her being upset by her neighbours, what with Michael being so unwell and everything.'

'She'll be fine. Tough as old boots, my mum is.'

'I don't doubt it.'

He stared at her a moment longer before raising his hand and starting to walk backwards across the road. 'See you again soon, Sylvia Roberts. Very soon, I hope.'

He turned around and Sylvia stared after him, her nerves stretched tight and her interest in Jesse dangerously deepened.

'Walked away pretty quick, didn't he?'

Rolling her eyes, Sylvia walked to her front door where her mother had reappeared, her shoulder propped against the door-frame and malicious glee in her eyes.

'Yeah, he did,' Sylvia said. 'Just as well, too.'

'Oh?'

'In you go, Mum. Nothing to see here.'

9

FREDA

'Sometimes, Nurse Parkes, I wonder whether you listen to me at all!'

Freda fought to stand firm and not give in to the perilous rebellion that wound through her as Sister Dyer glared at her. 'I thought it would be a good idea—'

'It is not your job to come up with good ideas, Nurse, it's mine. Do I make myself clear?'

'Yes, Sister.'

'Good. Now, finish giving Mr Humphries his medication and then you can go to the laundry and bring up all the required bedding for Markham ward. Seeing as you cannot be trusted to carry out the tasks I give you on this ward, I am putting you on bed-making duty elsewhere for the rest of your shift.'

The sister turned on her heel and marched down the length of the ward.

Freda stared after her.

It was the third time she had been on the sharp end of the sister's tongue in as many days. She scowled. She wasn't Sister Dyer's target as often as Sylvia seemed to be, but still the woman was proving herself to be strict and downright cold at times. Each of the newly qualified nurses were doing their best, yet she continued to look down her nose at Sylvia especially, and subtly implied to Veronica that she would report anything she did wrong to her mother.

Freda tried to focus on the job in hand and poured some water into a cup for Mr Humphries, but she still inwardly fumed. The woman seemed determined to keep Freda in her place and not allow her to veer off course from hospital expectations by thinking for herself or making unsolicited suggestions. Clearly, the frustration she sometimes felt being confined to the ward was beginning to show.

All she'd suggested was that Mr Humphries was more than capable, as certain other patients were, of taking his medication himself, rather than being fed the tablets as though he were an invalid. He and many of the other patients on the ward had gone through goodness knew what, faced dangers and saved the lives of children and animals, and now they were being treated as though they were minus a brain or backbone.

'You alright, love?'

She blinked and faced Mr Humphries, forcing a smile. 'Sorry, I was miles away.'

His gaze was dark with annoyance. 'That woman don't deserve your concern.'

'Maybe not, but we'd better get your medication taken before she comes back or I'll be in more trouble than I am already.'

'Yeah, well, to my mind, you shouldn't be in trouble at all,' Mr Humphries grumbled, shooting a glare at Sister Dyer as she scrutinised a clipboard at the end of another patient's bed. 'You are a diamond to stick up for me and the others the way you do. That woman would have us cleaned and dressed by whippersnappers and then put in bloody playpens out the way if she could.'

A smile pulled at Freda's lips. Despite suspecting Mr Humphries' summary of the sister was entirely accurate, it wouldn't be right to agree with him behind her back. 'She's nice enough, honestly. It's her job to keep me and the other newly qualified nurses in line. I shouldn't have spoken up the way I did.'

'Why not? You and your fellow nurses are the ones really running things around here and Sister Big Pants should know that after most likely coming up the ranks herself. She's throwing her weight around and I don't like sitting here watching her do it to a lovely girl like you.'

'I'm tougher than I look, Mr Humphries.'

'I have no doubt, sweetheart, but that woman is nothing but a bully.'

His rising voice aroused her guilt and her mother's disapproving face filled Freda's mind's eye. She should not have answered the sister back the way she did and she had no idea what she'd been thinking by doing so.

'Mr Humphries, please,' she said, giving him his tablets and a cup of water. 'Here, take these for me.' He took the medication and water as Freda darted a furtive glance in Sister Dyer's direction. 'Don't go upsetting yourself on my behalf. I am perfectly all right. Truly.'

He tossed the tablets to the back of his throat, followed by a mouthful of water. He swallowed. 'Rubbish. I saw the way you stepped back from her, looked across the ward. You are a good nurse, and I don't want the likes of her' – he sniffed and threw another glare at the sister – 'making you think you don't belong on this ward along with the other nurses, 'cause you damn well do.'

Freda took the cup from him. Did she belong here? Really?

'Uh-oh. What's with the glum faces?'

Freda jumped and turned to find Sylvia standing beside her, a teasing look in her dark brown eyes. 'Nothing. I was just about to leave Mr—'

'I'll tell you why we're looking glum, Nurse Roberts,' Mr Humphries interjected. 'That bloody uppity sister. Throwing her weight around, upsetting Nurse Parkes—'

'She didn't upset me,' Freda objected, hardly daring to look at Sylvia and have her friend riled up and jumping to her defence. 'Hush now before she hears you.'

'What happened?' Sylvia asked, her smile gone as she looked between Freda and Mr Humphries. 'What did the ol' battle-axe say to you this time? She can pick on me until the cows come home and I couldn't care less, but I won't have her upsetting you and Veronica. I consider us friends now and that means I've got your backs.'

Freda sighed. 'She didn't say any—'

'She's put her on bed duty.'

Freda closed her eyes as Mr Humphries filled in the remaining gaps in Sylvia's knowledge of the situation.

Sylvia narrowed her eyes as she followed the sister's progress through the ward. 'I see. Well, if I start to suspect she's picking on you for no good reason—'

'She was not picking on me.' Freda pulled her shoulders back and pinned Sylvia with a glare. 'And if she did, I am perfectly capable of handling her myself.'

Their gazes locked, until Sylvia raised her hands in surrender. 'Fine, but I won't stand by and have her take advantage of your good nature.'

Battling against her mother's voice as it seeped into her ears – *good girls are the best girls* – Freda turned away from Sylvia and Mr Humphries' watchful gazes and busied herself stacking the empty medicine paraphernalia onto a tray atop the bedside table.

'Right, so I'll presume that means this conversation is over,' Sylvia said with a sniff.

'It is.'

'Good. Then, if all is as it should be, I suggest we celebrate that with a drink at the pub after our shift. What do you think?'

Freda stilled. 'A drink?'

'Why not?' Sylvia's smile faltered. 'You have been in a pub before, right?'

Heat travelled up Freda's neck to her jaw and Sylvia's eyes widened. Freda looked at Mr Humphries, whose raised eyebrows almost brushed his hairline. She laughed and picked up the tray. 'Of course I have,' she lied.

'Good, then we'll—'

'But I won't be going to the pub tonight.'

'Why not?'

The disappointment in Sylvia's eyes quickly change to concern and Freda struggled for a viable excuse. How could she go to a pub? Her mother would have forty fits at the mere thought of her doing such a thing. Wasn't it better she sacrificed the small things in order to do the bigger things she wanted to do? Maybe if she built up enough praise for a job well done in one direction, her mother might occasionally turn a blind eye in the other. It was a somewhat shaky hope, but it was hope all the same.

'I...' Freda shrugged, the tray in her hands wobbling. 'I don't fancy it.'

'You don't fancy it?'

Just then Veronica passed them, pushing Mr Ingalls in a wheelchair. 'I'd get moving if I were you,' she warned. 'Sister's on the warpath.' She grimaced. 'No pun intended.'

Glad of the escape route, Freda joined her friend. 'I was just on my way to the laundry.'

'You'll come, won't you, V?' Sylvia asked.

Freda briefly closed her eyes and inwardly cursed in a manner that would've caused her mother to pass out.

Veronica frowned. 'Come where?'

'To the pub.' Sylvia winked. 'After work.'

Freda turned to Veronica. There was no mistaking the hesitation, the indecision in her eyes. 'I...' She looked at Freda. 'Are you going?'

'What is this?' Sylvia laughed and looked over her shoulder as Sister Dyer marched towards them, her arms swinging and her cheeks mottled. 'Uh-oh, time to skedaddle, lovelies. End of shift, the three of us are going to the pub. No arguments.'

Freda opened her mouth to protest but Sylvia and Veronica dashed away, leaving her no option but to make a run for it herself, or endure the sister's wrath for the second time that day. She strode along the ward to the double entrance doors, her heart beating fast. She couldn't possibly go to the pub. Her mother...

Yet, she couldn't stop smiling. Oh, to hell with it... Why not?

10

SYLVIA

'Well, I don't care what you say,' Sylvia said firmly as she, Freda and Veronica made their way through the hospital's main doors. 'Kathy Scott is not to be trusted as far as I'm concerned. She's got her beady little eyes on us day in, day out. Once a snitch, always a snitch.'

Veronica's eyes widened with interest. 'Did she snitch on you?'

'Yes, when we were training.' Sylvia scowled. 'More than once. She acts all sweetness and light, but underneath, she's as sly as a fox. Made out several times to the senior nurses that I was up to no good when I was too bloody busy trying to get my qualification to be up to no good.'

'Maybe she's jealous of you,' Veronica mused. 'Or maybe she even likes you.'

Sylvia sniffed. 'What are we, kids in the playground? She'll be pulling my hair next in the hope I chase her.'

Freda laughed. 'Oh, leave her be. Kathy has no reason to be bothered by us. She needs to keep her concentration on what she's doing, the same as the rest of us. One wrong move and Sister Dyer will come down like a tonne of bricks on any of us.'

'Hmm, I'm not so sure she would where Kathy Scott is concerned.' Sylvia looked around Freda at Veronica and her concern about whether she had done the right thing in pressuring her new friends to come to the pub deepened. Veronica looked far too pale, her lips pulled tightly together. Sylvia forced joviality into her voice. 'You alright, V?'

Veronica visibly jumped as she snapped her eyes to Sylvia's, her smile far too immediate to be genuine. ''Course. You?'

Sylvia raised her eyebrows. 'When am I not all right? I'm looking forward to this. It will be good for the three of us to have some social time away from the hospital.'

'I agree,' said Freda with a nod. 'You two have been my saving grace since we came onto the ward and I...' She looked at Sylvia and then Veronica and gave a tentative smile. 'I'd like to think of us as friends. I'd be as pleased as punch if you two felt the same.'

Sylvia grinned, entirely touched by Freda's unusual hesitancy and grateful to her, too. 'Well, I for one absolutely do. It's not an everyday occurrence that women offer me the hand of friendship, but I feel as though us three clicked from the start. What with Sister Dyer on our backs, working on the ward, driving back and forth on the country transfers...' She grinned. 'We are well and truly side by side in this job and that makes me very happy. What do you say, V?'

Veronica flashed what Sylvia surmised to be her first genuine smile since they'd left the hospital, her eyes shining with unshed tears. 'I'd like us to be friends more than I can say. Truly.'

Sylvia's heart twisted with caring for Veronica, a girl who seemed so lovely and sweet one minute and then distant and troubled the next. Vulnerable. That's how she'd sum up her new friend.

'Good, then...' She hitched her handbag onto her shoulder and pushed her hands into the crook of her friends' elbows, tugging them close. 'From this moment forward, we are friends looking out for each other, supporting each other and joining forces against the likes of Kathy Scott when necessary!'

'Sylvia!' Freda laughed. 'Leave the girl alone, will you?'

'I'm telling you. The truth will out about that one sooner or later. Mark my words.'

Veronica sighed as they continued to walk down through the long central street that ran through the centre of Bath. 'I have to agree with Sylvia, Freda.'

'Ah-ha!' Sylvia grinned. 'Pray tell your umbrage with Nurse Scott, dear V.'

'Well...' Veronica grimaced. 'I have overheard her talking about you – or us – at least half a dozen times since we've been on the ward. And Nurse Taylor told me that Kathy said that the three of us need to be watched, and anything she sees us doing that doesn't appear up to standard, Nurse Taylor was to report it to Sister.'

Sylvia stared at her in disbelief, her distrust of Kathy Scott multiplying. 'I knew it. Well, that seals the deal. I suggest we keep our distance and make sure we're on our best behaviour whenever Nurse Scott is anywhere near any of us.'

'But...' Freda frowned. 'We hardly know her. Don't you think it's a bit soon to assume she's bad through and through? She always seemed friendly with other nurses in training, although I never spoke to her myself.'

Sylvia bristled, knowing only too well what women of Kathy's ilk could be like. 'As I've said before, Freda, you have a good nature. Don't let yourself be fooled by the likes of Kathy Scott. Keep your guard up for the time being. The truth of her will out in the end.'

'But don't you think we should give her the benefit of the doubt for a while longer? I mean, if she does something to specifically upset one of us, that's different. But for now, I'm not going to jump to any foregone conclusions.'

Defensiveness burned hot in Sylvia's chest as she fought not to respond. It was clear Freda had never been on the receiving end of judgement about the way she looked, dressed... who her bloody mother was. She glanced at Veronica, and she shrugged. Possibly an indication she agreed with Freda.

Sylvia dropped her tense shoulders and blew out a breath. 'Come on, let's step up our pace, it's starting to rain.'

She led them down one of Bath's many cobbled side streets that would eventually lead to a small friendly pub she knew would be just the ticket for what she suspected was Freda and Veronica's first venture inside a pub. She smiled and temporarily buried her irritation with Kathy Scott. For this evening, she would celebrate having found two kind, generous and hardworking friends.

11

VERONICA

Veronica could barely hear Sylvia and Freda's conversation as they walked alongside her through Bath's dark backstreets towards whichever pub Sylvia had decided they would visit. It was gone eight o'clock on this October evening, and Veronica tugged up the collar of her jacket, her nervousness showing in the way her fingers ever-so-slightly trembled. The only reason she had agreed to this excursion was because of the way Freda had turned her pleading eyes on her earlier that afternoon.

It had been clear Freda was battling with whether or not to go to the pub and almost certainly would have refused if Veronica had also not agreed to go. But she wanted Freda to do what she really wished to do and if that meant Veronica stepped up beside her in comradeship, so be it. She sensed an inner fire in her new friend. A longing for more. Unlike her, who was happy to remain small and inconspicuous. She had accepted long ago that the haunting shadow of one particular harrowing afternoon would forever shroud her, keep her unremarkable in every way. She exhaled a shaky breath and prayed Sylvia continued to lead them in this direction. Each step they walked brought Veronica a step closer to her home address, so if – when – she needed to get away from the pub, she could do so amid familiar streets.

Trepidation curled through her stomach. There would be countless untold dangers at the pub. So many men. Her heart began to thump in her ears and Veronica fought to breathe deep. Why in heaven's name had she agreed to this? A burst of Sylvia's infectious laughter broke through Veronica's thoughts, and she jumped, the hammering of her heart suddenly overwhelming. 'I can't do this.'

'What?'

'What?'

She stopped. Had she said that out loud? 'I... um... just remembered I'm supposed to be somewhere else tonight.'

'Where?' Sylvia frowned. 'You never said anything this afternoon, or the whole time we were walking here.'

Veronica slid her gaze to Freda, the confusion in her blue eyes easier to handle than the potent suspicion in Sylvia's. 'I'm sorry, Freda. Go with Sylvia. Have fun. I'll come along next time.' She squeezed her hand. 'I'm sorry. Both of you.'

'But—'

'V, wait,' Sylvia said. 'Where are you going?'

Veronica hurried away and didn't look back. She turned into the closest street and out of her friends' sight. She had thought she could go out with them tonight. Had thought herself strong enough to start tentatively venturing out of her isolation, her loneliness. That she might be near being able to trust her new friends – trust herself – that she would not spend the rest of her life hiding. Sylvia's confidence and humour and Freda's quiet strength and kindness had begun to break down her self-imposed boundaries. Yet, the fear was still there, lingering inside her like a bruise. Or a stark and painful warning.

Every pub, club or coffee house they'd passed on the way to

their impromptu night out had pressed in on Veronica until her panic began to escalate to an uncontainable climax. Men, young and old, dirty and halfway presentable, had stood on the pavement outside every pub, tankards in their hands as they laughed and jostled one another. She had sneaked glances through the pub windows as she passed and saw male silhouettes laughing and drunkenly walking about like puppets with missing strings. She had not seen a single woman like her, Sylvia or Freda. Instead, she had seen good-time girls and older women with what she assumed to be glasses of gin in hand. Not that she was judging. There was a war on, damn it. Everyone, women included, was entitled to do what the hell they wanted, but for her, drinking and chatting in pubs was a step too far. For her, it was pretty much guaranteed to invite trouble. A stupid decision that she would regret.

But God, how she longed to be with her friends...

Tears burned the back of her eyes and slipped onto her cheeks. She angrily swiped at them. She wanted to be all Sylvia and Freda assumed her to be. Freda had once called her mysterious. Sylvia referred to her as enigmatic. Veronica smiled wryly. Oh, how little they knew her. She was a coward. Nothing more, nothing less.

Deep in her heart, she knew Sylvia would never expose her or Freda to trouble, and now she was missing out on the possibility of a fun couple of hours. Why? Because she was a fool who kept living the same life day-in, day-out, terrified of feeling a man's callused, hard, grasping, clawing hands on her again.

'Aye, aye! Hello, darlin'.'

A pathetic squeak passed over Veronica's lips as she came face to face with two men, their feverish gazes burning into her... through her.

'Hey, no need to look like we're bad 'uns, love. We're only passing the time of day with ya.'

Trembling from head to toe, Veronica brushed around the smaller of the two and picked up her pace, their laughter ringing in her ears. She had to get home. She had to be safe with the door locked and the curtains drawn. Why was she even out at night? Once again, her judgement had proven lacking. First, she'd made the mistake of agreeing to go out, and then she'd made the even bigger mistake of changing her mind and finding herself alone and open to abuse on the streets of Bath. Streets that were made all the more eerie and threatening by the complete darkness of the blackout every night. What in God's name had she been thinking? She hadn't been thinking, she'd been reacting. Just as she always did.

It wasn't until she was a couple of streets from home that Veronica's heart slowed and her breathing regulated. All was well. She was disappointed in herself – ashamed, even – but the next time Sylvia asked her out – *please let there be a next time* – she would not falter. She would trust her friends and her judgement, but for tonight…

'Well, this is an unexpected pleasure.'

The smell of stale sweat masked with cheap cologne assaulted her nostrils, and Veronica stopped. She looked up and his icy blue stare froze the blood in her veins. The man who had changed her life forever – the man who had raped her, stolen her virginity and hurt her – grinned, the gap in the bottom row of his teeth once again consuming her entire focus as she tried not to think or feel. She knew that looking into his eyes made everything he might say and do so much worse.

'Cat got your tongue, Miss Veronica?' He sniggered at his own humour and ran his callused finger along her jaw. 'You'd better get home. Won't do to set your ma to worrying, will it? How is she, by the way? Must be difficult for the pair of you without a man around the house. My Marlene and the kiddies would be lost without me, I'm sure. They'd be worried about all and sundry coming into the house. Got to be careful who you open the door to these days, haven't you?'

Hatred and anger rolled into a tight, hot ball in the centre of Veronica's chest and she slowly lifted her gaze to his.

'Ah, there's those pretty emerald eyes!' His eyes glinted with undisguised lust. 'You have such pretty eyes, Veronica. Such pretty everything.'

Perspiration burst along her hairline, her hands turning clammy. 'I'd better get home, Mr Riley.'

'Oh, indeed, indeed.' He stepped back and theatrically swept his arm out to the side, gesturing for her to pass him. 'You give my regards to your ma, won't you?'

'Of course.'

'That's a good girl.'

Veronica swallowed the bitter sickness that rose in her throat and quickly walked along the street, wishing she was in her uniform and cape rather than a skirt and heels. If anything should happen, it would be her own fault.

'Night night, love.'

Her breath caught at Mr Riley's shout behind her, and she pressed her hand to her mouth, trapping the scream that built inside her throat. It was over. It would never happen again. It couldn't. She was older now. Wiser. Yet, as she stood at her front door, her key in her hand, she shook so violently, she couldn't fit it into the lock.

The door suddenly swung open, and her mother stood on the threshold, glaring. 'What in heaven's name are you doing? Do I have to teach you how to use a key on top of everything else?' She turned back into the house. 'Heavens above, Veronica, you're always as jumpy as an alley cat. Where have you been? I finished my shift at the hospital hours ago and you told me you would be done by seven.'

'I was.'

'Well, where have you been then?' Her mother gave a dismissive wave. 'Don't answer that. Sometimes it's best a mother not ask too many questions. Or so I've been told. Your tea is in the oven. I'll be in the living room listening to my programme.'

Veronica shut the door and threw the latch and key chain into place before dropping her forehead against the wood, the sound of her mother arguing with whoever was talking on the wireless slowly thawing the ice in her heart. She was safe once more. She was home. But it was here, in this house, that her nightmare had taken place and where she feared it would stay forever.

12

FREDA

Carrying a pail of bloodied bandages destined for the bin, Freda walked towards the ward entrance just as Sister Dyer came through the swinging doors, her cheeks mottled and her gaze stern. Freda tried to avoid eye contact with her and bowed her head. She was not in the mood for the sister's nit-picking.

'Ah, Nurse Parkes, come with me.' She waved her hand at the pail of bandages. 'Quickly now, find someone else to deal with that. You are needed in surgery.'

'Surgery?' Freda's heart picked up speed. 'Me?'

'Yes, you,' Sister Dyer snapped. 'Do you want this opportunity to do more than what you are doing on the ward or not? Come along. Chop chop.'

Freda was quick to notice the glint of triumph in the sister's eyes. Well, she had another thing coming if she thought putting Freda in an operating theatre would break her. She pulled back her shoulders and looked around. Spotting Kathy Scott coming along the corridor, Freda made a beeline for her.

'Kathy, could you take these to be binned?' She thrust the pail into the other nurse's hands, adrenaline pumping through her blood. 'I've been called to theatre.'

'Theatre?' Kathy grimaced and took the pail. 'Rather you than me.'

Not wanting to contemplate what Kathy might or might not know about the arena she was about to enter, Freda turned and practically ran back to where Sister Dyer waited. 'Come along, Parkes. Honestly.'

'Sorry, Sister.'

Half afraid and half ecstatic to do something so entirely different, Freda's mind whirled with what ifs and maybes as she strode beside the sister along one corridor after the next until they arrived at one of the four operating theatres at the hospital.

Sister Dyer pushed open the door. 'I have Nurse Parkes for you, Mr Martin.'

The room was bathed in muted light except for the operating table itself, which was brightly lit, starkly illuminating the surgeon standing over a patient who lay on his back, blood completely drenching one leg and the man's torso scarlet red. There was so much blood Freda had no idea where it was coming from or where the poor man had suffered injury.

'Very good, thank you, Sister.' The surgeon's steel-grey eyes met Freda's over the top of his surgical mask. 'Get yourself washed up and masked, Nurse Parkes. I need use of your hands as soon as possible.'

'Yes, sir.'

'Parkes is one of my best-performing nurses,' Sister Dyer said. 'I am sure she will prove a perfect temporary help to you.' She prodded Freda in the back with her finger. 'Go on now, Nurse, wash your hands in the side room over there. Gowns, masks and gloves are on the shelves.'

Sister Dyer gave a firm nod to Mr Martin and left the theatre as

Freda made for the small room adjacent to the theatre. Sister Dyer considered her one of her best-performing nurses? Goodness. God only knew how she treated her lesser performing nurses if that was true!

By the time Freda had finished washing her hands and returned to the operating table, the tension in the theatre had escalated.

'Right, stand here, Parkes,' Mr Martin barked, strands of dark grey hair peeping from beneath his cap. 'I want your hands splayed over this part of the leg where I am indicating. Good, good. Now, press down and hold steady. I hope you're not in any way averse to the sight of blood, tissue or bone, Parkes. Otherwise, this is not your lucky day.'

Freda caught the eye of the female anaesthetist who gave her an encouraging nod and then turned away, intensely concentrating on her work at an intravenous drip and the other complicated machines next to her. A female anaesthetist! Who knew such a thing existed? The war was making roles for women that never could have been imagined just a few short years ago, and seeing a female colleague in such a responsible position sent a rush of empowerment through Freda. A horrible gurgling came from the table and she quickly focused her attention on the patient, just as a stomach-turning snap cracked through the room, followed by something indiscernible before fresh blood poured from the open wound in the patient's leg and flowed over her hands. She kept focused, doing everything Mr Martin asked of her, her heart pounding as she immersed herself in what was becoming the most exhilarating moment of her life.

Two hours passed before, at long last, Mr Martin stepped back and gave a satisfied nod. Freda instinctively blew out a breath, taking his cue that the worst of the procedure was over.

'Are you happy to stitch up, Parkes? I'm pleased with how

things went. Now we just wait to see how this chap does overnight.' The surgeon removed his mask and smiled at her. His gaze was kind, but his tiredness was evident in the lines around his eyes and the dark smudges beneath. 'I'd like Mr Kelly to be your responsibility on the ward, if that's all right?'

'Of course.' Pride swelled inside her. 'I want to see him through this, sir.'

'Very good. Well...' Mr Martin exhaled heavily. 'You did a fine job today. I may have need of you or one of the other nurses on the ward again tomorrow. Things are certainly getting busier. But for now, I'll leave you to it.'

He left the theatre, and the anaesthetist who hadn't spoken a word throughout the entire surgery stood and began doing whatever needed to be done with the machines she was in charge of. Concluding that there would be no conversation between them, Freda walked to the cupboards along one wall of the theatre and, after a quick search, located a suture kit so that she could close Mr Kelly's wound.

She returned to the table and set to work. After a few minutes, the anaesthetist broke their companionable silence.

'I'm Betty,' she said. 'Betty Wilson.'

'Freda.' Freda smiled, not taking her eyes from her stitching lest she mess it up. 'Pleased to meet you.'

'You handled yourself really well today after being thrown in the deep end like that.' Betty walked to a metal chest of drawers on wheels and opened one of the drawers. 'As things get busier around here, I think we're all going to be expected to think on our feet a bit more.'

'I agree.' Freda sighed as she clipped the last stitch. 'But as long as we keep in mind what our servicemen and women are having to do, we'll do well enough, I'm sure.'

'Have you got someone out there? On the frontlines?'

Freda straightened, her heart suddenly heavy with the loss of her brother and not knowing where her other brother, James, was. 'Yes. My brother. At least, I hope he's still alive. He's missing in action.' She looked at Betty properly for the first time and the sympathy in her eyes was unmistakable. Not wanting to deepen it by admitting the death of her other brother, Freda purposefully changed the subject. 'I have to say, it is very impressive what you are doing here. Have you trained as an anaesthetist recently? I had no idea women did the job you're doing.'

Betty smiled wryly. 'You can be pretty sure there aren't many of us, but once the bombing started in Bristol close on two years ago, Mr Martin chose to take me from the ward and have a male colleague of his train me up before he left to assist at one of the temporary airfield hospitals. Mr Martin is a wonderful man to work for, forward-thinking and has the patience of a saint. If you or any of the nurses are interested in surgery, it's to him you should look to further those aspirations.'

'Wow, that's good to know. He seems extraordinarily hard-working.'

'Oh, he is. And a fine surgeon. This war and playing our part in it deeply matters to him and if we can serve our country and its people better by adding female doctors, surgeons and anaes-thetists to our resources, he'll do all he can to make that happen.'

Freda smiled, excitement knotting her stomach. Betty's clear admiration for Mr Martin was palpable and reignited Freda's own passion to do more for the war effort. 'Well, let's hope we get more men thinking the same way during and even after the war. God knows there must be thousands of women up and down the country who will find the idea of their lives being nothing more than home and hearth deplorable once this war is finally over.' Freda blew out a breath. 'Right then, I'll get this lot packed away,' she said, gathering the kit and closing it. 'And make sure I thoroughly wash up before I return to the ward or Sister will be on my back again.'

Betty raised her eyebrows. 'Bit of a dragon, is she?'

'She can be. Other times not so much.' Freda walked to the storage cabinet. 'But I do think she suspects that I don't belong here. Can't blame her. I sometimes think the same.'

'You do?'

Freda looked away. What in God's name was she telling her that for? She didn't know Betty from Adam. She could easily tell tales on her to Sister Dyer, and then before she knew it, she would be doing nothing more than making beds and emptying bed pans as punishment for her ingratitude for the rest of the month.

She forced a smile. 'I'm only joking. Nursing is what I am trained to do and while this war is on, that is what I'll do.'

Betty's hazel eyes were bright with interest. 'And after the war?'

'I can't find a reason to think about the end of the war the way things are going. Can you?'

'No, I suppose not.'

They finished clearing up, then washed at the sinks before leaving the theatre together. As they walked along the corridor, Freda heading to the ward and Betty towards the hospital exit, Veronica approached carrying a stack of bed pans.

'Hey, you.' She smiled at Freda. 'Where have you been all afternoon?'

'I'll leave you to it, Freda,' Betty said. 'Nice to meet you.'

'You too. Have a good night.'

'Well?' Veronica said, habitual concern in her eyes. 'Where have you been?'

Freda grinned. 'Theatre.'

'Theatre?' Veronica's eyebrows shot to her hairline. 'You were involved in an operation?'

'Yep, and it seems any one of us will be soon enough, if what the surgeon said is anything to go by.'

'Well, I can't see Sister asking me to assist in any surgeries. She doesn't seem to have much faith in me past working on the ward and going on any necessary trips to the rural hospitals.'

'I wouldn't be so sure. She actually told the surgeon I was one of her best-performing nurses.'

Veronica's eyes widened. 'She did?'

'Yes, so maybe there is more to Sister Dyer than what she lets us see.'

'Hmm. Maybe.' Veronica blinked and her face lit with a smile, her green eyes shining. 'So, did you like working in theatre?'

'I did, but not enough that I'll be hankering to go back.' Freda sighed, her mind drifting to her writing ambitions. 'I'd much prefer to be able to talk to the patients who are conscious. A much better route to finding out what is really happening in this war, don't you think? I'd better get back before Sister comes looking for me.'

'And I'd better get on with delivering these.' Veronica held the pans aloft. 'See you later.'

As her friend hurried along the corridor, Freda stared blindly ahead. The intense atmosphere, the efficiency and speed, the precision and care when she'd been in theatre had given her a shift in purpose. Even though surgery was not where she wanted to work, it had shown her she was prepared for more intense exposure to the realities of war than nursing provided. She smiled and headed for the ward. She could not wait to get home and write up everything that had happened today, every emotion she had felt and every skill she had executed. She and the other nurses, surgeons and hospital staff might be on the home front, but somehow that blurred with the frontlines in a hundred ways.

There were already rumours flying around that two nurses on

another ward had quit, despite starting the same time as her, Freda and Sylvia just weeks before. Maybe they had found themselves unable to hack the pressure of the increasing stress on the ward, but for Freda she felt she hadn't even got her hands dirty yet. She could not waste her life adhering to her mother's well-meant but wholly domestic plans for her and Dorothy. She was made of tougher stuff than to serve and pander to a husband, see to a brood of kids and cook something – to quote her mother – 'delectable' every night.

But how was she to escape? Not just the hospital, but the guaranteed pain she would put on her already suffering mother if she veered from her expectations.

I'm sorry, Mum, but nursing is not it for me. Not by a long shot.

13

SYLVIA

Dusk was falling as Sylvia marched home, more than ready for a good and ugly set-to with her mother if she as much as looked at her in the wrong way. What a day it had been, and the bloody nerve of Kathy Scott getting all uppity and bossing her around the ward as though she owned the place! She'd even insinuated she'd been told by Sister to keep tabs on her, Freda and Veronica. Well, that had been the last straw.

'And I'm glad I told her she can do what the hell she likes,' Sylvia muttered, her arms swinging at her sides. 'Because if she upsets one of my friends on my watch, God help her.'

Sylvia blinked back the tears that pricked her eyes and fought to maintain her irritation rather than succumb to the horrible insecurity twisting inside her. Her inability to trust all women like she was coming to trust Freda and Veronica only proved what she knew to be true. That she wasn't good enough, worthy enough, for the likes of Kathy Scott or a hundred other women equally as forthright and confident enough to call her out. Sylvia swallowed against the lump in her throat. If she was truly destined to end up like her mother, as so many people from her past and present –

including ex-boyfriends and her stupid ex-fiancé – had presumed, she would have left Kathy a quivering mess with just a few choice words.

But she hadn't. Kathy had had the last word and it had been Sylvia who walked away. Albeit with her chin held high and her backside swaying.

She reached her front door and angrily swiped at her cheeks before pushing her key into the lock.

She took a deep breath and entered the house. 'I'm home.'

'In here,' her mother called out.

Sylvia entered the living room to find her mother standing in front of the mirror above the fireplace, putting on a set of fake gold clip-on earrings, a cigarette bouncing between her bright red lips. 'I've got to get to the pub. If you're hungry, you'll have to sort yourself out.'

Sylvia collapsed onto the settee and blew out a heavy breath. 'As opposed to you having been slaving over making a cottage pie from scratch and keeping it warm for me in the oven?'

'Oh, look, Miss Smart Mouth has returned from the wilderness.' Her mother finished with her earrings and spun around, snatching her handbag from the chair beside her. 'I don't know why you've got to act so hard done by all the time, my girl. You've got a roof over your head, which is more than thousands of others can say right now. Eat or don't eat, ain't no skin off my nose.'

Sylvia briefly closed her eyes, self-loathing crawling over her once again, before she opened them. 'Sorry. I'm being a cow.'

Her mother studied her. 'Bad day?'

'You could say that.'

The silence stretched, before her mother shrugged. 'Well, you know what I always say.'

'What?'

Her mother winked. 'Whether king or cad, sod 'em.'

She flounced from the room, leaving behind a blend of cheap perfume and cigarette smoke. Sylvia closed her eyes again and concentrated on breathing through her nose and out of her mouth, having remembered something in the newspaper last week about ways to calm yourself during a bombing, or upon receiving devastating news about a loved one. She had neither to worry about, and instead was feeling ridiculously sorry for herself.

'Get a grip,' she muttered and pushed to her feet. 'You're twenty-three, not bloody three.'

She left the living room and put her handbag on the stairs to remove her shoes in favour of her slippers.

Her mother came out of the kitchen and whipped her coat from the hook on the hallway wall. 'Right, I'm off,' she said, shrugging it on and buttoning it. 'Look...' Her voice softened a little. 'Why don't you pop down the road and get yourself some chips? Better than cooking for yourself this time of the evening, eh?'

A little of Sylvia's bitterness dissolved. For all her mother's faults and the tension that hovered between them more often than not, Sylvia rarely had any real reason to doubt their love for one another.

She sighed and halted untying her shoelaces. 'Maybe you're right. I'll walk out with you.'

'I bumped into Enid across the road on the way home from the shops this morning...'

The slow, languid lilt in her mother's tone alerted Sylvia that any maternal concern was over and had now turned to something meant to antagonise her.

Sylvia stood and hitched the strap of her handbag onto her shoulder. 'And?'

'And she reckons you've been spending a bit of time with the eldest Howard boy.' Her mother pinned her with an unwavering stare. 'I told her she must be mistaken.'

'Did you?'

''Course. I said there's no way my Sylv would risk her reputation—'

'My reputation?' Sylvia huffed a laugh. 'Unfortunately, you'd set my reputation in stone before my boobs came in.'

Her mother glared. 'Is that so?'

Sylvia shrugged.

'Then Enid bloody Ascot is right, is she? You're walking out with one of those who ain't the same as us regardless of all and sundry who might see you?'

Anger pulsed at Sylvia's temple. 'The Howards aren't the same? Why? Because they're black?'

'Why else?'

'Give me strength. Just stop talking, Mum. Please.'

'Hearing me say that upsets you, does it?' Her mother's mouth twisted into a sneer and she pointed her finger. 'Well, that's nothing to what others will say when they see you with him. What in God's name do you think you're doing messing about with anyone from that family, my girl? It will lead to nothing but trouble.'

'And how do you work that out?'

'That lot haven't got the same ways as us.'

Sylvia clenched her teeth and tipped her head back to look at the hallway's tobacco-stained ceiling. 'That lot? For the love of God, Mum.' She dropped her chin and glared. 'I advise you to get a grip on that vicious tongue of yours before I do it for you.'

'Are you threatening me, girl?'

'I won't stand here listening to you spewing bloody nonsense that draws lines between people when I work my backside off day and night helping men and women of every colour. People are people, Mum. No one is any different than anyone else.'

Her mother snorted. 'Listen to you. Don't waste your time

defending him, sweetheart. That boy is sniffing around to see what he can get from you before he kicks you away like all the others did... your fiancé included.'

'Do you know what, Mum?' Sylvia stepped around her and reached for the door before turning and locking eyes with her mother. 'Why don't you bugger off to work and leave me in peace?'

She yanked the door open.

Jesse Howard stood on her doorstep, his knuckles raised to knock on the door.

'Oh, perfect,' Sylvia muttered before slapping on a wide smile. 'Jesse. As I live and breathe.'

His gaze burned into her as he slowly lowered his hand, those intense dark eyes searing through her and making her want to grab his shirt and pull him forward so she could crush her lips to his. It had been one hell of a crappy day so she might as well finish it with a bang.

Her mother's cackle rippled between them and Sylvia spun around, her smile straining. 'Bye bye then, Mum. See you tomorrow.'

'What do you want?' her mother snapped at Jesse. 'I think your mother made it perfectly clear what she thinks of the rest of us in the street. Go on. Get away from my door. My daughter doesn't need your fun and games. Get back to where you were born, why don't you?'

Jesse Howard held her gaze. 'I was born in England, ma'am.'

'So you say.'

'Mum!' Sylvia cried. 'Knock it off.'

'What?' Her mother shrugged. 'I'm only saying what everyone else on Castle Street is thinking.'

'For the love of God, just go, will you?' Sylvia gripped her mother's elbow, urging her outside as Jesse stepped aside, his eyes fixed on her mother. Clearly, he had no intention of going anywhere... for the time being, anyway.

'Go, Mum. You're going to be late for work.'

Her mother didn't even look at Sylvia, but continued to glare at Jesse before giving an inelegant sniff and marching away, her chin high and her ample backside swinging beneath the hem of the fourth-hand mink jacket that Sylvia swore her mother would insist on being buried in.

'I'm so sorry.' She faced Jesse, her heart skipping treacherously at the way he stared at her. Pure, undisguised passion burned in his dark, dark eyes. A passion that was as attractive as it was unnerving. 'My mother is...' She shook her head, embarrassment and shame making her feel sick even as she forced a sassy smile. 'Anyway, what can I do for you? Another sibling suffering from sore tonsils?'

His eyes glittered with soft amusement as he stepped forward and put his hand high on the doorframe. 'Are you making fun of my worry over my kid brother, Nurse Roberts?' Before she could answer, he appraised her from head to toe and gave a low whistle. 'Seriously. It doesn't matter what you're wearing...'

Sylvia stood straighter but couldn't help appreciating his admiration considering she was still in her plain old uniform. 'Excuse me?'

'You're a knockout, Sylvia, and I don't mind telling you.'

'Is that so?'

'Yep.'

Their eyes locked and the seconds passed with each beat of Sylvia's heart. Warnings screamed in her head. *Don't go there! He'll bring you more trouble than tenderness! He's black, you're white, that will only lead to eternal harassment...* Yet...

She arched her eyebrow, purposely lingering her gaze at his

mouth before slowly raising her eyes to his. 'Well then, if that's the case, I suggest you take me out to dinner.'

His smile was slow and as tempting as hell. 'Now?'

'Well, not right this minute. A girl doesn't like to sit in a fancy restaurant in her work uniform. Even a man like you should understand that.'

'A man like me?' His smile faltered and the guardedness she'd seen in his eyes before flashed again. 'What's that supposed to mean?'

Defences rising, Sylvia held his gaze. 'It means: a man who is old enough and handsome enough to know what women do and don't like should know better. Now, I suggest you get yourself back home and wash up. Knock for me in half an hour or so and I'll be ready with bells on.'

'With bells on, huh?' He grinned and pushed away from the door. 'Sounds pretty fabulous to me. However…' He glanced at his house, his jaw tightening. 'I'll meet you at the end of the street.'

Sylvia laughed. 'Are you serious?'

'Trust me,' he said, walking backwards away from the door. 'It's easier this way.'

Her smile vanished as the warnings in her head grew louder. 'Is this about your mother?'

He winked. 'Half an hour.'

Her stomach flip-flopped.

For the love of God, Sylvia, don't you dare go falling for the man's charm. We don't want to go down that road again, do we?

14

VERONICA

Veronica pulled her cape tighter around her shoulders and waited at the open back doors of the ambulance as the patient she was accompanying to one of the rural hospitals was settled comfortably and safely onboard. The ambulance driver and a male porter carefully manoeuvred the gurney into place and the sound of the bolts being locked echoed from inside. The patient was an RAF pilot who had suffered horrendous burns from head to toe but was now well into the healing process and needed to be somewhere quiet to convalesce. She assumed they must be headed for one of the small community hospitals outside of Bath, but couldn't be sure as she'd yet to be given specifics by Sister Dyer.

Glancing towards the hospital doors behind her, Veronica frowned. Not only was the sister nowhere to be seen, but there was also no sign of Sylvia either. Sister had promised her that Sylvia would accompany her this evening as Freda had come with her the last three times. As Sister Dyer was still happy that the three of them alternated these journeys, it seemed she also appreciated how important it was that the nurses knew each other's ways well if optimum patient care was to be maintained.

'All safely onboard, Nurse. Shall we get going?'

As the porter brushed past her to return to his duties inside, Veronica turned to the ambulance driver and forced a smile. 'I'm just waiting for Nurse Roberts. Why don't you go ahead and get into the ambulance? You stand out here any longer and you'll be soaked to the skin.'

The older man tapped his fingers to his forehead in a salute. 'Right you are.'

Swift footsteps behind her turned Veronica's head towards the doors a second time. Sister Dyer approached, alone and carrying no hint in her harried expression that Sylvia would be joining her anytime soon.

'Are you all set to head off, Nurse Parkes?' she asked, her cheeks flushed pink. 'It's gone six o'clock, you should have been on your way by now. The driver has my instructions.'

'I'm waiting for Nurse Roberts.' A horrible foreboding knotted in Veronica's stomach. 'You said she would be accompanying me tonight?'

'Ah, yes. There's been a change of plan.' The sister gave a tight smile. 'You will be perfectly all right with the driver.'

Veronica stared as a wave of nausea swept through her. 'Alone?'

'Well, yes. Oh, don't look so entirely lost, Nurse.' Sister Dyer frowned and shooed Veronica towards the back of the ambulance. 'The patient – Captain Morley – is stable and just needs to convalesce. There is nothing about this transfer that you are not perfectly capable of overseeing on your own. Now...' She nodded in the direction of the ambulance. 'Off you go. The sooner you leave, the sooner you'll be back. We are expecting another seven patients from Bristol this evening. We do not have time to waste.'

Veronica's pulse beat hard and perspiration broke cold on her forehead. 'I'm really not comfortable...'

'Climb aboard, Campbell. Now.' The sister glared, the dark blonde curls peeping from under her cap bobbing with the force of her annoyance. 'The captain is hardly going to hurt you, and your driver, Mr Allen, is father to three girls.'

'But that doesn't mean—'

'Be sensible, Nurse,' the sister snapped. 'There is a war on and fuss over propriety and nonsense is almost certainly over for the time being.'

Veronica's legs shook as she climbed aboard and slid unsteadily onto the seat alongside a sleeping Captain Morley. Nurse Dyer slammed the door and the clang of metal reverberated through Veronica's entire body.

'Here we go then, Nurse,' the driver said cheerfully from the front seat. 'You all set?'

Veronica barely managed to nod as she kept her gaze on Captain Morley, his face relaxed in slumber, his closed eyelids flickering with his dreams. She wondered what he dreamed of and wished she could disappear into blessed sleep too and not have to face what was going to be one of the hardest journeys of her life. She turned and stared at the back of Mr Allen's head, her heart pounding.

She was alone, driving from the city into the country. There would be a myriad of long, deserted lanes and blacked-out streets. He could stop the van whenever he chose to, pull over, drag her from the back and... Veronica closed her eyes but failed to stop her tears escaping. Mr Riley – her rapist – was a father, too. She'd thought him harmless, let him into her home, made him a cup of tea and given him a slice of cake. They'd chatted at the kitchen table, laughed at something on the wireless. His smile wide, his gaze alight with friendliness...

And then he'd lunged at her and her entire world had turned on an axis, never to regain equilibrium again.

Veronica's breaths rasped against her throat and she squeezed her eyes tightly shut, her fingers curled around the edges of her seat.

He'd tackled her to the ground, ripped her tights, and shoved her skirt high onto her hips, his hand over her mouth and the light in his eyes no longer friendly but manic, wild with lust. And then... then... a sharp pain had shot through her most intimate place to the pit of her stomach as he took what he wanted.

Veronica sucked in a breath and pressed her fist against her mouth to trap her cry as, once again, she experienced every second of her innocence being ripped from her by a man who still lived with his wife and three daughters just along the street from her house...

'You all right back there, Nurse?'

Veronica snapped her eyes open.

In the darkness, Mr Allen appeared to be staring ahead, but somehow she felt his gaze on her through the rear-view mirror.

She swiped at her cheeks and lifted her chin, forced her shaking shoulders back. 'I'm fine, thank you.'

'Only it can't be much fun sitting back there with a sleeping patient.'

'I'm not here to have fun.'

'I know but while he's getting some shut eye...'

His voice trailed off, insinuation hanging dark and dangerous in the air. Sickness coated Veronica's throat and she gripped the seat harder. 'I need to stay right here for the entirety of the journey, Mr Allen. I'm a nurse and my duty is to devote myself to the captain's care.'

Drawing in a strengthening breath, Veronica slowly released it, pleased that her voice had sounded so calm. A few seconds passed in silence, but she could sense the cogs in Mr Allen's brain turning and she stared hard at the captain, willing him to wake up so she might attend to him. Should she pretend he'd awoken? Perhaps even accidentally jolt him awake?

'Why don't you come and sit up the front with me, eh?' Mr Allen asked. 'Just for a little while. I promise you'll have a lot more fun than you are right now.'

'Please…' Veronica squeezed her eyes tightly shut. 'Just concentrate on the road and leave me be.'

'Oh, come on, darling. Everyone knows you young nurses like to let loose now and then. All I'm asking for is a bit of company on a wet and lonely drive.'

The first whispers of anger seeped into Veronica's blood, diluting a little of her fear, and she snapped her eyes open. Captain Morley stared at her, his eyes canny and dark with anger. His fingers gently touched hers, and he slowly shook his head, reassuring her. Veronica stared, unsure what to do or say.

She was with not one, but two men.

Alone in an ambulance.

'She won't be going anywhere near you, Driver,' the captain said loudly and clearly, his eyes on hers. 'And if you make such a suggestion again, you will give me all the provocation I need to prove that occasionally killing another man is justified. I have killed before and will again if it means protecting this young lady. Now, as she said, concentrate on driving this vehicle safely to our destination while I think about whether or not to report your behaviour to whoever is in charge when we get to the other end.'

Veronica held Captain Morley's gaze as his fingers slipped from hers and he settled his head back on the pillow. 'You're all right, Nurse,' he said quietly. 'Nothing will happen to you. Not on my watch.'

She swallowed. 'Thank you.'

He nodded and closed his eyes.

Veronica did not look anywhere else but at the captain even as the penetrating heat of Mr Allen's glare bore into her from the rear-view mirror. The journey to the community hospital was likely to be the longest of her life.

15

SYLVIA

Sylvia unpinned her cap, then shook out her hair, enjoying the blissful feeling of her long, auburn hair flowing freely over her shoulders. 'My God, why does letting my hair down at the end of the day feel just as good as when I take off my bra?'

'Sylvia!' Freda grinned as she opened her locker in the hospital staff room. 'Some of the things you say would send my mother reaching for the sherry bottle and she doesn't even drink.'

Sylvia screwed up her nose, finding the idea of not enjoying a glass or two of something you fancy thoroughly criminal. 'She doesn't drink?'

'Nope, not even a sip at Christmas time.'

'Wow, then maybe our mothers should meet up and discuss the right and wrong way of living one day soon. The half-cut state of my mother most of the time and a mouth that is so filthy no amount of soap could clean it, compared to your la-di-da mother and the la-di-da life you've told us she wants for herself and you, I reckon they'd get on like a house on fire.'

'Yeah, of course they would.' Freda laughed. 'They're like two peas in a pod, clearly.'

Sylvia continued to gather her things together and then pulled a lipstick from her purse, her smile fading as the horrible foreboding that had been ebbing and flowing through her stomach over the last couple of hours rolled through her again.

She glanced at the wall clock. 'Have you seen Veronica since she headed off for that patient transfer? I thought she would've been back by now. She went hours ago.'

Freda pulled on her cardigan as they readied to leave for the night. 'She got back about twenty minutes ago.'

Relieved, Sylvia dropped her tense shoulders. 'You've seen her?'

'Yes.'

'And she was all right, was she?'

Freda frowned. 'Yes, why?'

'Oh, nothing.' Sylvia gave her lips a quick slick of colour before combing her hair through as she purposefully stared into the mirror on the back of her locker door in a bid to avoid Freda's ever-present astuteness. 'I thought Sister was going to ask me to go with V this afternoon, but she didn't.'

'So, who did then?'

'Who did what?'

'If you didn't go with her,' Freda said, 'and I didn't go with her, then—'

'It was probably Kathy.' Sylvia's uneasiness gave another roll through her stomach. 'I bet they got on perfectly fine and V's insistence it's just us that go with her on the drives will be a thing of the past from now on.'

Sylvia started to hum a tune to fill the ensuing silence.

She could practically hear the cogs in Freda's brain working and was pleased that her friend would soon catch on to why Sylvia had asked questions about Veronica and the transfer. As the weeks wore on, it had begun to bother Sylvia more and more that they had never got to the bottom of why Veronica had wanted Sister's agreement that one or both of her friends always went with her on the ambulance transfers. There had been something not quite right about her reaction that day, something that Sylvia felt deep in her bones that she and Freda should be aware of if they had any chance of being the friends Veronica needed them to be.

'She was perfectly all right,' Freda mused, her eyes glazed in thought. 'She arrived back in the ward and then took off again pretty sharpish, saying she had something to tell the surgeon she helped a week or so ago and would catch up with me tomorrow.'

'I see. So as far as you could tell...'

Footsteps approached the staff room door and then Veronica appeared in the doorway.

Sylvia intensely appraised her friend's face and then, although immensely pleased to see her, turned back to her locker and pulled out her coat and hat. Veronica was as white as a sheet and Sylvia's uneasiness reared again.

'So, the wanderer returns,' Sylvia said, feigning nonchalance as she abruptly faced her friend and lifted her eyebrows. 'Everything all right, V?'

Veronica returned her stare, her gaze wary before she blinked. 'Of course.' Her smile strained. 'Why wouldn't it be?'

Sylvia shrugged. 'I was expecting to come along with you tonight, that's all. It seemed Sister had other ideas. She told me I was needed on the ward. At first I thought she was being spiteful, but we had four pilots arrive from Bristol in a bit of a mess, so I was forced to give her the benefit of the doubt.'

'I see. Well...' Veronica flashed her a brief smile, a distinct nervousness about her as she walked across the small room to her locker. 'No harm done.'

Inexplicable tears pricked the back of Sylvia's eyes and she quickly blinked them away as she closed her locker. Veronica had taken an unfairly large piece of her heart since they'd met, maybe even more than Freda. Freda's confidence and belief in herself grew every day, but the almost palpable vulnerability in Veronica stubbornly remained. It was as though she never really walked anywhere without checking over her shoulder, her eyes seeming to dart here, there and everywhere looking for God-only-knew what.

Sylvia pulled her coat from its hanger. In other words, there was something going on with Veronica that she couldn't work out and that was incredibly frustrating. If she didn't know what she was watching out for, how could she look out for her friend should Veronica need her?

She looked across the room and caught Freda's gaze, widening her eyes and silently asking her what she thought about Veronica's demeanour. Something wasn't right. Freda lifted her shoulders, her brow creased. Veronica might have given them each a smile, but she was far from happy. Her colour and jerky, uncertain movements indicated a nervousness that Sylvia hadn't seen before. She studied Veronica where she sat on one of the chairs, taking off her shoes. Having removed her cap, her dark hair had fallen forward, hiding her face. Sylvia met Freda's concerned gaze and tilted her head towards Veronica, urging Freda to speak up. Sylvia didn't trust herself to execute the gentleness the situation warranted, whereas Freda had a knack of knowing exactly how to coax the best from people, whatever the circumstances.

Freda cleared her throat and hitched her handbag onto her shoulder. 'Did Kathy come with you on the transfer, V? Or was it one of the others?'

'Um... no. I went alone. It was fine.' Veronica continued to focus her attention on her shoes, seemingly tackling an imaginary problem with one of her heels. 'A nurse I didn't know from the hospital came back with me though. She'd had an issue with a transfer earlier in the day and needed to grab a lift back. She was really nice, chatty. We talked about all sorts, and do you know what?' She laughed. 'I forgot to ask her name! How daft is that?'

Questions bit at Sylvia's tongue as Veronica's garbled speech came to an end. It was no good, she couldn't keep shtum. 'Were you all right, V?' she asked. 'Going in the ambulance alone? Only—'

'Ooh.' Veronica abruptly stood, her eyes too bright, too wide. 'Why don't you tell us all about your date with Jesse?'

'I just asked you if you—'

'I told you, it was fine.' Veronica waved dismissively. 'Tell me about your night out! I heard the place he took you was pretty fancy.'

Sylvia narrowed her eyes. Subtly changing a subject clearly wasn't Veronica's forte. She glanced at Freda who shrugged again. Great.

'To use your word of the day...' Sylvia said pointedly. 'It was *fine*. Jesse's a gentleman, I like him, but there will not be anything going on romantically, so you can both stop looking at me that way. Men are off my wish list for the time being and, to put it frankly, long may it stay that way.'

'Really? Only you seem pretty keen on him to me,' Freda said, her eyebrows raised. 'You get this look in your eyes whenever you talk about him.'

'What?' Rare heat warmed Sylvia's cheeks and she huffed a laugh. 'Since when?'

'Since the first time you mentioned him to me.' Freda grinned. 'You know, when you showed me the cake he gave you...'

Sylvia planted her hands on her hips, her defences rising. 'Which his mother made.' Sylvia swallowed against the sudden dryness in her throat. Were the feelings that she was battling so bloody hard out there for all to see anyway? For the love of God. She turned to Veronica, who stood from her seat and grinned too. As much as she was pleased to see a genuine smile from her friend and some colour back in her cheeks, she and Freda were still annoying. 'Like I said, Jesse is nice, but that's it. No romance for me. No, siree.' She walked back to her locker mirror and pinned her hat in place, steadfastly avoiding looking at her friends in the reflection. 'I have one hundred per cent learned the lesson that men are never what they seem. Ever.'

She turned around and grabbed her coat where she'd left it on the arm of the rather worse-for-wear settee, but the silence only continued. She looked up to find Freda still smiling at her. She was about to tell her friend to mind her beeswax but then she noticed Veronica had paled once more.

Sylvia took a step towards her. 'V? What is it?'

'Nothing.' Veronica's fingers slightly trembled as she tucked a stray curl into place. 'You stick to your guns. Do what you want to do. If this Jesse or any other man is not for you then that's your right to say so.'

Once again, Veronica's rapid speech and edginess raised warning signs, but Sylvia merely nodded, knowing that pushing Veronica now would not only be futile, but possibly unkind, too. Further unease tiptoed along Sylvia's spine, as she fought the urge to give Veronica a great big hug. Would that be the right thing to do in that moment? She wasn't so sure.

So, she forced a wide smile and adopted her carefree, never-failed-her persona. 'Exactly!' She laughed. 'Right, coats on? Let's get out of here, shall we, ladies?'

They walked out of the staff room and into the corridor, heading for the hospital exit.

'I know what you're saying, Sylvia,' Freda mused. 'But love is something you can't really control.'

Sylvia rolled her eyes. She should've known Freda wouldn't drop the subject of Jesse. She was like a dog with a bone once a story got in her head. Real or not. 'What in heaven's name are you talking about?'

'You, actually. You're lively, vivacious, fun. I would've thought you, more than anyone, would enjoy every moment of happiness for however long it lasts. We're in the middle of a war. If you're lucky enough to have a man want to court you, a man who makes you smile, why push him away?' Her bright blue eyes were filled with curiosity, but also care. 'Or is there more to this Jesse fella than you're telling us?'

Guilt seared Sylvia's cheeks knowing it wasn't just her losing battle with her feelings for Jesse that stopped her talking to her friends about her date with him. It was also that she had yet to tell them he was black, for fear of their reaction. She liked Jesse. A lot. And her friends' rejection of him because of the colour of his skin had the potential to change everything between them. She could not be friends with anyone that narrow-minded. No matter who they might be.

She forced a smile. 'Of course there isn't.'

Damn Freda and her unwavering inquisitiveness. It was usually Sylvia doing the nosing, the pushing, until she found out what her friends were thinking and feeling. Being on the receiving end of Freda's growing confidence wasn't quite as fun as it had been watching it emerge. Sylvia strode forward, but unfortunately Freda and Veronica kept pace alongside her. 'I've just been hurt a couple of times before. Worse, I was dumped by a man I thought I was going to marry.'

'What?'

'Oh, Sylvia.'

'No. No *Oh, Sylvia*'s, Freda.' She waved her hand. 'I'm old enough and ugly enough to know these things happen. And it happened a long time ago. It's fine.'

'There's that word again...' Veronica sighed. 'Now I know for sure you're still hurting.'

Sylvia looked away. She had no wish to say more. At least not yet. Her past was her past and she had no more clue today than she did yesterday if Jesse would feature in her future, so what was the point in poking and prodding at that particular can of worms? 'But you don't know it will be the same this time,' Freda pressed. 'Don't push Jesse away when deep down you know damn well you li—'

'I think you should leave Sylvia be, Freda,' Veronica said.

Surprised, but grateful for Veronica's firm intervention, Sylvia gave a curt nod and winked at V. 'Thank you, my lovely friend.'

'And I will,' Freda said, seemingly unperturbed, her gaze burning a hole in Sylvia's temple as they walked outside into the cold night air. 'Once I'm convinced she's going to stop lying to herself about not wanting a man in her life when I've seen her going ga-ga over those romance novels she reads on her breaks when she thinks no one's looking.'

Sylvia bristled under the accusation – even if it was true – and stared ahead. 'They are stories, Freda. Stories...'

'All right then, I'll leave you be when you convince me you don't want to fall in love, get married and have kids of your own one day. I've seen that look you get whenever you're with mothers at the hospital, Sylvia Roberts. You love hearing about their families, their little ones. Don't deny it.'

Sylvia glared as her heart treacherously filled with longing. She did not like how entirely exposed she felt in that moment. Did Freda have some sort of special power that she could see inside people's hearts and learn their deepest desires? 'What look?'

'The look of a romantic.'

'A roman—'

'And long may it last.' Freda linked her arm through Sylvia's and then pulled Veronica close and did the same with her. 'Now, let's see if we can share a taxi home, shall we? It's starting to rain.'

Sylvia glared at Freda's turned cheek. Romantic, indeed.

16

FREDA

'You're showing exemplary patience feeding me like this, Nurse.' Corporal Ferris cleared his throat, his frustration palpable. 'Never in a million years did I think there would be a day I wouldn't be able to feed myself. Then again, I never thought I would lose my sight either.'

Freda's heart broke for so proud a man – an army corporal, no less – as he lay in bed, the whiteness of the sheets stark against the sallowness of his skin. The tone of his voice and his hardened jaw, the tight curl of his hands where they lay defunct on the bed, illustrating all he had endured.

She dipped the spoon in the leek and potato soup she was feeding him and forced a smile. 'Don't you know how much I prefer sitting chatting with you all afternoon than doing some of the more unsavoury jobs that need doing? Your company is always a pleasure, Corporal.'

'If you really think that, then the company you keep must be far below par.'

The smile she'd been hoping for at the end of his sentence didn't come and she laid the spoon onto the tray on her lap and placed her hand gently over his, relief whispering through her when his fingers relaxed a little.

'Things will come right in the end,' she said quietly. 'You need to give yourself some time. The burns on your arms will heal and the use of your hands will return. As for your eyes, didn't the doctor say this morning there is every chance you'll have your sight back in the next few weeks? You have to give your body time to recover. Have faith that all will be well.'

'Never been one for the guy upstairs, I'm afraid, Nurse Parkes.'

'Then don't call it faith, call it hope. That's just as powerful. Just as life-affirming. We can all find something to be grateful—'

'Stop,' he barked, his cheeks mottling. 'Don't go telling me there are things to be grateful for. Not in wartime. I'm sorry, Nurse, but you have no idea what you're talking about.'

Hurt and feeling entirely inadequate, Freda slipped her hand from his, as her shame for not really knowing what the corporal had been through quashed any offence she might have taken at his snappishness.

'I don't even know if I want my sight back after what my eyes have seen,' he continued. 'But, then again, even if it doesn't come back, the images will still be in my head, won't they? So, what difference does it make? At the end of the day, I'm stuck with all I remember and all I felt for the men – my men – who fell before me, who died in the air or on the ground, some left to drown in their own damn blood!'

Bitterness singed his words, his resentment tangible. Freda stared at the bandages bound over his eyes and around his head, wanting to see deep inside his mind, to know what he had seen. Self-disgust unfurled inside her for her relentless thirst to know more about the other side of the war. The war being experienced by those beyond the home front. What did that desire say about her as a woman? As a human being?

'You can take that soup away, Nurse. I'm no longer hungry.'

Freda put the tray on the wheeled table beside her and pushed it to the side before pulling her chair closer to the corporal's bed. He could not have been any older than thirty, his strong jaw and thick dark hair hinting at his handsomeness, even if most of his face was obscured and criss-crossed with deep lacerations that would undoubtedly scar. Sadness twisted inside her to see such a good, hardworking and honourable man brought so low. He deserved a future, a happy future... just the same as every man and woman who had been injured, maimed or killed under the dark cloud of war over the last two years.

'If you want to talk to me about what you've seen, what you've had to do in service, you can, you know,' she said quietly, fighting her fear she might be pushing the sergeant too far. 'I understand you were one of many in charge of transporting weapons to the frontlines. Is that right?'

'Yeah, transporting sounds like nothing, but it's a dangerous job, Nurse. What with the landmines and German air drops, I've lost more comrades – more friends – than I can count.' He collapsed further into the pillow at his back as though remembering exhausted him. 'It's not just the endless death, it's the smells, the sounds, the metallic taste that coats the inside of your mouth and throat and never disappears, not even when you're eating or drinking.'

Freda ran her gaze over the shirt of his striped pyjamas. It was at least two sizes too big, hanging off his shoulders like a shirt on a wire coat hanger. Having no wife, his mother had brought him in some things two days before and her shock at the sight of her thin and injured son had been so severe, it had sent her wailing from the ward, yet to return.

Clenching her jaw against her annoyance with the woman, Freda drew in a long breath and laid her hand over the corporal's a second time. 'Tell me about the smells and sounds. Tell me every-thing you can. It will do you good and help me to understand a darn sight...' She grimaced. 'Sorry, bad choice of words.'

A small smile twitched his lips. 'Apology accepted.'

Relief pushed the air from her lungs and Freda gently touched his hand again. 'Please. If I can't do anything else, I can listen. How can I, and so many others, really understand this war when we are here, at home in safety? I have the comfort of a home in un-bombed Bath and I work shifts in an un-bombed hospital, I have enough food to eat and a pillow to lay my head on.' Guilt pressed down on her as her tirade slowed. 'Albeit I've lost a brother to this war, and another is MIA.'

The silence grew longer and longer as the muscles flexed and relaxed in his jaw.

Freda stared, her heart heavy. 'Please, tell me what it's really like.'

'All too soon, you'll know more than you want to know. Every hospital from here to Newcastle will soon be brimming with the injured. Mark my words. This war is not ending any time soon.'

His conviction sent tremors along Freda's spine. Unbeknownst to him, his surety had only fuelled her deep need to see with her own eyes what the government was trying to hide from everyone at home. How long would this war go on? Months? Years? If years, then what? How would people survive? What of the food rations and fuel for heating as winter drew ever closer? What of the men killed and the women stepping in to do their jobs?

Her stomach tightened.

'Why do you want to know about it, Nurse?'

She blinked. 'What?'

'Have you got a hankering to get in amongst the danger? The risk?' Corporal Ferris' jaw tightened again. 'Is that it?'

Freda swallowed. 'Maybe.'

His eyebrows lifted above his bandages. 'Maybe? Damn it, young lady, I wasn't serious.'

Indignation rose warm in her cheeks, and she snuck a glance left and right along the ward. 'I'm made of stronger stuff than I'm given credit for, Corporal.'

'So I've heard, but being in the line of fire is no place for a woman. Nurse or no nurse.'

Defensiveness raised her hackles. No doubt everyone on the ward thought her 'suited to a job fit for a lady' and little else, just like her mother. 'And what have you heard about me exactly?'

'Don't go getting your knickers in a twist,' he grumbled. 'It's all complimentary.'

'Good, because no one, including me, should be taken at face value.'

'Well, you'll forgive me if I have to assume that face value considering I can't see a bloody thing right now.'

She briefly closed her eyes. Was she intent on putting her foot in it?

'So what?' Corporal Ferris sniffed. 'You're thinking of nursing out there?'

Freda hesitated. If she didn't start telling people what it was she really wanted to do, nothing would ever change. Besides, being honest with such a lovely man, a corporal no less, might lead to her gaining some insight that no one else would be in a position to give her. Then again – she drew in a long breath – no doubt more and more officers, sergeants and every other rank of military would be passing through the hospital soon enough.

'Nurse? You haven't gone to sleep, have you?'

She smiled. 'No.'

'Then am I right? Is this about you wanting to go out into the field to nurse?'

'No, I want to write.'

His brow creased. 'Write?'

'Yes.' Freda sat a little straighter in her seat, embracing the pride that rose from having the courage to share her ambitions with someone other than her parents. 'I think Bath, maybe the whole of England, would benefit from hearing more about this war from a woman's point of view. A woman willing to write the stories of the men and women facing unimaginable horror across Europe.'

'I see.'

Ignoring the scepticism in his voice, Freda pressed on. 'The people at home, the country's womenfolk and children deserve...' She swallowed past the unexpected lump that rose in her throat as she glanced along the ward towards Sister Dyer's desk, relieved to see her distracted as she spoke to Kathy Scott. Freda faced Corporal Ferris. 'They deserve to know the real stories, the human stories of the people serving. Outside of my care for my patients, writing about this war is all I think about.'

Once again, silence fell and the seconds passed like minutes. Freda fought not to fidget, not to fill the silence like she would have at home when her parents' judgement pressed down on her.

'Let me guess,' the corporal said quietly. 'Nursing was decided for you. You didn't choose it, right?'

Freda dropped her shoulders. Even with his eyes bandaged, he had managed to really see her. 'Yes. By my mother.'

'Hmm, the army was chosen for me, too. But thankfully, there is nothing else I'd rather do... or rather would have done. I was lucky in that, at least.' He drew in a shaky breath. 'Your life isn't your mother's, Nurse Parkes.' He winced as he eased himself forward, tightening his fingers on hers. 'It's yours. Do what you are called to do while you can. We are in the midst of a second world war; who's to say there won't be a third? A fourth?'

'Oh, don't say that.' Freda closed her eyes, sickness unfurling inside her. 'You can't even think such a thing. None of us can.'

'If you can truly imagine this world without another war, another conflict, then you're right... you don't know anything.'

He pulled his hand from hers and turned his cheek into the pillow and the action slapped her face with its perceived rejection. She sat immobile, stunned for a moment, before she slowly stood and stared down at Corporal Ferris as a deep, dark determination built inside of her. Her days of being a good girl were over. Come what may, regardless of whom she might upset, including her mother, she had to learn and write about the real war Britain was fighting to survive. The real war, past the blood and bandages of the lucky few who found themselves being cared for in Bath, how thousands were being killed or severely injured in circumstances like those that would haunt Corporal Ferris for the rest of his life.

17

VERONICA

Veronica nervously chewed her bottom lip as she, Sylvia and Freda made their way across the city centre. Luckily, all three of their houses were no more than twenty minutes' walk from the other in any direction, and tonight that served Veronica well as she hoped her friends would stay out to talk a little longer before they headed home together.

Honesty and loyalty.

Those were the things that mattered in friendship and if theirs was to grow from strength to strength, she needed to show complete integrity... or at least as much as she was capable of right now. She had no idea how Freda and Sylvia had managed to burrow so quickly and deeply into her heart and evoke the need to share her attack with them, but they had, and now that need felt more like the opportunity for escape, for finally being able to begin to heal by no longer carrying her shame alone.

They had enjoyed their day off together with a wander around the shops, each treating themselves to a little something. A fountain pen for Freda, a purse for Sylvia and, for herself – Veronica smiled – the most beautiful scarf she had ever seen. The day had felt like her first taste of liberty in four long years, and it could only be because of how much she enjoyed being with her new friends.

She had no doubt her mother would have something to say about her being out all day, but she imagined Freda would have things a lot worse when she got home. As for Sylvia, she wouldn't care less what her own mother had to say. Oh, how she wished she could be more like her vivacious friend!

Well, maybe tonight she could take a small step in the direction of beginning to fully live again.

'Do you need to get home straight away?' she asked as they walked through Charlotte Square. 'Only, I thought we could go to the park, have a wander along Royal Crescent?'

'Well, you know me.' Sylvia grinned. 'The longer I can stay away from my mother on my day off, the better. Another couple of hours and she'll be starting her shift at the pub and be out of my hair for the night. A walk definitely sounds good.'

Veronica peered around Sylvia at Freda. 'Freda?'

'Well, my mother will surely have my guts for garters when I get home, considering she accused me of' – she rolled her eyes and adopted a sing-song voice – '*acting as though I expect the world to bend to my every whim and ignore everyone else*, last night.' She sighed. 'So, yes, a walk sounds good to me, too.'

Veronica and Sylvia laughed just as the air raid sirens blasted through any possibility for further conversation. They walked beneath the stone archway that served as the entrance to Victoria Park, two lions perched high on their stone pillars above the space that had once housed two huge iron gates, since taken down for use in the war effort.

Sylvia shook her head and tutted, her gaze skywards. 'Here we go again. Bristol's in for another terrible night.'

Minutes later, the familiar rumbling started in the pink-tinged sky and Veronica looked upwards at the gut-churning sight of a large formation of enemy planes flying in the direction of Bristol. Her throat dried and she sent the people there her silent prayers. The German attacks on the city had been relentless recently and there was no indication the bombers intended moving on anytime soon.

'As the weeks go by, it feels more and more likely your dad was right, Freda,' Sylvia shouted above the noise as she stared at the sky. 'But I'll tell you this for nothing, if Bath is bombed, we'll weather it just as we know the Bristolians are.'

Freda's jaw was tight, and her brow furrowed as her stare followed the planes. 'We've escaped attack so far and can't possibly know the true toll of living in war as others do, but if we have to learn the hard way, we'll be ready.' She shook her head. 'Which is why I will keep asking questions of those who have been injured and are now recovering at the hospital. The more aware of reality we are, the more we can prepare ourselves. Goodness knows we're entitled to know how bad things really are and not what the government chooses to tell us.'

Veronica looked at Freda as the planes disappeared and the sky fell silent once more. 'You seem so passionate about knowing the truth.'

'I am. When I listen to the officers' stories – or even the women's who have lost their homes, their children – I realise their experiences go beyond what their injuries can tell us. The real wounds are in their hearts and minds. That's where they keep the real stories, hidden away like shameful secrets.'

'But they've got nothing to be ashamed of!' Sylvia protested.

'I know that, and you know that, but some of these people are struggling with so much self-blame, Sylvia. It's just heart breaking.'

Veronica frowned. 'But what else can we do but nurse them?'

'Well...' Freda's eyes burned with determination. 'I intend to write their stories.'

'What?'

'Write them?'

Freda nodded. 'I believe people on the home front – us – need to know everything they've had to endure. What they've had to do, what they've seen and heard. How else will we truly understand everything the injured have been through? How else will we have any hope of them believing us when we tell them how proud we are of them, how much we care?' She drew back her shoulders. 'Nursing isn't enough for me. I want to write.'

Veronica's heart swelled with admiration for her friend. 'When you say write, do you mean for the newspaper?'

Freda gave a firm nod. 'Yes.'

A moment of silence stretched before Veronica grinned and squeezed Freda's hand. 'Well, I think that's fantastic.'

Sylvia nodded. 'Me too. I wish you all the luck in the world.'

Freda smiled. 'Thank you. It means a lot to have your support when my parents dismiss my writing dreams over and over again.'

'I think our parents' input in our lives is by the by, don't you?' Sylvia raised her eyebrows. 'We're in charge of our own destinies, ladies. Nobody else.'

Veronica inhaled a shaky breath, her friends' strength deepening her need to share her secret with them. 'Come on, you two, we should pick up our pace, we won't reach Royal Crescent before blackout at this rate.'

Once they reached the expanse of grass at the edge of the park that gave a magnificent view of the Crescent, Veronica sighed at the phenomenal sight of the houses built with Bath stone, their butter-yellow colour glowing in the semi-darkness. Who knew if they would still be standing by the end of the war? She swallowed. Who knew how the people of Bath would fare and if demolished historical buildings would even be thought about when there was so much more to worry about? Such as England's future rather than its past – no matter how great that might be.

She glanced at her friends as they stared ahead.

The time had come to talk openly and honestly.

The time had come to take a leap of faith.

The ambulance journey a few nights ago and the terror she had felt at the driver's propositions had haunted her ever since. She just hoped that, by telling Freda and Sylvia about Mr Riley's attack on her, the iron bars of her own personal prison would finally be broken wide open and she could start to walk towards freedom. Freedom from the memories that had haunted her day and night for far too long.

Veronica pointed to a wooden bench beneath some trees alongside the cobbled walkway. 'Could we sit on that bench over there? I'd like to tell you something and I'm scared if I don't do it now, I never will.'

Freda and Sylvia exchanged a-not-so veiled glance before Freda pushed her hand into the crook of Veronica's elbow and led her forwards. 'Of course.'

They reached the bench and Veronica's heart beat hard as Sylvia and Freda sat either side of her and waited for her to begin. *Oh, God, where is the beginning?*

Sylvia put her handbag on the seat and took Veronica's hand. 'We know something's been bothering you, V. We want to help, but if you feel you're not ready to talk to us, there's no pressure. As long as you know we're here for you, that's enough. Right, Freda?'

'Absolutely.'

Veronica looked between the two women who had become the best part of her life after her nursing. As a sister at the hospital, her mother's encouragement and love for the job had meant Veronica had always known she wanted to follow in her mother's footsteps one day, but she could never have known she would make friends with two of the best women she had ever met. Before Sylvia and Freda, before working on the ward, her entire life had been dominated by debilitating fears and her mother insisting that now Veronica's father had been killed in battle, it was just her and Veronica together forever.

Her mother's love was precious to her, yet she had never confessed her secret to her and that spoke volumes. But the claustrophobia she often felt at home and living on the same street as her rapist was becoming too hard to tolerate.

Veronica breathed deep and closed her eyes. 'I just can't go on living as I have been. You have both inspired me to believe I deserve more.' She opened her eyes and, for the first time in a long time, she let her true feelings flow. 'You have been such good friends to me from our very first day at the hospital, and even though I suspect I will never be as strong or inspiring as you both are, I am ready to start standing up for myself.'

'Standing up for yourself?' Sylvia's face hardened. 'Has someone been bullying you? Is it Sister Dyer? If she's picking on you, you aren't alone. I swear she wakes up in the morning, looks at her staff list and sticks a pin in the name of her chosen victim for the day.'

'It's not the sister.'

Freda had produced a handkerchief from somewhere and pressed it into Veronica's hand. 'Then who is it, V?'

Veronica's heart beat fast as she dabbed at the tears she didn't know had escaped. She stared at her friends, habitual shame rising inside of her. 'When I said start standing up for myself, I mean it's time I started standing firm in my decisions and instincts. I don't trust myself and haven't for a long time. I think that's part of why I like nursing so much.'

'What do you mean?' Freda asked.

'The constant instruction and supervision means I don't have to be truly responsible. If things go wrong, the buck stops with my superior rather than me.'

'But we are always making decisions, V,' Sylvia said. 'We have to think on our feet, and you have proven yourself as capable of that as anyone else on the ward.' She winked. 'Granted, you might not be quite up to my standard, but then who is?'

Freda swatted Sylvia behind Veronica's back. 'You keep telling yourself that, but you know I give you a run for your money every day.'

Veronica tried to smile and join in her friends' banter, but her shame and humiliation were like pinpricks that had slowly leaked the meagre self-confidence she'd had before she was raped, leaving barely a scrap behind to build on. Everything that had happened to her fought to come out and she refused to keep it locked inside a minute longer.

'I'm so sick and tired of not being sure who I can trust, what I can trust.' Her voice cracked. 'I can't do this any more. I want to start trusting myself and other people again.'

The concern in her friends' eyes added to Veronica's guilt, illuminating her weakness when Freda and Sylvia had shown time and again how strong they were.

'Whatever, or whoever, is making you feel this way,' Sylvia said, holding her hand, 'it stops today. You're shaking, V. Let us help you.'

Freda inched closer, slid her arm through hers. 'Is it something or someone?'

'It's someone. A man who lives on my street,' she said. 'He's a neighbour, and one day four years ago I invited him into our home. I was seventeen, alone and...' Royal Crescent blurred through her tears even as a fire ignited deep in Veronica's stomach.

'He raped me. It was in the kitchen. Before I knew it... he had me on the floor and he raped me.'

There was a sharp, dual intake of breath.

'Oh, V...'

'My God.'

Sylvia's and Freda's hands gripped hers, their gazes running over her face, their eyes glinting with tears before they dropped their heads onto her shoulders.

Veronica continued to stare blindly ahead as the remembered fragments of that fateful day played like a jumbled, revolving kaleidoscope in her mind's eye. 'Once he... was finished, he patted my cheek and left. I couldn't open my eyes, couldn't think, or hear or see. There was just... nothing left.'

'Didn't you tell your mum?' asked Freda quietly. 'Anyone?'

Veronica shook her head, aware that Sylvia's hand now trembled around hers, no doubt with anger, if she knew her friend at all.

She swallowed. 'I have a vague memory of a draught coming along the hallway from the front door. He must have left it ajar when he left. Every now and then I think I remember a voice, someone talking to me, but I have no idea what they are saying or who they are.' She exhaled a shaky breath and opened her eyes. 'I must have imagined it, because when I finally got up from the floor, I was alone. I somehow made it to the front door and closed it. Then I... sorted myself out and never said another word about it to anyone.'

'Oh, V,' Freda whispered.

Sylvia lifted her head and when her eyes met Veronica's, they burned with fury. 'And this... monster still lives on the same street as you?'

Veronica swallowed. 'He does, yes.'

Sylvia's trembling started again. 'We have to do something

about that. You can't live like that any more. It's madness. It's horrible.'

Swiping at the tear that ran over her cheek, Veronica tried to smile. 'It won't be forever and he disappears from time to time anyway. He goes away, comes back, goes again. It wasn't long after my attack, maybe a week or so later, that the neighbours were gossiping that he was in hospital for some reason.' She gave a wry smile. 'I hope someone had given him the once over he deserves, but I doubt it.'

'I honestly haven't got the words to help you right now,' Sylvia said, shaking her head. 'But I'm here and Freda's here.' She squeezed her hand. 'Whenever you need us. Always. When this has sunk in, we'll talk again, all right?'

Veronica nodded and then allowed herself to cry like she'd never cried before but, being there in that moment, her friends' comfort seeping into her blood, Veronica knew for the first time in a long time that she was home and safe.

18

SYLVIA

Sylvia's mind continued to reel with Veronica's confession an hour after she and Freda had left their beautiful friend at her door, Veronica insisting they didn't need to come into the house with her. It seemed to Sylvia that insistence had as much to do with her mother knowing nothing of her daughter's attack as it did Veronica's reluctance at the prospect of having to introduce her mother to her friends.

Swallowing against the bitterness coating her throat, Sylvia upped her pace towards home, the night's revelations somehow making her so much more aware of the invisible dangers that lurked on the streets.

How on earth had Veronica kept such a trauma to herself all this time? She'd said she and her mother were close, but she could never find the right moment to share what happened. Plus, her shame and culpability often overrode the need for her mother's care. Culpability! *God, what I'll do to the man who hurt her if I ever get my hands on him...*

Having left Veronica at her front door, Sylvia and Freda had walked so far together, Sylvia filling the time with a tirade of abuse towards Veronica's un-named rapist, while Freda had marched alongside her, her face set in stone and keeping her thoughts to herself.

As Sylvia entered Castle Street, her shock gave way to anger. It was time women took control of their lives and openly declared what was best for them once and for all in this stupid messed up world.

And, with that decision made, she headed straight for Jesse's front door rather than her own. It had been over a week since their dinner, and she had been under the illusion – or maybe disillusion – it had gone well. Conversation had flowed, albeit both of them seeming to sense discussion concerning their home lives was out of bounds. The food had been the best she'd had since rationing started, a couple of glasses of something nicely alcoholic served below room temperature, and they had shared a more than satisfactory kiss on the way home. Since then? Not a word from him. Nothing. Nada.

She stood at his closed front door and before her sanity returned or her state of mind altered, she lifted her knuckles and rapped three times on the painted wood.

Through the arch of glass above the door, the hallway light flicked on, catching her unawares. Sylvia pulled back her shoulders, annoyed by the treacherous nerves that took flight in her stomach. The door opened and she came face to face with Mrs Howard, immaculately dressed and groomed as always, not a paisley housecoat or metal hair curler in sight.

Sylvia planted on a smile even as the other woman's eyes shot daggers at her. 'Good evening, Mrs Howard. Is Jesse in by any chance?'

Mrs Howard's gaze remained cold and hard, her mouth twisted in disdain. 'No, he's at work and even if he was here, I would tell you the same thing.'

Sylvia held her gaze, her smile straining. 'Have I done something to upset you, Mrs Howard?'

'You upset me? I don't think so.'

'Only, the last time I saw you it was because your eldest son invited me into your home to look over your younger son. I believe – thanks to my advice – Michael is now better.'

'Jesse did not have my permission to get you involved.'

'Maybe not, but I'm glad he did and your gift of the most beautiful and delicious cake afterwards led me to believe you felt the same.'

Mrs Howard narrowed her eyes, but from the way she shifted uncomfortably, Sylvia knew she had beaten her at her own game. Clearly, her baking had been a knee-jerk reaction to Sylvia's ministrations and now she considered her generosity as some kind of misplaced weakness. Well, be that as it may, she did not deserve the woman's derision. Not by a long shot.

'You aren't any better than me, my girl,' Mrs Howard snapped, standing taller. 'Just because you have a bit more worthiness about you than your mother, I'm still keeping an eye on you.'

'Do you mind if we leave my mother out of this? Only, she's still my mum and I love her, so it wouldn't do to start flinging mud at her, would it? Now...'

'I think this conversation is over.' Mrs Howard stepped back, but as she put her hand on the door, it ever-so-slightly trembled. 'I'd very much like you to sling your hook and stop sniffing around my Jesse.'

Sylvia studied her, spotting a hint of uncertainty in the other woman's dark brown eyes. Guilt whispered through her conscience. Hadn't Jesse mentioned something about his mother not being herself since his father was killed? *What if her terseness isn't about me at all, but something I can neither see nor understand?*

'Well? Are you going to get off my doorstep or not?' Mrs

Howard appraised Sylvia from head to toe, her eyes narrowed. 'My Jesse would never be interested in the likes of you. You're not good enough for a man like him. Not in a month of Sundays. So you can get any such imaginings out of that daft head of yours.'

Sylvia fought to keep hold of her compassion in the face of Mrs Howard's sharp slice at her worst insecurities. She was more than aware of how high the chances were that Jesse's interest in her wasn't heartfelt. Just as the interest of any man before him had proven to be eventually. She lifted her chin. Receiving disdainful reactions from other women was hardly something new in Sylvia's experience – especially when they discovered she was Eileen Roberts' daughter – but what was new was Mrs Howard's dislike of her, despite Sylvia helping her little boy. That didn't make sense at all, and she wasn't leaving until it did.

'Can I ask why you think that?' Sylvia crossed her arms.

Mrs Howard narrowed her eyes. 'Think what?'

'Why Jesse would never be interested in me.' She glanced along the row of houses as though bored with the conversation. 'Because, to my mind, if that was true, he wouldn't constantly find excuses to talk to me as I come to and from the hospital.' She faced her. 'He wouldn't light up like a candle when we spend a bit of time together and he wouldn't—'

'Light up like a candle?' Mrs Howard smirked a second time. 'My Jesse wouldn't *light up* – as you put it – for anyone but his family.'

Sylvia smiled, despite knowing by retaliating with a game of tit-for-tat she was playing straight into Mrs Howard's presumptions about her. But how the bloody hell was she supposed to stop when the woman continued to wear such an expression of complete and utter contempt? 'He wouldn't have taken me to dinner last week either.'

Mrs Howard's smile vanished, and she stepped back as though

Sylvia had slapped her. 'He took *you* out? My Jesse?' Her eyes bulged as she held on to her pristinely clean doorframe like a crutch to stop her falling. 'I don't believe you.'

Unease tip-tapped along Sylvia's spine, as the knowledge she had just told tales on Jesse echoed in her conscience. Would she never learn to keep her mouth shut? Hadn't Jesse's insistence that they meet at the end of the street been warning enough he did not want his mother knowing he had been fraternising with her? Familiar hurt burned inside her. What was she? Public enemy number one? Hitler's sidekick?

She slumped her shoulders. 'Mrs Howard—'

'Don't you "Mrs Howard" me. Just because you helped my Michael, that doesn't make you some sort of saint. My family means everything to me. How was I supposed to know how ill he was? I haven't got your fancy medical training, have I? But that doesn't give you the right to stand on my doorstep looking down at me.'

Heat warmed Sylvia's cheeks. She didn't look down on anyone. Ever. 'Mrs Howard—'

'Ever since we arrived in this street, we've been made to feel like second-class citizens because of our colour. Well, I won't have you adding insult to injury by using your nursing against me.' She flung her arm out. 'Get out of here! And if I catch you around my Jesse again, God help you.'

The door slammed shut with such force that Sylvia swore the glass in the bay window to the side of it shook, despite the tape protecting it from a potential bomb blast. For a long moment, she didn't move. Instead, she stared at the closed front door, half expecting Mrs Howard to open it again and douse her in tar and feathers. Or else for Jesse to appear tied and gagged, before Mrs Howard dragged him back inside by his shirt collar.

Purposefully forcing a smile, Sylvia battled the tears pricking her eyes and slowly walked onto the street. When her first tears escaped, she tilted her chin. She would not wipe them until she was in her own home with the door firmly shut. God only knew if any number of neighbours had witnessed her and Mrs Howard's exchange. The woman might not like her, but Sylvia had nothing against her at all, and the last thing she wanted was one of the housewives coming outside to find out what had been said between them. She and her mother were hardly the most popular neighbours on the street, but they almost certainly fared higher than Mrs Howard and her family, and Sylvia would not add to their struggles by allowing any gossip to start.

But that didn't make it any less frustrating that Mrs Howard wouldn't give her the benefit of the doubt. What was wrong with her? Why was she never good enough for anyone? First her father left her, then her fiancée, and now the mother of a pretty wonderful man she was terrified to like but liked all the same thought her beneath him, too. What did people see when they looked at her? Nothing more than Eileen Roberts' daughter? A waste of space playing dress up in a nurse's uniform? She would be the first to admit to her mistakes, but as far as her past relationships were concerned, she still couldn't see where she had gone wrong, or how she deserved such complete abandonment. She might be a little mouthy from time to time; her mother had taught her to stick up for herself and others, after all. But, if truth be told, she was honest, loyal, hardworking and once someone had her love, they had it forever, through good times and bad... unless they left, of course.

A sharp, unexpected sob caught in her throat and Sylvia upped her pace, her front door feeling a hundred miles away rather than a hundred feet. At last, she reached it and took her time pulling her key from her bag, her back straight as she drew her gaze along the blackened windows of the houses opposite, daring someone to taunt her. From where she stood, they would not be able to see the tracks of her tears as they slowly slid down her cheeks, landing salty on her lips.

Turning, she pushed her key in the lock.

One of her friends had been attacked and raped and in struggling with that God-awful reality, all Sylvia had wanted was to feel Jesse's comforting arms around her, his warm, soft lips brushing hers. Just a moment's comfort, a moment's strength, until she proved herself in control and could be whatever Veronica or any number of patients and casualties needed her to be during this seemingly endless war.

Only once her front door was firmly closed did Sylvia allow herself to crumble as she sat on the carpeted bottom stair and cried.

19

FREDA

Freda stood a short distance from the front window of the *Bath Chronicle* newspaper office and fought to gather her courage. Clutching her newly typed article in her gloved hand, sealed in an envelope to keep it protected from the morning's rain, her heart beat an erratic concerto. If she didn't get this over with soon, she would be late for her shift at the hospital.

She closed her eyes, inhaled deeply and then, snapping her eyes open, strode the few steps to the office's front door and pushed it open.

The dark, wood-panelled, rather gloomy space was ineffectually lit by opaque glass lamps on four desks that faced one another in a square in the centre of the room. Further weak light came from a couple of wall sconces and the bare lightbulb hanging from the ceiling. The varnished floorboards were bare, but the maroon-coloured settee and two armchairs set before a low table in one corner somewhat softened the staid atmosphere.

She walked forward, her gaze on a man in his late forties speaking to another man maybe twenty years younger sitting at one of the four desks. Another man sat at the third desk, but the last desk – much to Freda's relief – was occupied by a woman, who looked to be around her age. She suddenly looked up and a smile immediately lit her face as though she had been waiting for something – or someone – to appear and break up her day.

She came forward, her blonde curls bouncing and her high-heeled shoes – the exact same shade as her dark green skirt suit – clip-clopped along the floorboards.

'Good morning. Can I help you?'

'Um, yes.' Freda forced a smile, cursing the trembling in her knees. 'I'm hoping that an article I've written might be considered for publication in the paper. I'm a nurse. At a hospital here in Bath and I...' She briefly closed her eyes. *Stop babbling.* She thrust the envelope at the woman. 'Here.'

'Well, I'm Barbara, general secretary come lackey...' She winked. 'Or so I let the boys in the office think. Unfortunately I'm not the person you need to speak to regarding articles or anything specifically to do with the paper.' She cupped Freda's elbow and led her forward. 'But I am the person who can get you a cup of tea while you speak to the gentleman who *can* help.'

Barbara's friendliness dissipated a little of the tension in Freda's shoulders and she smiled. 'Oh, I can't stay, I have to get to work. I just wanted to leave this with someone.'

'Right, then I'll quickly get someone to help you.' Barbara turned to the square of desks and approached the youngest of the men, who now worked alone, his brow furrowed and his fingers tapping ferociously on the keys of a typewriter. 'Richard? This lady would like someone to look at an article she's written. Can you spare a minute?'

The man looked decidedly harassed as he looked first at Barbara and then past her to Freda. She stood a little taller and fought to hold his steady, emotionless gaze.

His sigh floated across the space separating them before he stood. 'Of course.'

Barbara shook her head and leaned close to Freda's ear. 'Don't be put off by his dramatics. He's a pussycat once you get to know him.'

The man came to a stop in front of them and slowly appraised Freda's entire face before he held out his hand. 'Richard Sinclair. Nice to meet you, Miss...'

'Parkes. Freda Parkes.'

'Shall we take a seat at my desk?'

'Well, I can't stay—'

'Go on.' Barbara's finger gently prodded Freda's back. 'You're here now, you might as well sit down.'

A whisper of a smile lifted Mr Sinclair's lips, his gaze softening. 'She's right, you know.' He waved towards his desk. 'After you.'

Swallowing against the sudden dryness in her throat, Freda forced her feet to move, her entire being alert with inexplicable awareness. Richard Sinclair had the most incredible dark blue eyes, and his hair was the darkest jet black. At best, she had thought someone would take her article from her and tell her when she could expect an answer. At worst, she thought she'd be laughed out of the office in two seconds flat. She had not considered a scenario of her sitting at a journalist's desk while he leaned his bottom up against said desk and stared down at her, arms crossed and pinning her with a rather beautiful, but expectant, stare.

A shiver ran through her and Freda blinked, warmth heating her face and neck.

'So, Miss Parkes...' He nodded at the envelope in her hand. 'Is that the article?'

'Um... yes.' She held it out to him. 'I'm a nurse at the hospital on Upper Borough Walls in the city centre. The article touches on my experiences there and how much I am learning from the injured about the reality behind the war. Many of the patients have been transferred from Bristol, both civilians and officers returned from fighting.'

He withdrew her typed pages from the envelope and scanned the first page, turning to the next. His brow furrowed as he protruded his bottom lip, his reading stopping towards the bottom of the page before he turned to the third and final page.

'Well.' He looked up. 'A quick look has certainly been enough to catch my interest, Miss Parkes.'

Freda smiled, her shoulders coming down from around her earlobes. 'Really?'

He smiled at her for the first time and her stomach flip-flopped.

'Indeed. Although, that interest does mean I'll need a little longer to properly consider the piece.'

She fought to keep her face impassive as though impervious to his looks and charm. 'Of course.'

He looked back at the pages, piled the sheets together and pushed away from the desk. 'Leave this with me. Your address is on the top of the covering letter. I'll be in touch as soon as possible.'

Freda stood, clutching her handbag so tightly in front of her, her knuckles ached. 'Thank you, Mr Sinclair.'

'You're welcome.' His gaze lingered on hers for a moment before he turned away. 'Barbara? Could you show Miss Parkes out, please?'

Duly dismissed, Freda followed the lovely Barbara to the door and bid her goodbye before hurrying along Bath's sodden streets towards the hospital, her heart swollen with happiness and pride, her mind a mess of thoughts about Richard Sinclair and the possible acceptance of her article. Being knocked off kilter by a handsome journalist had been the last thing she'd expected to happen this morning. What was wrong with her? What if he detected her attraction? An attraction as discomfiting to her as it undoubtedly would be to him. But the simple fact was with those looks – and those eyes – Richard Sinclair would almost certainly gain admirers wherever he went – no doubt a useful weapon to have in the field of journalism.

Twenty minutes later, Freda rushed into the hospital staff room and blew out a relieved breath to see Sylvia still pinning her cap in place in front of one of the mirrors. At least that meant she wasn't late, as Sylvia was always on time.

Her friend turned. 'There you are. I was getting worried.' Sylvia's brow was creased with a rare frown, her gaze shadowed. 'I barely slept last night thinking about Veronica, I'd be even more of a mess if you suddenly went missing without us knowing why.'

Freda's selfish happiness burst like a balloon. She hung her coat in her locker and reached for her cap on the shelf above. 'I didn't get much sleep either. What are we going to do?'

'About V?' Sylvia sighed. 'I don't think we should do anything for the time being. She needs to lead the way with this. She has kept what happened to her a secret for four years. She does not need us telling her what to do next.'

'I agree.' Freda's stomach knotted with care for Veronica. 'As long as she knows we are here for her and will do whatever she needs us to do, that's what matters.'

Sylvia clipped on her nurse's badge. 'Exactly. But...' Her eyes blazed with anger. 'One day in the not-so-distant future, the man who hurt her will pay for what he did. It might take some time for V to tell us exactly who he is, but when she does...'

Freda nodded, fury burning hot in her stomach. 'We'll do whatever we must to see justice done.'

They lapsed into silence before walking from the room and along the corridor towards the ward.

'Guess what else I did on my way home last night, on top of worrying about V,' Sylvia asked.

Freda glanced at her. 'What?'

'Instead of going straight home, like I should have, I made the stupid mistake of knocking on Jesse's door.'

'And?'

'And his mother answered and she was not pleased to see me on her doorstep. It was pretty clear by the end of our conversation that the woman doesn't want me to have anything to do with her precious son and thinks me far from worthy of him.'

'Despite you caring for her little boy?'

'Yep, and giving Jesse the advice that meant his brother is now fully recovered from what was a nasty case of tonsilitis.'

Freda bristled, her defence of Sylvia igniting. 'Well, that seems entirely unfair of her. What did Jesse have to say about it?'

Sylvia's frown deepened. 'He wasn't there, and I hadn't seen him for a while before I spoke to his mum. No doubt he'll have plenty to say to me when he finds out I had crossed words with her.'

Freda blew out a breath as she hooked her hand around Sylvia's arm and squeezed. 'I wouldn't worry about it too much. You know as well as I do that mothers can be the bane of their children's lives. Maybe Jesse will take your side in this fight for his affections?'

'Fight for his affections?' Sylvia scoffed, two spots of colour darkening her cheeks. 'Who said anything about affections? You need to keep your head out of the clouds, Freda Parkes.'

Sylvia snatched her arm away and marched ahead of Freda into the ward.

Freda smiled. If Sylvia wasn't falling for this Jesse fella, she'd eat her hat.

20

SYLVIA

Leaving a patient who had arrived from Bristol earlier that morning to get some much-needed sleep, Sylvia glanced at Freda and Veronica at the other end of the ward where they were working, side by side, distributing cups of tea. She had managed to have a quiet word with Veronica an hour or so before and it had warmed her heart no end when Veronica told her how comforted and supported she felt after sharing her trauma with her and Freda the night before.

Sylvia drew in a breath and slowly released it as she watched Veronica smiling and laughing. Her quiet yet brave friend had managed to burrow deep into her heart before her confession, but now Veronica was well and truly settled there – which meant Sylvia would do her darndest to protect her against further hurt for however long their friendship lasted. Which she hoped would be for a long time yet.

'It's always so cheering to see your lovely smile, Nurse,' called Mrs Harlow, a mother to three children who had all – thank goodness – been staying with their grandmother in Corsham when their house just outside of Bristol's city centre had been hit by a bomb, reducing a third of her home to rubble. Unfortunately, Mrs Harlow had chosen to stay behind, the same as thousands of other residents, afraid what the result of leaving their homes might be.

That decision meant she now suffered a broken arm and ribs, plus high levels of smoke inhalation that were taking time to shift.

'You remind me so much of my sister,' she said. 'She always manages a smile for all and sundry, no matter the circumstances.'

'Well, considering Hitler and his cronies are showing no sign of letting up, smiling is the best way to show him we won't be beaten. Don't you think?' Sylvia came to Mrs Harlow's bedside and plumped her pillows. 'But how are *you* feeling? It will soon be time for you to go back to your mother's, I should think. Do you want me to ask Sister if she has any better idea of when that might be?'

'Oh, would you?' Mrs Harlow's eyes brightened and then widened as she was wracked with a barrage of coughing. 'Oh...'

Sylvia quickly stole her arm around the poor woman's shoulders and held her. 'It's alright. There now, the more you cough, the more we can hope the nastiness is leaving your lungs. There you go... how's that?'

The coughing stopped and Mrs Harlow sipped the water Sylvia held to her lips. 'Better, thank you, Nurse.'

'You're welcome.'

Mrs Harlow collapsed back against the pillows, unshed tears making her blue eyes glitter under the ward's overhead lights. 'It's only the thought that I will be back with my babies soon making things easier to cope with. Our home in Bristol is wrecked, but my mother is a godsend, someone I can really rely on with Bill being away, but still, children need their mother, you know?'

'I do,' said Sylvia, her smile faltering as she thought of the times she had wished her mother was more maternal. 'Would you like a cup of tea? Or maybe I can refill your water jug?' she asked, reaching for the empty jug on the wheeled side table beside the bed. 'While I'm gone, I'll track down Sister Dyer and see how the land lies for you going home.'

'Oh, that would be wonderful. Thank you.'

'A cup of tea and fresh water coming right up.'

As Sylvia walked away, she pulled back her shoulders, drawing in as much strength as possible to approach Sister Dyer with her questions. The sister more often than not looked down her nose at her or else accused her of being far too friendly with the patients and nurses alike. Sylvia lifted her chin. Well, she had no intention of changing, so one way or another, she and the sister needed to find a way of rubbing along. Sylvia grimaced. She had a feeling their upcoming conversation would not be the catalyst to that happening.

She nodded at Freda as she passed her talking to Mr Humphries at his bedside, a grandfather of four who had thought nothing of forgoing his place in the family Anderson shelter so a neighbour's two children could take refuge instead. As payment for his generosity, he was injured by a piece of flying metal slicing through his leg, the wound thankfully missing vital veins and nerves, but severe all the same. Sylvia suspected he was by far Freda's favourite patient and she his favourite nurse. Freda's smile was wide and contagious, and Sylvia smiled right along with her as she walked towards the ward exit.

'Well, well, here's the nurse of the hour.'

Sylvia's smile strained, her happiness wavering. 'Good morning, Kathy. How are you?'

'I'm well, Nurse Roberts. I hear you and Nurses Campbell and Parkes have been spending more and more time together away from the hospital.'

Sylvia's inherent impatience with Kathy ignited once more. There was something about her that niggled, even though both Freda and Veronica insisted she was harmless enough and that maybe Kathy's occasional need to take little jabs at their deepening friendship might be shrouded in a little envy.

'We're friends, Kathy. We enjoy spending time with each other if we are lucky enough to have time off together. Maybe' – she swallowed past her next words as they caught in her throat – 'you could join us sometime in the future. Who knows?'

Kathy shrugged, her gaze tinged with what looked to be forced nonchalance. 'I just find it a little strange, that's all. I'm not sure I'd want to spend time with people I work with outside of the hospital.'

'Well, live and let live.' Sylvia moved to walk past her. 'I really need to get on. Excuse me.'

'No one is bothered by the three of you gossiping and laughing together, you know.' Kathy sniffed. 'In fact, most of the nurses on the ward think your friendship's far from normal, and Sister certainly isn't impressed that the three of you seem joined at the hip half the time.'

Sylvia pinned her with a stare. 'Is that so? Well, never mind. Talking of Sister, do you know where she is? I was hoping to have a word with her.'

'She was heading off to speak with Sister Campbell when I last saw her. I imagine she'll be back on the ward any minute.'

'Perfect. See you later.'

Sylvia walked away, feeling as though Kathy's glare was burning holes in her back. She would keep being as nice as possible to her for Freda and Veronica, but God above, Kathy had a way of pushing her buttons. Leaving the ward, she walked along the corridor and entered the kitchen, her nerves giving a little jolt to find Sister Dyer at the sink. Kathy had clearly got it entirely wrong where Sister was going. Just another reason to find her annoying.

She cleared her throat.

'Oh, hello, Sister.'

Sister Dyer turned from the sink and gave what might or might not have passed for a smile; it was so fleeting, it was hard to be sure. 'Nurse Roberts.'

'I was just coming in to make a cuppa for Mrs Harlow and replenish her water jug.'

'Very good. Don't let me stop you.'

Sylvia headed to where the kettle and tea-making bits and pieces were, pleased that the kettle was full and she wouldn't have to ask Sister to move from the sink for the time being.

She set the kettle on the stove to boil. 'I was hoping to have a quiet word with you about Mrs Harlow as it happens.'

'Yes?' The sister re-dunked her hands in the soapy water. 'Is everything as it should be?'

'Yes, in fact, I think she's looking a lot better today.'

'Do you?'

'Yes, and to that end, I told her I'd ask you if there is any indication of when she might be able to leave the hospital. She's missing her children terribly.'

'That may be so, but her going home is out of the question for the time being. She is still very unwell.'

'But her arm is set, and she's moving much easier, despite her ribs still healing. Surely it won't hurt for her to convalesce at her mother's so she can spend time with—'

The sister spun around, her brown eyes bulging. 'Why do you insist on this infernal backchat? You asked me a question and I told you the situation. Yet still you feel you know better than me.

Mrs Harlow will remain at the hospital until whatever time I see fit. Is that clear?'

Sylvia trembled with the effort it took not to further challenge the sister's decision. After all, what harm would it do to Mrs Harlow's recovery if she was in a clean and happy home, one where she would be surrounded by the recuperative love of her own mother and children?

Unless... Sylvia cleared her throat. 'I apologise, Sister. I'm just concerned, that's all. Would it be possible... that maybe the children and her mother could come here? To the hospital?'

'What?' The sister's cheeks mottled. 'The hospital is no place for young children to see their mother when all around her there are men and women on the ward suffering terrible injuries, burns and goodness knows what. Heavens above, Nurse Roberts, use your head.' Sister Dyer continued to glare at her as she whipped the tea towel from her shoulder and dried her hands. 'This conversation is over. Mrs Harlow will be going nowhere anytime soon. Now, get on with making her tea and get back to work.'

Sylvia bowed her head. The sister was right. Right now, the hospital wasn't a place any child should be unless they needed medical attention. 'Yes, Sister.'

Sister Dyer threw an audible tut in Sylvia's direction before gathering the cleaned paraphernalia from the countertop and striding, nose in the air, from the room.

'Bloody hell,' Sylvia muttered as she set about making a cup of tea for Mrs Harlow.

There had to be something she could do to ease the poor woman's pain. Maybe... No, she couldn't. Could she? Maybe with Freda and Veronica's help, then...

A slow smile curved Sylvia's lips as her mind reeled with the beginnings of an idea that would almost certainly bring a much-needed burst of joy to Mrs Harlow's heart – but might also land Sylvia and her friends in a whole load of trouble if they were caught. But surely Freda and Veronica would be onboard with her idea if it meant Mrs Harlow's guaranteed, if brief, happiness? Sylvia lifted the whistling kettle off the heat. This war was taking too much, and if she and her friends could just do a little extra now and then, it would get them all through the hardships a little easier. Right?

21

FREDA

'Sylvia, what in heaven's name is this all about?' Freda demanded as her friend dragged her and Veronica by their elbows into the ladies' toilets. 'I haven't got time for fun and games. I've already been on the sharp end of Sister's tongue this morning and if she catches us in here, she'll—'

'Shh. I just need to talk to the pair of you for two minutes.'

Freda exchanged a look with Veronica as Sylvia made her way along the row of five cubicles, pushing at each door, presumably to check they were empty. Crossing her arms, Freda waited while Veronica darted anxious glances at the closed main bathroom door.

'Right. Good. We're alone.' Sylvia grinned, her pretty brown eyes alight with suspiciously excited intent. 'I have a plan to do something for a patient of mine, but I need your help.'

Freda frowned. 'And who is this patient, might I ask?'

'Mrs Harlow.'

'Mrs Harlow?' Veronica echoed. 'But she's getting better every day, isn't she?'

Sylvia nodded. 'Exactly. Which means the woman is well

enough to cope with what I have in mind to do for her.' She looked from Veronica to Freda. 'Something that will undoubtedly give the poor woman just the boost she needs to get through the final days of her recovery.'

Inexplicable unease tiptoed along Freda's spine, yet the happiness in Sylvia's eyes was hard to dismiss. 'Alright, you've got our attention. What are you up to?'

Veronica smiled and planted her hands on her hips. 'And why do I feel as though Freda and I are going to run for the door the minute you tell us?'

'Mrs Harlow is suffering more and more the longer she is away from her children,' Sylvia said, her voice soft with care. 'She needs to see them. Be with them... even if it's only for a while.'

'And how can we help with that?' Freda asked, trying to fathom what her friend had planned. 'Children aren't allowed on the ward.'

'Exactly.' Sylvia grinned, her eyes flitting between Freda and Veronica. 'But if the three of us work together, we could ensure Mrs Harlow gets to see her kids for an hour this evening.'

Veronica laughed nervously. 'How?'

Freda dropped her arms and narrowed her eyes. 'I really don't like where this is going, Sylvia.'

'Just listen to me.' Sylvia glanced at the bathroom door and then back at Freda. 'All three of us are on duty this evening.'

Freda's unease only escalated at Sylvia's distinctively conspiratorial tone. 'And?'

'And, I'm hoping it won't come to it, but I'm sure I could drive an ambulance as well as I can a car if needs be.'

'You can drive?' Veronica asked, her eyes wide. 'I love that!'

Sylvia grinned. 'So do I. We've got to keep adding strings to our bows, V, and driving was one I wasn't going to miss out on. I learned as soon as I could afford to.'

'Which is very admirable,' Freda said, still not at all keen where this was heading if her suspicions were right, but knowing she had to hear what Sylvia had to say. 'But what does you driving an ambulance and Mrs Harlow have to do with one another?'

'Well...' Sylvia pulled back her shoulders, her gaze alight with determination. 'I thought we could sneak Mrs Harlow out for an hour or so. Her mother lives in Corsham, which isn't much of a drive from here. She could visit with her children for a while, and we'll bring her back. Fingers crossed, Sister Dyer will be none the wiser.'

Freda stared in disbelief. 'Fingers crossed? My God, Sylvia.'

Veronica's breath hitched. 'We can't do that. It's impossible.'

Sylvia continued to smile as though she had come up with a solution that would have Hitler strung up by his manhood outside Bath Abbey come morning. 'Nothing's impossible, V. I've already been down to the ambulance bay and I'm really hoping Keith will agree to drive the ambulance rather than me, but if not, he'll at least be willing to cover for us if I take a van for an hour or two.'

'You've involved a driver in this, too?' Freda cried. 'Have you lost your senses?'

Her friend shrugged. 'Keith's a good sort. He doesn't mind.'

'He doesn't mind? Can you hear yourself?'

'Yes, Freda, I can.' Sylvia's smile vanished and her eyes flashed with annoyance. 'You and I can find a way to get Mrs Harlow into an ambulance. All we need to do is wait for Sister to go for her break, which we all know she takes at the same time, to the very minute, every shift. Then V can stretch out that time by joining her and becoming a royal pain in her backside by asking one question after the other, doing whatever she can think of to delay the sister's return to the ward. I'll take care of getting Mrs Harlow away from the ambulance bay, and you can return to the ward and do whatever necessary to distract the other nurses' attention from our missing patient.'

Freda's heart beat a little faster knowing that what Sylvia was suggesting was madness, yet maybe – just maybe – the three of them could make this happen for Mrs Harlow. The risks were huge, of course. Their jobs would almost certainly be in jeopardy if Sister Dyer uncovered their reckless adventure, but wasn't that what living was all about? Risk? Taking your chances? Fun?

Veronica nudged Freda from her thoughts with her elbow. 'What are you thinking?'

She dragged her gaze from Veronica to Sylvia, whose eyes pleaded with her in such a way that Freda knew she was beat.

'Maybe this could work if we have Keith's help and I manage to keep the other nurses busy, but...' She stared at Sylvia. 'Are you really so worried about Mrs Harlow that you're willing to take such a risk? For all three of us to take such a risk?'

'I'm not asking you to do anything you don't want to do, but yes, I am.' Sylvia clutched Freda's arm. 'Mrs Harlow is a wonderful lady, Freda, and as far as I'm concerned, she could be sent home to her mother, but Sister is having none of it. Just a few minutes with her kids will do Mrs Harlow wonders, I know it will. Please say you'll do this with me.' She looked at Veronica. 'Both of you. I need you with me in this.'

Freda's heart twisted with compassion for both Mrs Harlow *and* Sylvia. She turned to Veronica. 'What do you think?'

Veronica had somewhat paled, but determination darkened her green eyes. 'If Sylvia feels this strongly, I think we owe it to her to try. Who knows when something might matter to one of us this much and we call on each other for help?'

Freda slumped. She could hardly argue with that.

'Yes, we're taking a big risk and if we're caught' – Veronica's jaw tightened – 'we could be in big trouble. But I think having friends you'll do anything for and they'll do anything for you means more than any job, right?'

Freda faced Sylvia and her heart softened to see tears shining in her friend's eyes as she looked gratefully at Veronica.

Blowing out a breath, Freda threw her hands up in surrender. 'Fine. We're in. Let's hear more about this plan, Sylv.'

22

SYLVIA

A few hours later, albeit entirely exhausted in both body and mind, Sylvia could not stop grinning as she walked through Bath's dark, residential streets towards home. Her plan to enable Mrs Harlow to visit her children had gone off better than she could have hoped. Unbeknownst to her and Freda, Veronica was quite the actress – which made sense considering what she had gone through – and she kept Sister Dyer distracted and busy from the minute she'd accompanied her to the canteen. With the coast almost clear – admittedly it would have been preferable if Kathy Scott wasn't on shift; her eyes barely left the three of them for five minutes at the best of times – Sylvia had managed to wheel Mrs Harlow from the ward without having to explain herself to anyone.

Freda had been waiting at the ambulance and helped Mrs Harlow aboard before waving Sylvia and Keith off on their clandestine outing.

After a brief forty-minute visit with her precious babies, Sylvia had helped Mrs Harlow back into the ambulance – the woman grinning like all her Christmases had come at once, happy tears rolling down her cheeks. A job well done, and made even better by Mrs Harlow's safe return to the ward. Fingers crossed, no one was any the wiser to what Sylvia, Freda and Veronica had managed to pull off that evening and it felt so damn good!

Sylvia sighed happily and then flinched.

Up ahead of her, a certain someone leaned against a neighbour's front garden wall watching her, his hands shoved into his pockets and his collar turned up in a way she found far too sexy.

Her heart kicked.

The beams of the bright full moon seemed to be directed entirely on Jesse like he was an ethereal being.

'Bloody man,' Sylvia whispered into the darkness.

Swallowing hard, she tilted her chin, proud that there had not been – and never would be – as much as a blip to her gait when she'd seen him. As she came closer, he stood away from the wall, his hands still in his pockets as he slowly strolled towards her.

They stopped barely two feet apart and Sylvia was forced to tip her head back to meet his dark eyes. 'We're going to have to stop meeting like this.'

A soft smile lifted his lips before it slowly faded. 'I understand you spoke to my mother a few days ago.'

Dread crawled around her heart. His face was so sombre, a muscle flexing in his jaw, his eyes burning into hers. 'I did.'

'You shouldn't have done that, Sylvia.'

Annoyance caught deep inside her. 'Why not? I was friendly enough.'

'You told her we went out.'

'Because we did.' She crossed her arms against the guilt that whispered through her, her handbag pressed uncomfortably against her knotted stomach. 'I don't lie, Jesse. Never have, never will. Lies hurt people and I've never been in the business of hurting people.'

He looked past her and, as the seconds ticked by, Sylvia became more and more uneasy. More and more irritated. Possibly more with herself that she was still standing there than she was with him.

'I was friendly enough,' she said a second time, defiance lacing her words. 'I don't understand why she has such a problem with me. She doesn't know me from Adam.'

'Who you are has nothing to do with it.'

'I beg to differ. The woman obviously caught one look at me – and quite possibly my mother – when you moved in and decided there and then neither my mother nor I were people she or her family would befriend.' Sylvia pinned him with a glare. 'But what makes my recent exchange with your mother worse is that I came into her home and did all I could, both personally and professionally, for a very sick little boy. Her son. Which I have no regrets about, Jesse, none at all, but to have her thank me with the most beautiful cake I've ever seen or tasted and then, days later, she slams the door in my face. Well...' She glared. 'Did she tell you she did that?'

'She did.'

'And what did you say to her about it?'

'I told her you were different.'

Sylvia frowned. 'Different? Why am I different to anyone else?'

'Oh, you're different all right, Sylvia Roberts. Different to any woman I've ever met.'

His gaze grazed over her face, his eyes smouldering in such a way that she barely managed to stem the shiver that treacherously rippled through her core.

'If you don't know that,' he said, quietly, 'I have no idea how you've been interpreting the attention you get from me whenever I lay eyes on you.' His intense study lingered on her lips. 'It's not something I've found myself doing to other women as a rule.'

Sylvia stood tall and battled the urge to grab the lapels of his jacket, yank him forward and plant a good, hard kiss on his lips. 'What is your mother's problem with me? I want to know.'

His gaze bored into hers before he looked down and kicked a stone. He met her eyes once more. 'I've told you. The problem's not you.'

Familiar insecurity bit at her heart, threatening her bravado. Of course it was her. It was always her. Didn't her history with men tell the world as much? 'So who is then, Jesse? You? What's coming next? The "it's not you, it's me" chestnut?' She huffed a laugh. 'Save your breath. I've heard the same old story a hundred times before.'

His gaze hardened. 'I mean it, Sylvia. It's not you.'

'No? So, it's not the way I dress? Not because I wear makeup? Not because I'm the wrong class? Live on the wrong side of the street? Give me a break. It's always something about me.'

She pushed past him and strode forward, tears pricking her eyes before his hand gripped fast on her elbow and he spun her around. 'For the love of God, it's none of those things.'

'No?'

'No.'

'Then—'

'It's because you're a nurse. Because you're confident and beautiful. Because you're kind, competent and came to my brother's rescue when Mum didn't know what to do for him.'

She barely resisted stumbling backwards from the intensity of his gaze and voice. 'What?'

He closed his eyes, pain etched on his face. 'She's struggling. Really bloody struggling.'

Words escaped her and Sylvia pressed her lips together, tears smarting her eyes to see the pain etched on Jesse's face.

She swallowed and tentatively reached forward, gently placed her hand on his forearm. 'I'm sorry. I didn't realise…'

He dropped his chin and when he opened his eyes, they pleaded for her understanding. 'Dad was killed almost two and half years ago, but instead of growing stronger, she weakens in her mind every day. Obsessively cleaning. Over the top worrying where her kids are. Barely eating. Refusing to ask for help.' He swallowed. 'It's bad, but I don't know what to do to help her.'

Sympathy and care for this wonderful – from what she'd had evidenced so far – good and kind man seared deep in her heart. 'Listen, it's good you told me,' she said quietly. 'I'll look out for her if that will help. Do what I can to get the snooty housewives off her back and at least try to convince your mum I'm all right, that she can rely on me...' She winked and smiled, hoping to provoke one from him. 'Once she gets past my pain-in-the-arse attitude, of course.'

His chest rose as he inhaled a long breath, no smile forthcoming unfortunately. 'Thank you, but this, you and me. It's already making things worse for her. Our talking – going out – clearly isn't the best idea.'

She spent her days and nights comforting and caring for those suffering; the thought she was in any way adding to his mother's pain was like a punch to her stomach. 'I don't understand. Why are we making it worse?'

He held his hand to the back of his neck, his gaze unwavering. 'Surely you feel it, don't you?'

Her heart picked up speed as he stared at her in that intense, incredibly sexy way of his. She pulled back her shoulders as her worry gave way to stupid, dangerous hope that he implied what she was beginning to feel for him was stirring in him too. But what a fool she'd be to allow herself to go there. Again.

He stepped closer, lifted his fingers and tucked a fallen curl behind her ear. 'My mum is afraid of this. Of us. I like you, Sylvia. A lot, and I've told her as much.'

'You've told your mum you like me?'

'Yes, and it's only made her worse. But, like you, I don't lie and when she asked if I had feelings for you...' He dropped his gaze to her mouth. 'I said yes.'

Her heart beat faster at the very real possibility Jesse wasn't rejecting her, but warning her of what lay ahead of them should she agree... to what? She was afraid to ask him to specify exactly what his feelings meant and break the moment. Especially when he stood inches away from her, looking at her as though she was Rita bloody Hayworth, rather than just good old Sylvia Roberts.

He leaned closer and his lips touched hers, and God help her, Sylvia took a chance and curled her fingers around his muscular biceps, felt the bliss of his mouth on hers, his tongue searching, demanding. She kissed him back with every ounce of passion, every inch of her heart until arousal simmered inside her, just as it did every time they were together, every time he looked at her. Oh, if only she didn't know what she knew. If only she could trust that this man would fight for her, but he wouldn't. Not in the end.

After she'd taken what she could from him, branded what she could to her body and memory, Sylvia eased him away.

'Romance is complicated enough, Jesse, without adding a mother who wants nothing to do with me to the list. Whatever this is between us, it ends now. I won't do this again.'

'Do what?'

'This. Take a chance on something possibly growing between us. Not after what you've just said. I've been let down and hurt too many times, too deeply, to walk along that road again.'

'Sylvia—'

'No. I've got my friends. My good friends.' She hitched her bag onto her arm and stepped past him. 'For the time being, that's all I need.'

The heat of his stare followed her all the way along the street, and it wasn't until she was out of his possible sight that Sylvia released her held breath. She had meant what she said. All she needed was Freda and Veronica but, damn, it felt good to acknowledge Jesse wanted to court her, even though it would almost certainly be proven – given time – that he wouldn't want her for his wife. They never did.

23

FREDA

Freda hitched the belt of her dressing gown tighter and yawned as she wandered downstairs, her eyes itchy from lack of sleep. She and her friends' gargantuan level of rule-breaking the night before had meant she had dozed for the last seven hours rather than slept, wondering if or when her, Sylvia and Veronica would have to face the consequences of their actions. Yet, throughout the night, she had not once regretted going along with Sylvia's plan. How could she, having seen the delight and happiness in Mrs Harlow's eyes and face upon her return to the ward?

There was every possibility that Mrs Harlow herself would unwittingly arouse Sister Dyer's suspicions, considering her complete change in demeanour, but there was little use in worrying about that now. The deed had been done.

The letterbox in the front door clattered and three envelopes fell onto the hallway mat. Freda yawned again as she bent down to retrieve them. One for her father, one for her mother, one for...

She stopped and slowly raised her hand to cover her mouth, the other envelopes forgotten as they fluttered to the floor. Her heart hammered. The newspaper's stamp above her address was there in black ink for all to see. Her hand trembled as she put her finger under the seal and pulled out the typed note.

Dear Miss Parkes,

I have read your article and feel that it would be of avid interest to our readers. With so many women left at home while their husbands, sons, brothers and uncles serve in our Forces, to give them opportunity to read about the care and attention of the nursing staff here in Bath would be cheering. More than that, the empathy that you propose in the re-telling of the serving officers' stories in such a raw and truthful way will encourage public morale and belief that people know the truth of what their loved ones are enduring.

Therefore, the Bath Chronicle would very much like to publish your...

'Freda? There you are!'

Freda started and whipped the letter behind her back, adrenaline coursing through her.

'I was just about to call for you,' her mother exclaimed as she emerged from the kitchen, wiping her hands on a tea towel, the clipped curls on her forehead dipping as she frowned. 'Is that the post? Letters are taking longer and longer to arrive, but I'm grateful for anything we receive. Is there any word from your brother?'

The hope in her mother's eyes clawed at Freda's conscience as weight of her mother's wish for her to be 'a good girl' and provide her with eternal peace of mind twisted like a knife inside her. Freda hesitated. The natural thing for her to do would be to bend down and pick up the envelopes she'd dropped, but if she did that, her mother would almost certainly see...

'What are you hiding behind your back?' Her mother came closer, her eyes clouded with suspicion. 'Let me see.'

'It's nothing. Just a letter from a friend.'

'Then there shouldn't be a problem with me seeing it.'

There was no escape. Her mother would harangue her mercilessly, but now was not the time for her to learn about the article. Once it was in print, maybe, just maybe, there would be a small chance her mother might feel a little pride in her eldest, if errant, daughter.

'Mum, please.'

Her mother held out her hand. 'Now, Freda.'

Freda drew back her shoulders and held her mother's angry gaze. 'No.'

'What?'

'It's private.'

'Private?' Her mother snapped. 'It's from someone I wouldn't approve of, isn't it? For goodness' sake, give it to me. Right now!'

Dorothy came out of the kitchen, followed by their father, and Freda embraced the rush of determination that swept through her. Her sister's eyes were alight with malicious glee, her mouth stretched in a grin. Well, Dorothy could relish what was building in their hallway all she wanted because there was no chance Freda was giving up this dream opportunity to finally see her writing in print.

'What's going on?' her father demanded. 'It's barely eight o'clock in the morning. I will not have raised voices between my wife and child before I head off to work. Now, what on earth has happened?'

'She is hiding a letter from me, Clive,' her mother cried, her cheeks mottled. 'I won't have my girls keeping secrets from me. Good girls do not lie and hide things from their mothers.'

'Mum, I'm an adult.' Freda sighed. 'I have every right to keep my correspondence private if I choose to do so.'

'See? Insolence!' She snapped her gaze to her husband. 'Tell her, Clive. Tell her to give me that letter.'

'No.' Freda glared. 'I won't! It's my own business.'

Dorothy's gasp was loud… as was the exaggerated drama of it.

'Why you—' Her mother stepped forward, her hand raised.

Freda froze. She could not remember a single time her mother had slapped or smacked her. Was this what the war was doing to people? Turning man against man? Mother against child?

'Mary, don't you dare!' her father boomed, making Freda and Dorothy jump and his wife freeze. 'What is the matter with you? You are willing to strike your daughter over a letter she has every right not to share with us? We have lost one son and the other is missing. A thousand sons are missing. What does a letter to Freda matter, when the entire world is in turmoil and grief? My God, I am ashamed. Entirely ashamed!'

'Oh, Clive. Don't say such things!'

Her mother promptly burst into tears and Dorothy rushed to embrace her, throwing a protective glare at Freda.

'Is it not true?' her father shouted.

Freda looked at each member of her family and waited for her guilt, her deference, but neither came; instead, she held her father's gaze with complete confidence and conviction. Her writing was the one thing she had of her own and she would not allow her family or anyone else to take it away from her. Tears burned behind her eyes. War or no war. A brother gone or a brother alive.

'I just want the best for my children,' her mother whimpered. 'All of them.'

Her father lowered his shoulders and turned his sombre gaze on Freda. 'And what do *you* want, Freda? God knows, I suspect often enough you are far from happy.'

Freda stared in surprise. 'You do?'

'Of course, I am your father and I am not blind.' He pointedly glanced at his wife. 'Neither is your mother.'

Freda looked around her family's expectant faces as they stared at her, her heart swelling with love for her father, in particular. That he would ask her what she wanted, that he had noticed her frustration, was like forgiveness for all the resentment she had harboured against her mother for the last couple of years.

She inhaled a long breath and drew the letter from behind her back. 'It's like I told you before, Dad, I long to write for newspapers and magazines. I want to be a writer.'

'Oh, not this nonsense again,' her mother protested. 'Freda, you cannot—'

Freda's father sharply raised his hand, cutting her mother off, his gaze on Freda. 'And I'm guessing that letter contains something that pertains to your wish to write?'

'Yes. It's from the *Bath Chronicle*.' She steadfastly kept her gaze on her father rather than her mother or Dorothy. 'They want to publish an article I submitted to them last week.'

'You sent them an article? About your work at the hospital?'

'And the serving men who have come into the hospital from Bristol. I've also acknowledged the mothers who have lost children, or the ones who have been injured saving their children from harm, or even death.' Her heart beat faster, her passion emerging as she finally looked at her mother and sister. 'Men and women doing what they can to survive and help others. To feed one another and save lives.' She faced her father. 'This is just the beginning of what I want to do, Dad. If I can get my writing published locally, who knows what my future might be. Maybe I will write for a city paper one day. If the war continues, I might even...' Freda stopped, her heart pounding.

Her father's face was etched with concern, his eyes dimmed with apprehension. 'You might even what, my love?'

Encouraged by the endearment, Freda smiled, hoping it would go some small way to allaying his fears that she hadn't completely lost her mind. 'Report from where the real danger lies.'

He closed his eyes. Her mother emitted a small squeak before putting her hand to her mouth. Dorothy's eyes were so wide, Freda feared they might roll right from their sockets onto the hallway carpet.

She walked forward and put her hand on her father's arm. 'But that is in the future, Dad. Not yet. The fact the newspaper wants to publish my very first article gives me encouragement that I can truly write. If I can write more pieces for the *Bath Chronicle*, that is enough for now. I promise.'

The atmosphere was thick with tension. So much so, even Dorothy had been silenced.

Then, after a long moment, her father opened his arms and Freda stepped into them, inhaled his familiar smell of soap and pipe smoke, hoping his embrace was a sign of his understanding. Maybe even his blessing.

24

SYLVIA

Sylvia pushed a final pin into her hat and reached for her coat just as Kathy Scott entered the staff room.

'Oh, hello, Sylvia,' Kathy said in her usual sing-song voice. 'How are you?'

Planting on a smile, Sylvia closed her locker and turned. 'Good. How are you?'

'Oh, happy as always.' Kathy's bright blue eyes twinkled, her smile wide as she walked to her locker and opened it. 'Why don't you hang on a minute, and I'll walk out with you?'

Sylvia inwardly groaned but managed to keep her smile in place even if her cheeks were beginning to ache from the strain of it. 'Sure.'

She had promised Veronica and Freda she would make a bit more of an effort to get along with Kathy and bury her so-far unfounded suspicions that the woman wasn't to be trusted. There was just something about her that Sylvia couldn't shake but, considering Sister Dyer – in her wisdom – had decided to change the rota up a bit, it meant she would be working more closely with Kathy for the foreseeable.

Tension stiffened Sylvia's shoulders as she watched Kathy unpin her cap and let her blonde hair tumble over her shoulders before she rummaged around in her handbag and finally produced a hairbrush. She turned to the mirror hanging on the inside of her locker door. After a lot of brushing and fluffing, she swiped on some lipstick, dropped it in her purse after her brush and spun around, all smiles and teeth. 'Right. I'm good to go. You?'

Sylvia continued to smile. 'As I have been for the last seven minutes.'

Kathy's smile wavered as she pinned Sylvia with a stare before she looked away. 'Good, then let's go.'

They walked along the corridor in silence for a minute or two, but as they left the hospital through its double doors and emerged into the early morning air, Kathy blew out an exaggerated breath.

'I suppose you're wondering why I asked to walk out with you when I never have before...' she said, suggestion lacing every carefully delivered word.

Sylvia sharply turned, her every instinct on high alert. Why hadn't she asked herself as much? What she knew of Kathy Scott told her that everything the woman did, she did with an agenda. 'And?'

'It's about what you, Freda and Veronica got up to the other night.'

Dread dropped like a stone into Sylvia's stomach. 'What do you mean?'

'Oh, come on, Sylvia. I'm talking about the three of you blatantly disobeying rules and illegally taking a patient out of the hospital.'

If such a thing were possible, Sylvia could have sworn she felt the blood drain from her face. 'I've got no idea what you're talking about.' She held Kathy's smarmy gaze for a moment before looking towards the hospital entranceway. 'I'd better go. See you tomorrow.'

Kathy's hand shot out and gripped Sylvia's elbow.

Anger simmered in Sylvia's stomach as she slowly turned, her gaze on Kathy's hand and her mouth pursed until Kathy – intelligently – released her.

'Look...' Kathy sighed and plumped her curls with her cupped hand, her hazel eyes roaming over the people walking back and forth around them. 'I'm not going to do anything about what I know – at least not yet – but I wanted you to know I know.'

Sylvia glared, her fingers itching to slap the sanctimonious look from Kathy's face. 'Why?'

'Because it's about time you three stopped swanning around the ward as though butter wouldn't melt, and silently telling the lot of us that no one's allowed to impinge on your little friendship circle.'

She huffed a laugh. 'We have never done any such thing. Me and my friends are open to getting to know anyone... nice, on the ward.'

Kathy sniffed and looked past Sylvia for a heartbeat before turning her cold gaze to hers once more. 'I don't like how you think you're better than everyone else and I told Sister Dyer as much. That's why she put the new rota in place. She agrees that all the nurses should be regularly swapped with one another through their shifts in order to forge good relationships and build unwavering trust between us. Even you must see the sense in that?'

Sylvia trembled with suppressed annoyance. 'Of course.'

'Good.' Kathy beamed. 'You three won't be able to remain as you are forever, after all.'

Sylvia crossed her arms. 'And why's that? I really hope you don't think this little game of keeping what you think you know about us to yourself is going to make us like or trust you, Kathy.

You do realise holding this nonsense over us only reinforces what I've suspected about you all along.'

Kathy smirked. 'Which is?'

'That you are a nasty piece of work and jealous of me and my friends. That you wish you were as popular with the officers who come into the ward as we are and, more importantly, you were as good at your bloody job as we are!'

Colour darkened Kathy's cheeks and she stepped back, her eyes narrowed. 'I'd be very careful if I were you, Sylvia. If the wrong people find out about your little escapade the other night, it could mean losing your job, your career... Freda and Veronica losing theirs, too. Maybe you should start being a little bit nicer to me, include me a bit more in your lives. Especially if you want me to keep schtum.'

Sylvia smiled, but her heart picked up speed, belying her nonchalance. 'Why don't you take me and my friends out of the equation and give some thought to Mrs Harlow, huh? It's the patients that matter in everything we do. Not us.'

'Maybe, but there's a war on. Who knows if any of us will come out of it in one piece?'

'Bloody hell, Kathy, if we can't hold on to the belief that we will get through Hitler's rampage alive, how in God's name are we supposed to instil that belief in our patients?' Sylvia glared. 'This job isn't about you, it's about helping others and there is no reason any of us shouldn't survive this war. Having you imply otherwise helps no one.'

'All I'm saying is, I hope I, if not all of us, eventually fall in love, get married, but in the meantime, who knows how long we'll be stuck here working together? We should make an effort to befriend one another. The three of you barely glance at Carole and Martha and only speak to me because I give you little choice about it. Why don't you think about making some changes before the information I have does it for you?' She hitched her bag onto her arm and turned away. 'See you tomorrow.'

Sylvia muttered a curse as she glared at Kathy's retreating back, wishing the bloody woman would walk faster and open the space between them. Guilt writhed inside her. There were elements of truth to what Kathy had said and maybe it was time she, Freda and Veronica opened up a little more to the other nurses on the ward. Did others feel the same about them as Kathy clearly did?

Worrying her bottom lip, Sylvia left through the hospital entrance and hurriedly picked up her pace towards home. Who knew how long Kathy would keep quiet about the trip away from the hospital with Mrs Harlow? There was no doubting she knew the truth of it. It was written as plain as day in her eyes and across her smug little face. Sylvia swallowed. What if she lost her job? God, what if her friends lost their jobs, too? All because they'd done what she'd asked of them.

Sylvia blew out a shaky breath through pursed lips. One thing was clear. Kathy Scott held the upper hand over all of them. For now…

As she was more and more prone to do these days, when Sylvia got close to her own house, she glanced across the street towards Jesse's house and slowed her walk. The blackout curtains were still drawn, which was hardly surprising considering it was barely seven in the morning. God, how she longed to talk to him, even if it had been her who'd called a halt to anything that might have had the chance to start between them.

Doing her best to bury memories of Jesse's kiss, Sylvia sighed. The bombing that had echoed across the miles between Bath and

Bristol for most of her night shift convinced her more and more that the Germans would soon target Bath.

Surely it was only a matter of time before their beautiful city and every other small city and town in Britain was drawn into the war. How could they not be? But the one thing Britons wouldn't do was surrender, which meant the entire country would become embroiled in an inevitable struggle of attack and counterattack.

Reaching her front door, Sylvia fought to draw a halt to any more thoughts about the war and Kathy Scott. Both problems would still be there in a few hours. Getting some sleep was what mattered now. She pulled her key from inside her purse. She planned to devour a couple of slices of bread and jam, followed by a thorough strip wash at the sink and, finally, collapsing into bed and sleeping for England. Fingers crossed, her mother would not get in the way of those, quite frankly, humble plans. Considering Eileen Roberts didn't usually rouse from her bed before midday if she'd had a shift at the Garrick's Head the night before, Sylvia sent up a silent prayer that she'd find the house in blessed peace.

She entered the hallway and strained her ears for any noise.

All seemed quiet except for... What in God's name was that?

The scraping and stumbling coming from behind the ajar kitchen door set Sylvia's every nursing instinct to high alert. Dropping her bag to the floor, she rushed for the kitchen and pushed open the door.

Her mother jerked and stumbled back and forth, her eyes wide with panic and her fingers clawing at her throat, the skin around her mouth the palest blue.

Sylvia ran forward. 'My God, Mum, are you choking?' She moved behind her and abruptly forced her mother forward. 'Work with me, all right?'

Her heart pounding in her ears and her blood pumping, Sylvia raised her hand and slapped her mother hard on the back, once, twice... 'Come on, Mum. You're not going out in a blaze of bloody glory, you're bloody choking, for crying out loud.' Three, four... Her panic rising, Sylvia gritted her teeth. 'Come on, let's be having you!'

Mustering all her might, Sylvia brought her hand down hard on her mother's back and a tiny piece of something creamy-white flew from her mouth and landed with a resounding 'ping' against a metal dish on the table. Her harried breaths joined with her mother's, as the kitchen clock continued to count the seconds, before her mother straightened and splayed her hands on the table, sweat beading her brow.

'Christ alive. That'll teach me for trying to better myself and get my arse out of bed of a morning and eat a bit of fruit for my breakfast,' she gasped. 'Didn't I always tell you fruit is the devil's food, right alongside vegetables?'

'Fruit?' Ever-so-slightly trembling, Sylvia leaned around her mother and screwed up her nose as she tentatively inspected the morsel on the table. 'Is that apple?'

'Yep, and it's safe to say I'll never be tempted to eat one of the buggers again.' Her mother closed her eyes, took a deep breath. 'Well, that started my morning off a bit differently than expected, I can tell you.'

'And damn well ended my day with a slice of drama I could've done without.' Sylvia blew out a breath and sat down in one of the chairs at the table. 'Grab yourself some water. Do you feel all right now?'

'Right as rain,' her mother said as she walked to the sink. 'That was... good of you to... you know.'

Sylvia smiled at her mother's turned back. It was the best she could hope for in way of a thank you. 'All part of the service.'

Her mother returned to the table with a mug of water and sat down. Sylvia assessed her and breathed easier to see the colour returning to her mother's cheeks, the horrible blue around her mouth gone.

'Well, despite the unconventional welcome home this morning, I'm glad normal life is resumed,' Sylvia said firmly as she pushed up from her chair and walked across the kitchen to the bread bin. 'I'm going to have something to eat and get myself to bed. I can hardly stand up after all the excitement since I've been home.'

The legs of her mother's chair scraped over the floor tiles as she stood. 'Yeah, I think I'll go back to bed for an hour, too.'

'Good idea.'

'You know people are talking about you and that fella over the road, don't you?'

Sylvia stiffened and slowly placed two slices of bread on a plate. 'Are they? Let them. It's no skin off my nose.'

'Come on, I'm owed more than that, aren't I?'

Sylvia walked to the larder and pulled out the butter dish and a jar of gooseberry jam.

'I don't owe you anything, Mum. All I will say is this. Jesse Howard, although easy on the eye' – she glanced over her shoulder and winked, bringing a smile from her mother – 'is dealing with issues I want no part of, thank you very much.'

'Issues? What issues?'

Sylvia walked to the kitchen counter and stuck her knife in the butter. Why had she said that? Now her mother would no doubt be investigating the answer to that question for days. 'Wrong word. Not issues, just things I want no part of. All I want, no...' She faced her mother. 'All I *need* from now on is my work at the hospital and my friends. Nothing else.'

'I see. So, the fact he was out on his doorstep last night having a set-to with his mother and shouting that he's falling in love and, no matter what she says, he's going to do whatever he has to do to get the girl concerned to feel the same way about him, is neither here nor there, is it?'

Sylvia's mouth dried and her heart beat faster. 'What?'

Her mother smirked. 'Don't know what it is about you, my girl. You don't half choose them. Only this time, I think you might be turning your back on a good 'un. Even if he is coloured.'

And with that, her mother walked out of the room, leaving Sylvia staring after her and wondering what the hell she was supposed to do next. She was better off without a man, any man, but God, Jesse made her heart sing. Maybe she could take a risk again, after all. She softly smiled and turned back to her bread and jam, stubbornly ignoring the warning bells that were ringing in her head.

25

VERONICA

Veronica strode back along the white-tiled corridor towards the ward, nodding hello to a couple of orderlies as she carried a fresh load of towels from the laundry. She was so looking forward to a night out with Freda and Sylvia later. Not working with her friends again today had been horrible. Lord only knew how she'd feel by the end of the week if—

'You there!'

Veronica spun around.

'Yes, you.' The surgeon waved his mask at her as he spoke, his gaze intense. 'Put down those towels and come with me. Right now!'

'But I'm—'

'I don't care! I need an extra pair of hands and yours are the first I found. Now come on. Quickly!'

Veronica reeled left and right and then dumped the towels on a stretcher to the side of her before racing after the surgeon. She caught up with him as he pulled his mask over his nose and mouth and pushed open a set of double doors that led to a darkened corridor through to another set of doors.

'In there,' he said, pointing through the open doorway of a small room with a metal sink and glass-fronted cupboards on the walls. 'Get washed up and then put on an apron, gloves and mask.'

'Wait.' Veronica stared at him. Had he lost his mind? 'I've never stood in on a surgery. Not ever.'

'Well, today's your lucky day then, isn't it? Theatre is just next door. Quick as you can.'

The doors swung closed behind him.

Veronica froze, her mind racing before she blinked from her stupor and turned to the sink. She grabbed the soap and started to scrub her hands and wrists. What on earth had she got herself into now? What made it worse was that she could've sworn there had been a glimpse of amusement in the surgeon's eyes, as though he was entirely revelling in her shock.

She stopped scrubbing and slowly narrowed her eyes. More bullying.

Well... She recommenced scrubbing with significantly more gusto than before. He had picked on the wrong nurse today. She'd show him that, whatever his demands might be, they would be nothing compared to what other men had demanded of her. Moreover, she'd survived those demands and was still standing.

Once she was washed and fully dressed in surgical garb, Veronica strode from the washroom into the operating room. Her steps immediately faltered, her forced bravado wavering as nerves knotted her stomach. Masses of tubes, machines and surgical paraphernalia of which she had no idea of their name or function littered the room in every direction. Her body trembled with the effort it took not to turn and flee back to the safety of the ward... or maybe even home.

'Good. You're here. I'm Mr Martin.' The surgeon nodded to the patient lying on the table, a breathing apparatus over his mouth and nose and an open wound surrounded by green cloth on his abdomen. 'This is Sergeant Russell and that' – he tilted his head towards a masked woman sitting at the sergeant's head – 'is Nurse Wilson, our highly skilled and quite lovely anaesthetist.'

Veronica turned and stared into the most astonishingly big, bright hazel eyes she had ever seen in her life. Her heart gave a hard, inexplicable jolt, as the curve of the nurse's cheeks rose pink above the top of her mask when she smiled. Veronica merely nodded, seeming to have entirely forgotten how to curve her own lips.

She snapped her gaze to the surgeon who was talking again. 'Right then, Nurse. So all I need you to do is keep one hand firmly pressed here and then...' He pulled a tray that glinted with silver surgical instruments closer. 'Hand me the instruments I ask for, as and when.' He winked. 'You'll be out of here before you know it.'

But she wasn't. Far from it.

She had no idea how much time passed with adrenaline coursing through her body at a rate of knots, her heart thumping with unexpected joy and excitement; no idea how she managed to keep up with the doctor's instructions until it felt as though she had worked with him a dozen times before. The rush of seeing Mr Martin work, the efficiency and knowledge that flowed from his mind to his hands, how he realigned complex nerves, veins and goodness knows what else, all added to Veronica's euphoria. Although her hands and apron were smattered and smeared with blood, and rivulets of sweat rolled over her forehead and into her eyes, she had never felt more alive.

'And we're done,' Mr Martin said with curt satisfaction as he pulled down his mask. He stepped back and smiled. 'You can stitch him up whenever you're ready, Nurse.'

Veronica grinned. 'Absolutely.'

'You have done a fine job today. Thank you.'

Veronica stared, pride bursting inside her, as the doctor left the room. In all the time she had worked with Sister Dyer, not once had she thanked any of her nurses for their efforts or contribution. It felt incredibly good to have someone offer even the smallest amount of praise. She slid a glance at Nurse Wilson, but her back was turned as she worked at one of the machines. Veronica gathered all she needed to stitch up Sergeant Russell's wound from the tray beside her, happiness humming through her. She could not wait to tell Freda and Sylvia all about what had been, quite frankly, the most impulsive, highly stressful, completely wonderful day ever.

Once her stitching was finished, Veronica put the instruments she'd used in the designated tray for cleaning and then walked to the room at the side of the theatre, secretly hoping to find Nurse Wilson there. Veronica swallowed against the dryness in her throat. Lord only knew what she would talk to her about but, for some reason, she wanted to at least tell the pretty anaesthetist her name. But, when she pushed opened the door, the room was empty, Nurse Wilson nowhere to be seen.

Burying her disappointment – and whatever that disappointment might mean – Veronica removed her apron and mask, tossed them in the bin and then washed her hands and arms before heading back to her ward.

She turned a corner and walked straight into Sister Dyer's path.

'Nurse Campbell! Where on earth have you been?' she demanded, her eyes flashing with annoyance. 'I have been looking for...' She stopped and appraised Veronica from head to toe through narrowed eyes. 'There is blood on the skirt of your uniform.' She rubbed the edge of Veronica's collar between her thumb and finger. 'And here, too.'

'Mr Martin commandeered me to theatre, Sister,' Veronica explained. 'I had no choice but to do his bidding.'

'Is that right?'

'Yes, he was most insistent that I follow—'

'I am your senior, Nurse Campbell. You report to me, not Mr Martin. Why he seems to think he can pluck my staff from the ward whenever he sees fit, I have no idea.' She glared along the corridor in the direction of the theatre before turning her steely gaze on Veronica once more. 'But you should be ashamed by the state of yourself. Go to the laundry and see if there is a spare dress and apron. Re-pin your hat and' – she slapped her hand along each of Veronica's shoulders – 'smarten yourself up. You are a disgrace!'

'Is there a problem here I can help with, Sister?'

Veronica inwardly grimaced and slowly turned around.

Mr Martin and Nurse Wilson approached, the anaesthetist's extraordinary beauty no longer hidden behind a mask. Veronica's entire body burned with awareness, a strange tingling whispering through her until she forced her gaze to the surgeon.

'Is this reprimand my fault, by any chance?' he asked. 'Only I gave Nurse...' He looked at Veronica and raised his eyebrows.

She pulled back her shoulders. 'Campbell, sir.'

He smiled and faced the sister. 'I gave Nurse Campbell no choice but to work with me this afternoon. A patient was brought in from Bristol with temporary stitching that had ripped open down to the tissue, during a rather perilous journey. It was a delicate procedure that I could not have done alone. Nurse Campbell's work was exemplary.'

'That may be so,' Sister Dyer snapped. 'But she is a member of my staff, not yours, and I insist that, from now on, you refrain from commandeering any of my nurses without my prior permission.'

'Of course.' The doctor dipped his head in somewhat ironic deference. 'However...'

'However?' Sister Dyer glared.

Veronica bit her bottom lip to trap the smile pulling at her lips, but when she sneaked a look at Nurse Wilson she grinned at Veronica from behind Mr Martin, and Veronica's smile broke.

'However...' Mr Martin continued, then looked at Veronica as she quickly wiped her smile. 'You performed remarkably well today, Nurse, and I wonder if you would like to work alongside myself and Nurse Wilson more often? I have worked with a handful of other nurses from the wards, but none have taken to theatre support as effortlessly as you. It was hugely impressive, I must say.'

'Oh, gosh.' Veronica grinned. 'I'd love to.'

He returned her smile.

'Excuse me,' Sister Dyer cried. 'Am I not standing here? Do I have no say in what happens with regards to my staff? Mr Martin, I suggest you send me a note with a suggested date and time to discuss this properly rather than in the middle of a corridor when myself and Nurse Campbell are needed back on the ward. This is most unacceptable.' She faced Veronica. 'You will remain on the ward until I have fully discussed this with Mr Martin, so I suggest you take that silly smile off your face and return to your work. Right now.'

Her belly trembling with suppressed laughter and absolute joy, Veronica gave a curt nod to the sister and surgeon, smiled at Nurse Wilson and rushed back to the ward feeling like her life had finally begun to take her on a new and wholly welcome path.

26

FREDA

Freda pegged a last pillowcase on the line in her back garden and picked up the empty washing basket. The familiar thundering of planes that had sounded in the distance just moments before grew infinitely louder and she lifted her hand to her brow, shading her eyes against the sun. Eight planes flew overhead in formation, but she had no idea what sort of planes they were, or even if they were German or British. Her ignorance was shaming. If she was serious about a career in journalism, she had to make a dedicated and concerted effort to read up about the technicalities of the artillery and machinery that both Britain and Germany had in their arsenal. She must ask more questions of the servicemen she came into contact with at the hospital. After all, the injured patients under her care deserved their stories to be told with absolute accuracy.

'Come on, Freda,' Dorothy called from the open back door, interrupting her thoughts. 'We're about to sit down for breakfast. Dad's only got a little while until he starts his shift.'

'Coming,' Freda said, hurrying inside.

She entered the kitchen and walked through to the hallway to store the washing basket in the cupboard under the stairs. Closing the door, Freda breathed deep, bracing herself for another family meal that would undoubtedly bring further questions and complaints from her mother about Freda's future intentions. Her father's voice drifted through the open kitchen door, and her heart swelled with love. He had been so supportive since the morning she received the acceptance letter from the *Bath Chronicle*, telling her that his love of policing and the fact he had been called to the vocation when he was barely into his teenage years meant it would be unfair of him if he did not encourage his daughter in what might be her calling. His words had led her to telling him that nursing had never entered her mind until it had been drummed into her by her mother as a suitable *pastime* until she married.

Her father had merely smiled and told her he would not repeat this confession to her mother.

Taking a deep breath, Freda took her place opposite Dorothy at the kitchen table. Their mother and father sat at each end, every member of the family in the same place, every day, since she'd been old enough to be promoted from her highchair to chair.

'So...' Her father smiled a thank you to his wife as she spooned some porridge into the bowl in front of him. 'What time do you start at the hospital today, Freda?'

'I'm due in at ten.' She reached for the teapot. 'I'm working with two nurses I don't know all that well, so I hope it goes smoothly. I work so effortlessly with Veronica and Sylvia, it's sometimes a challenge to get used to how some of the other nurses work.'

'Well, it's important you work well with everyone and everybody right now. This war is separating families, friends and colleagues. We all need to embrace unwavering comradery. I'm sure you know that well enough.'

Despite knowing her father was absolutely right, she hated that she would not be working with her friends for at least a week, possibly more. She was all too aware of how petty such a problem was in the scheme of things, but still it rankled that Kathy had been in cahoots with Sister Dyer and had successfully managed to separate her, Sylvia and Veronica.

'I do know, Dad. I just think the world of my friends.'

'Hmm,' her mother said, giving her a pointed look. 'But not enough that you refrained from going to the newspaper looking for another job behind their backs… and ours.'

Freda opened her mouth to respond when a second lot of distant rumbling silenced her. She locked gazes with her sister as another formation of planes flew overhead, rattling the china crockery and teapot. Yet, Dorothy's eyes were almost blank and entirely unreadable. Concern twisted in Freda's stomach. Usually, her sister's dramatic reactions to anything and everything meant Freda could read Dorothy like an open book, the majority of her thoughts rarely straying from the topics of boys, marriage or homemaking. Yet, for the first time, something else lingered in Dorothy's eyes. Something worrying.

The planes passed and Dorothy quickly looked at her plate, a faint blush on her cheeks.

'No more talk about Freda's writing for the paper, please, Mary,' her father said brusquely. 'I have given her my blessing and, while this war continues, I will have no more conflict in the house over matters that will never override the importance of lost lives.'

'There is no need to remind me about the importance of lost lives, darling,' her mother said stiffly, tears glinting in her eyes. 'After all, hardly an hour goes by that I do not think of David. Our son.'

Freda dragged her gaze from Dorothy's bowed head and sadness squeezed hard in her chest as her father covered her mother's hand with his where it lay on the table.

She looked at her father, hating the anguish etched on his face as she cleared her throat. 'Your support of my writing means the world to me, Dad.'

He lifted his hand from her mother's and dipped his spoon into his porridge. 'Good. Although, it is only one article so there is no need for any of us to lose our heads over it.'

A quiet foreboding whispered through Freda at her father's tone, which had been laced with a distinct air of dismissiveness. As though, deep down, he believed it was unlikely his daughter would succeed in having a second article published and his wife's concern over what she had called Freda's rebellion in a past argument was all a fuss about nothing. Maybe he wasn't encouraging her as much as she'd thought.

They began to eat, and Freda pushed a slice of toast around her plate, before forcing herself to take a small bite. If she had any hope of her parents accepting she had every intention of creating her own life rather than the one they had planned for her, she must speak out.

She put down her toast. 'Dad, I know you said no more talk about the paper, but I need to make it clear that my writing is not a passing fancy. I am serious about it. War or no war, it's something I've wanted to do forever but...' She looked at her mother. 'I have always been told that any route other than marriage was a sure route to either purgatory or debauchery, depending on Mother's mood.'

'How dare you?' her mother cried, eyes wide. 'Clive, are you going to let her get away with speaking to me like that?'

Freda turned to her father, her heart beating with pride. 'I'm sorry, Dad, but it's only right that you and Mum understand it's my intention to do all I can to make journalism my job rather than nursing.'

'Do you never intend marrying, Freda?' Dorothy asked quietly.

Freda looked at her sister. Her tone had not held any of its usual derision, only distinct sadness. 'I have no idea how I'll feel in the future, but right now, I have no intention to marry whatsoever.'

Dorothy slid her lowered gaze to her mother and back to Freda. 'Marrying and having children is all Mum has ever wanted for us so how can you not—'

'Our lives are our own, Dorothy.' She faced her mother. 'I'm sorry, Mum, but Dorothy and I are adults, and there are women younger than us putting their lives on the line every day through their will to contribute to the war effort. I honestly believe what you deem as a perfect life of domesticity will not sit well for a lot of women ever again once this war is over. So, if I were you, I would start opening your mind to a new way of life. Especially for your daughters' generation.'

'What is the matter with you? Clive, say something!' Her mother's cheeks were red, her eyes bulging as she looked from her husband to Freda. 'Where is my good little girl? I hardly recognise you sat there, raising your voice and telling me what's what.'

'I am hardly raising my voice, Mum, and I am speaking the truth. The war will change everything and if you don't—'

'Freda, stop.' Her father's voice cracked across the table like a whip. 'Right now.' He glared at her. 'I told you not to mention your writing at the table and you've done it anyway. I give you my support, yet you continue to argue with your mother. You have disappointed me.' He drew in a long breath, focused on his plate. 'So much so, I would very much like you to leave us to finish our meal in peace. I'm sure you can find something to eat at the hospital.'

Sickness coated her throat as Freda slowly pushed her plate away from her. On slightly trembling legs, she rose and first met her mother's triumphant gaze and then Dorothy's shocked one. Finally, she turned to stare at her father's turned cheek as he concentrated on eating his meal, as though she'd already left the room.

Swallowing hard, Freda jutted her chin and strode into the hallway, embracing the knot of pride that unfurled inside her. She had just told her parents where her true ambitions lie, that she had ideas for a future that went far beyond anything they might have planned for her. For the first time ever, she felt like her own person. Her own woman. And she vowed in that moment that she would never go back to who she'd been before.

27

SYLVIA

'You going out then?'

Sylvia turned from the hallway mirror and faced her mother, who squinted at her through a swirl of smoke, her cigarette bouncing on her bottom lip.

'I told you. I'm meeting Freda and Veronica for a drink.'

'Well, don't go to my place, will you? Been no fun in the Garrick's Head lately.' Her mother took a long drag on her cigarette and exhaled. 'Non-stop talk about this bloody war is all that fills the place these days.'

Sylvia barely managed to stop from rolling her eyes. They had been getting along surprisingly well since the choking incident and the last thing she wanted was to start things off between them again with an impulsive facial movement. 'That's hardly surprising,' she said, reaching for her coat from the hook beside her and slipping a sealed envelope into one of her pockets. 'I wouldn't be surprised if war talk is all there is in every pub up and down the country. People are saying Hitler isn't going to give up until he gets his murderous hands on the whole of Europe.'

Her mother sniffed. 'Yeah, well, we'll see about that. He's got no idea what he's dealing with. Us British don't bow down to anyone.'

Images of the wounds and infections, grief and pain she dealt with on a daily basis pushed at Sylvia's heart. She was grateful her mother wasn't subjected to any of it.

'I should get going. I'm going to be late,' Sylvia said, grabbing her handbag from the bottom stair and making for the door. 'Don't wait up.'

'Have a good one. See you in the morning.'

Sylvia walked outside and closed the front door behind her, giving a quick glance at the living room window to check the blackout curtain was in place. She and her mother might be getting along for the time being, but the last thing she needed was having her mother spot her walking across the street to the Howards'. Having seen Jesse head off to work a couple of hours ago from her bedroom window, Sylvia smiled, safe in the knowledge she'd have the chance to talk to his mother alone. Well, possibly, assuming none of Jesse's siblings came to the door instead.

Striding forward, she walked purposefully to Jesse's front door and knocked before she could change her mind. Her heart hammered and, despite the decidedly chilly night, her hands were clammy around the handles of her bag. It had turned out to be impossible for her to push Jesse from her mind and heart so here she was, laying her heart open to being broken once again. She wanted to give whatever this thing was growing between them a chance, which meant he, *and* his family, had her unyielding loyalty. So, if they stood the slightest chance of getting their relationship off to a hopeful start, she had to find a way to get his mother on side.

The door opened and Sylvia braced herself... only to look down into the beautiful, melted-chocolate eyes of Jesse's youngest sister. A girl of no more than eleven or twelve.

'Hello.' Sylvia smiled. 'Is your mum home, sweetheart?'

The girl grinned. 'You're the pretty lady who lives in the house with the green door.'

'Well, thank you for saying I'm pretty, and yes, I live at the house with the green door.'

'I'm Patricia.'

'Sylvia.'

'Jesse likes you.'

Rare heat seeped into Sylvia's cheeks. 'Does he?'

'Yes. He likes you, but Mum says you're...' She frowned. 'I don't know how to say the word.'

Sylvia's smile vanished and she cleared her throat, thinking whatever the word might be, she didn't need to hear it. 'Maybe that's for the best, eh? So, is she in? Your mum?'

Jesse's sister turned inside. 'Mum! The pretty lady you don't like is here!'

Half hoping the ground would open up and swallow her whole as Patricia trundled upstairs, Sylvia briefly closed her eyes. But, when she opened them again, she was still stood in front of Jesse's open front door with trepidation knotting her stomach at the sound of determined footsteps coming along the linoleum hallway floor.

Mrs Howard appeared, drying her hands on a tea towel, her eyes blazing with resentment. 'What do you want?'

Inhaling a strengthening breath, Sylvia held the other woman's hostile gaze. 'I want to clear the air between us.'

'There isn't any air between us to clear. You have your life and I have mine and I'd prefer it to stay that way. So...' She gave a curt nod towards the opposite side of the street. 'If you don't mind...'

'Mrs Howard, please. I really like Jesse and I know he's told you he likes me. There's a war on and all of us are doing our best to survive it. Is this dislike of me really necessary?' Sylvia slumped her shoulders, her heart twisting with sympathy. 'Jesse told me what happened to your husband and I'm sorry. I really am, but to decide you don't like me when—'

'Jesse had no business telling you or anyone else about my Ronald.' Pain flashed in Mrs Howard's eyes before they gleamed with annoyance. 'And don't stand there telling me who I should and shouldn't like neither. I don't want some Florence Nightingale turning up on my doorstep every five minutes.' She gripped the door. 'Just stay away from my family.'

Before she could even consider the repercussions, Sylvia slapped her hand to the door and held it there. 'Mrs Howard. Please. There are a lot of good people living on this street. Women all too willing to help each other out, whether their husbands are serving... or they are widowed. Don't you want to make friends here? Have people close by you can rely on? I know first-hand the war is getting closer and closer to Bath. Who knows when we'll be targeted? I want you to have a community around you. Don't make enemies unnecessarily.'

Unmistakable tears gleamed in Mrs Howard's eyes, her gaze hard, but Sylvia's heart ached with care. Yet, how was she to break down barriers between her and Mrs Howard when the woman's were rooted in such obvious pain?

Sylvia dropped her hand from the door and lowered her voice. 'Don't you want Jesse to be happy?'

'Don't you dare,' Mrs Howard said quietly. 'Every one of my children means everything to me. I've dedicated my whole life to their happiness.'

'And I'm glad, but right now, I truly believe it would make him happy if he had your blessing to explore whether there could be something real between us.' Sylvia's heart beat fast, but as much as she recognised the pain in Mrs Howard's eyes, she had also treated enough people suffering from long-term shock and grief to know that she needed people around her. 'I just want to get to know your son, get to know you, his brothers and sisters. Please, Mrs Howard. Give me a chance.'

Silence stretched, each second exacerbating the tension until Mrs Howard released her grip on the front door and took a step closer to Sylvia. 'I will always want Jesse to be happy, Nursey, but not with the likes of you. Got it?'

Battling against her ghosts, the horrible surge of unworthiness that rose inside of her, Sylvia tilted her chin. 'The likes of me, huh?'

'Yes, that's what I said.' The older woman arched an eyebrow. 'Do you want me to say it a little louder?'

'And who am I, Mrs Howard? Someone who does all she can to help her fellow man and woman? A person who is loyal to her friends and family, no matter what? A woman who longs to love and be loved...' Sylvia swallowed. *What the hell did I just say?* 'I am just asking for a chance, that's all. Not just for me, but for Jesse, too.'

Seconds ticked by until the derision in Mrs Howard's eyes slowly dimmed into something more akin to consideration. Grabbing the moment while it lasted, Sylvia quickly pulled the envelope from her pocket and thrust it towards Jesse's mother before the woman could recalibrate for a second character assassination.

'Could you please give this to Jesse? Read it if you like. There's nothing in there I don't mean. Whether you like it or not, your son and I deserve a chance, Mrs Howard. It would be really nice if you and your family could be a part of that.'

Without waiting for a response, Sylvia turned on her high heels, walked away from the Howard house and hurried along the street, gasping for a drink with her friends.

28

FREDA

December broke with a brisk wind that whipped along Bath's streets making people slap their hands to their hats and dash for cover. Freda bowed her head against a particularly powerful gust, her fingertips gripping the brim of her hat as it fought for release against its pins. By the time she reached the *Bath Chronicle* office, she would look as though she'd been pulled through a hedge backwards.

Turning onto Milsom Street, she started down its steep descent, praying her heeled shoes did not let her down and that she'd end up on her behind, while simultaneously hoping her second meeting with the paper's journalist, Mr Sinclair, proved less stressful than the first now that he'd accepted her article. His latest letter asking that she stopped by the office that morning with an outline for a second article had come as a surprise, albeit a welcome one.

With Sylvia now biting the bullet and embarking on a relationship with her handsome neighbour regardless of his mother's distrust of her, Veronica poised to work as a surgical nurse and – Freda smiled – her possibly being invited to write for the newspaper on a regular basis, it felt as though her and her friends' futures were looking up. They might be embroiled in a war that stretched across Europe, but there was still room for hope and there always would be.

She reached the newspaper office and, steadfastly ignoring the nerves jumping in her stomach, pushed open the door. Once again, she took a moment to allow her eyes to adjust to the grey, cigarette smoke semi-darkness that lingered throughout the space before walking across the wooden floorboards.

Just like before, the first person to notice her was the paper's secretary, Barbara, whose entire face lit with a smile. 'Miss Parkes! It's so lovely to see you again.'

'Good morning, Barbara, and please, call me Freda. How are you?'

'I'm as well as can be expected.' The secretary's smile faltered. 'But my parents recently received news that my older brother has been injured in France. We don't know how badly yet. I just pray he somehow finds his way back home. My mother's in pieces and we don't even know the full extent of things yet.'

'I'm so sorry.' Freda touched her arm. 'If there is anything I can do...'

'I'm doing all I can, as everyone is at the paper, to see if we can at least get him brought back to a Bath hospital to recover. It would be so much easier on my mother if she knew he was close by.'

'Well, I promise if he comes into my ward at the hospital, I will personally look after him and make sure I come to see you with any updates. How would that be?'

'That would be wonderful. Thank you.' Barbara's smile was strained and her eyes glazed with tears as she looked across the office. 'I assume you're here to speak to Richard?'

'Yes. Yes, I am.'

Barbara turned. 'Ah, there he is. Richard? Miss Parkes is here to see you.'

Freda met Richard Sinclair's eyes across the room as he walked towards her, her stomach treacherously flip-flopping as he came closer. Damn, if those ridiculous blue eyes didn't hold her where she stood.

He offered her a small smile. 'Miss Parkes.' He held out his hand. 'Nice to see you again.'

'Thank you, you too.' She took his hand, the skin-to-skin contact only escalating the perturbing chaos going on inside her. 'And, please, call me Freda.'

'As you wish.' He slid his hand from hers and gestured towards his desk. 'Come and take a seat.'

He had not offered her to call him by his first name and Freda immediately began to fret she had acted unprofessionally. The last thing she wanted was to lose even an ounce of his respect. If she was going to make a success of herself in a such a male-dominated field, she had to show she was by no means less serious about her work than he was about his... which was why her attraction to him was frustrating and damn annoying.

'Good lord. Always the charmer.' Barbara gave an inelegant snort beside her. 'I'll bring you both a cup of tea.'

Freda bit her lip to stop her smile as Richard glared after Barbara. Completely oblivious to his annoyance, the secretary nonchalantly sashayed across the room in the direction of the tea-making facilities as Freda sat on a wooden chair in front of his desk.

Once he was seated, he leaned his forearms on his desk and laced his fingers, his gaze on hers. 'So, you came back.'

'I did,' Freda said, unsure why he would make such a statement when it was him who'd invited her here. 'As per your letter.'

'As I didn't receive a response, I wasn't sure you were still interested in writing for us.'

Determined to settle her nerves and meet Richard Sinclair head on in order to convince him that she was capable of working with him – of learning from him – she lifted her shoulders. 'I concluded from your decidedly curt request that you weren't expecting an answer. It was more a case of "be here today at this time".'

'Is that so?'

'Yes.'

'Miss Parkes—'

'Freda.'

A slight blush darkened his cheeks. 'Freda, if you felt my tone was curt, then I apolo—'

The tip-tap of Barbara's shoes interrupted him as she approached with their tea. 'Here we go. One pot of tea, two cups with matching saucers, sugar and milk. No biscuits today, I'm afraid.' She looked at Freda. 'Our editor managed to finish off the batch I made yesterday and until I get my next lot of rations...'

Freda smiled. 'Tea is fine. Thank you.'

Barbara looked at Richard and quirked her eyebrow. 'Shall I pour?'

'No, thank you. I think we can manage.'

Once again, Freda bit her lip, deciding that she enjoyed Barbara's tormenting Richard Sinclair as much as Barbara clearly did carrying out the torment. The man could definitely do with relaxing a little. Freda inwardly grimaced. *Look who's talking...*

Barbara dipped a somewhat ironic semi-curtsy and returned to her desk.

Freda faced Richard as he came around to her side of the desk to pour the tea.

'Sugar?' he asked.

Freda blinked and met his eyes. His proximity was such that she could smell the woody, masculine scent of his aftershave. 'Two please.'

Barely resisting the urge to inhale deeply, she turned away, only to meet Barbara's amused stare across the office. The secretary wiggled her fingers, her eyebrows almost touching her auburn hairline. Heat seared Freda's cheeks and she quickly looked away.

Richard finished stirring the tea and passed her a cup, before taking his own and leaning up against the desk in front of her. 'So, what have you got for me? Did you manage to come up with a second article?'

Realising that he had no intention of returning to his seat, and opening the space between them so that she might breathe a little easier, Freda silently emitted a curse that would have sent her mother to bed for a week and reached for her bag that she had placed on the floor beside her.

'I'm not sure you'll agree,' she said. 'But what I propose next is a series of articles. I want to cover an issue I strongly believe will matter to a lot of women who are trying to do their best right now.' She held out her outlined article. 'A lot of mothers have come through the hospital over the last few months, and I've learned so much about their concerns. I think this article will interest those left feeling they're floundering at home, while their husbands and the fathers of their children are so far away, leaving their wives alone to protect and provide for their children.'

'And you think there are a lot of women who feel that way?'

'Oh, most certainly.' Her heart filled with passion for the many women she and her friends had cared for and comforted over the last months and weeks. 'More often than not to the detriment of their own health and safety. Not one of them has admitted to such, of course, all wanting to keep a stiff upper lip, keep strong for their children, make their husbands proud, but...' She shook her head. 'Their suffering is real, and I would like to produce a series they can draw strength from, that makes them feel less alone and helps them to realise they are no less perfect than the rest of us as we struggle through what is now our third year of war.'

His gaze was intense and indecipherable on hers. 'Sounds interesting, but you'd have to find a way to write this that will provoke public support rather than cause people to think women are in any way grumbling when the rest of Europe is in no better a position than us. Some infinitely worse.'

He took the pages and started to read. Freda sipped her tea, praying that he didn't immediately dismiss the idea. She may not be entirely familiar with the female readership of the paper yet, or what reaction her words might or might not cause, but the issue of mothers being sole carers to their children over the last two years was one that affected thousands, if not tens of thousands, of women throughout the city. The stresses and strains were unlikely to come to an end anytime soon and starting a public conversation about it would certainly do no harm, and may even bolster women to do more than they currently believe themselves capable of.

Richard finished reading and laid the pages on the desk beside him. He faced her, his brow furrowed. 'It's good. Very good.'

She smiled, relief lowering her tense shoulders. 'Really?'

'Yes, but...' He stared at her for a moment before lifting the pages again, his gaze flitting over her words. 'I think it needs something more. It would make a lot more impact with a couple of quotes from members of the public.'

'Quotes? You mean print their names in the paper?' Freda shook her head. 'Based on the female patients and mothers I've treated, the last thing they'd agree to is being publicly named. These women already feel they are failing their children, failing their husbands.' She glowered and took a sip of her tea. 'Which is complete nonsense, of course.'

'Well, you know these women and this issue better than I do, but I'll have a think.' He put her notes back on the desk and picked up his tea. 'William and I agree that—'

'William?'

'Keating. The *Chronicle*'s editor.' He turned and nodded at a rotund, balding man sitting at a desk at the back of the room. 'He likes the idea of you sharing what you are learning through your interactions at the hospital. We both agree that, with your writing style and obvious integrity and care, your articles could have the potential to be highly informative, evocative and ultimately provide a much-needed boost to women's morale in the city.'

Your unique writing style... Integrity and care...

Pride mixed with excitement as Freda battled to stay in her seat and not dance a jig. It was far too early to celebrate. Only one article had passed muster with Richard and clearly the paper's editor, too. There was a long way to go before she could celebrate or hope that she might have her foot in the door at the newspaper.

'But...' Richard mused. 'We are at war, Miss Parkes... Freda... and that means the paper needs to cover more than what is happening in Bath. We have to bear in mind those suffering further afield.'

'I understand.'

'As you are taking in patients from Bristol, that certainly places you in a good position to appreciate this war on a more human level than people living in Bath, who – thankfully – have yet to experience anything as traumatic as buildings being bombed or finding themselves exposed to machine gun fire. However...'

Freda sat straighter in her chair. 'However?'

He smiled and her stomach treacherously knotted.

'However, before we can really use your experiences and writing for public good, you need to convince me that writing for the *Chronicle* on a regular basis is really what you want.' His smile dissolved and his gaze turned sombre. 'Journalism during wartime must be about more than the home front. It must be about more than the injured coming from Bristol to Bath.' He drew in a deep breath. 'We can't offer you a regular position here right now, but we would certainly like more work from you as and when we ask you for it. Would that suit you?'

'That would be perfect. The last thing I want is to give up nursing during a time when nurses are needed more than ever, but I would happily deliver something you'd like to commission.'

'That's wonderful. However, even that basis needs commitment from you. We cannot afford to rely on you, for it then to become clear that you are not up to the grizzlier parts of the job.'

Her defences immediately rose. Such an assumed possibility would not be directed towards a man in her position, she was sure. 'I'm a nurse, Mr Sinclair, and I deal with blood, broken bones and burns as a matter of course, day in, day out. I'm also exposed to God-awful anguish, fear and loss. I am made of stronger stuff than you give me credit for.'

Seemingly unperturbed by her words or tone, he raised his eyebrows. 'And all of that is admirable and more than most could cope with, but are you prepared to be exposed to the real brutalities of this war, Miss Parkes?'

Annoyed and even a little saddened that he'd returned to addressing her by her surname, Freda held his unwavering stare. 'What are you referring to exactly?'

What was he looking for with his questions? Was he testing

her? Did he think her no more capable of serious writing than her parents? Did he think her soft-hearted and soft-minded?

'What do you mean by the real brutalities of war?' she demanded. 'Isn't nursing servicemen who have suffered truly horrendous injuries, or comforting people who have lost not just one or two loved ones, but their whole families, exactly that?'

His gaze still on hers, his jaw tightened. 'The people you are treating at the moment, they are all brought into the hospital from Bristol, correct?'

'Yes.'

'Then does it not make sense that, in order to garner a true idea of just how bad things are becoming, you might need to go to Bristol? Perhaps we could go together. So that you might see, hear and feel what the women there are living through, the decisions they are forced to make every minute of every day. All while coping with the heart-wrenching pain of their children being evacuated and their husbands goodness knows where.'

The horror of what she might witness played on a cinefilm in her mind as Freda pondered how on earth she'd be able to accompany him to Bristol as he so easily suggested.

'Look...' He leaned closer, his gaze intense on hers. 'We want these women's stories, but right now we have a responsibility to do all we can to make people understand what could soon be on its way to us. Bath needs to be shown what is happening in places where Hitler is already spreading horror left, right and centre.'

The passion in his words, in the deep, deep blue of his eyes drilled through her. 'You want us to go to Bristol? Together?'

He nodded, a soft smile playing on his lips and his eyes kind. 'Will you?'

Her body tingled with possibility. 'I...'

'Trust me, Freda. It's the only way to take your writing to the next level. If you really want to be a female writer, writing for women in wartime, then—'

'Yes.' She pulled back her shoulders and grinned, her heart racing. 'Somehow, some way, I will come with you to Bristol, Mr Sinclair.'

He blew out a breath and winked. 'Then, from now on, I must insist you call me Richard.'

29

SYLVIA

Sylvia ate another bite of potato and looked at Jesse across the restaurant table, his eyes annoyingly on his plate rather than her. It had been three weeks since her set-to with his mother and this was the fourth time they'd stepped out together since deciding to give their relationship a chance. She wanted to believe things were going well, but tonight the atmosphere was laced with unspoken words and tension – *his* unspoken words and tension.

She had been talking nineteen to the dozen, her entire body braced as though waiting for a blow. Something was definitely wrong. Unable to bear his brooding, tight-jawed silence a moment longer, Sylvia put down her knife and fork and reached for her water.

'What's going on, Jesse?'

He looked up from his food, his beautiful brown eyes glazed as though he'd forgotten she was there. 'Hmm?'

More than a little irritated, Sylvia glanced around the restaurant, taking a moment to steady her tendency to fly off the handle. 'Something's wrong,' she said. 'Is it your mother? One of your brothers or sisters? Work?'

He gave a derisive sniff, his gaze now fully alert and burning with undisguised frustration. 'Work? Work is mad all day, every day. Cargo is coming through Bath station at a heavier, faster rate every day, with the bosses expecting us to break our backs loading and unloading, preparing cargo to send on to London. It's bloody exhausting work and a word or two of encouragement from the upper echelons wouldn't go amiss from time to time.'

Sylvia studied him. Every instinct told her that his ranting was not about work. The one thing she was learning about Jesse Howard was how much his family meant to him and, as envious as she was to imagine how it would feel to have a constant loving relationship with her mother, she also knew him being out with her like this must be causing a strain between him and his mum even if he hadn't told her as much.

And Sylvia wasn't daft enough not to realise that, if it came to it, Jesse would undoubtedly walk away from her, not his family.

The silence stretched as they resumed eating, Sylvia casting occasional glances at him.

He suddenly looked up, met her eyes. 'Would you ever consider moving away from Bath?'

She stilled. 'What?'

'Maybe move to the country? Possibly somewhere further afield. It's just something I've been thinking about.'

Sylvia stared. Why was he telling her this? Was he suggesting she go with him? He couldn't be. They'd barely known one another more than two or three months.

'Obviously, I'd have to try my best to find work at one of the railways wherever I ended up,' he mused. 'Or possibly manual work on a farm. Maybe an airfield. There's not much I can't turn my hand to. I like being of use on the home front so would pursue something un-conscripted, if I can.' He looked her straight in the eye, his gaze filled with passion. 'Not that I wouldn't sign up if I was needed.'

She swallowed, hating that a horrible hollowness filled her at his words. 'Of course.'

'What about Wales?'

'Wales?' Sylvia's eyes widened. Her rambling to fill the silence during their meal had been nothing compared to the garbled rate of Jesse's speech a moment before. What on earth was going on in that wonderful head of his? 'Is this abrupt need to leave Bath about the stress at the station or something else entirely? Only my friend Freda's dad is a policeman, and he reckons the war will soon make its way to Bath. Is that what you've heard, too?'

His Adam's apple moved as he swallowed, his jaw tightening. 'This isn't about the war.'

'Then—'

'I just want to live my life how I see fit, Sylvia. Make my own decisions without answering to anyone else. Day after day, week after week, I've got people at work asking me questions about this, that and the other, my mother struggling on to do anything and everything for us kids and the damn house. So much so, I am breaking my back trying to take over her chores in the hope she might take a break, but she never does. I'm twenty-six years old and I've been out to work since I was fourteen, yet still I can't go about my business and do as I like. I'm sick to death of it.'

She carefully watched him, trying to read between the lines of what he was saying. 'Jesse, this sudden conversation about moving away has to be about more than your work or mum.'

He glared. 'Why?'

She put down her cutlery and took a fortifying sip of water. 'I know how hard you work and how much it matters to you that you do all you can for the war effort. I also know your mum and family mean everything to you and there's a huge possibility that going out with me is the first time you have done something for yourself rather than your family.' She softened her voice and gently covered his hand with hers where it lay curled around his fork on the table. 'What is it? What's wrong?'

'I just want to be away from the city, away from Bath. Start my own life, on my own terms.'

'But none of our lives are on our own terms right now.' Sylvia sighed and drew her hand from his. 'The war has put paid to that.' She looked deep into his eyes. 'You can't leave your mum. Deep down, you know that. Especially as she is right now. She needs you.'

His gaze burned into hers before he scowled at his food. 'She's got my brothers and sisters. She won't miss me.'

Sylvia laughed in disbelief. 'And I'll be better off without my left arm. 'Course she'll miss you. She adores you!'

He glared. 'I need... we need... to get away from here if this is going to work.'

'We?' Sylvia widened her eyes.

'Yes, we. Did you think I was just talking about me?' He shook his head. 'I'm talking about us.'

'My God, Jesse...' She huffed a laugh, trying to hide the panic thundering through her veins. How could he even think about such a thing happening? 'I'm already tarred with the same brush as my mother. Now you want me to add to that wonderful reputation by doing a midnight flit with you?'

She shook her head, her stomach knotting with trepidation of the beginning of the end. Again. Sickness coated her throat. What was wrong with her? Why wasn't she enough for any man to stick around for more than two minutes? Why did they all end up walking away from her? What a fool she was to convince herself Jesse was worth risking her heart for again. Why had she been taken in by his eyes, his kindness, his care for his family...

She lifted her chin and held his gaze. 'No, I won't do it,' she said. 'Bath is where I belong.'

'Do you know how many times I've moved homes in my life?'

The horrible, imminent loss of him twisted inside her and treacherous tears burned the back of her eyes, but Sylvia blinked them back.

She picked up her knife and fork, feigned interest in her food.

'Five. Five times, Mum and Dad have moved me and my siblings from one place to another.'

'I assume that was for your dad's work in the army?' she asked, trying to continue her charade of nonchalance despite the ache in her heart.

'No, it wasn't his work.'

'Then...' Sylvia stopped. The angry resentment in his eyes told her all she needed to know. 'Because of your colour?'

His jaw tightened. 'Yes.'

'I see.'

'Do you? Really?' His gaze burned with frustration. 'I want to find a place where I can fully be myself, but I'm not sure such a place will ever exist. This war might be breaking down some boundaries, some prejudices, but we've still got a bloody long way to go.'

Sylvia dipped her head as memories of the fracas outside the Howards' home and the part her mother played in it came flooding back. 'I agree. We do. And it might take one person at a time, but the world has to change eventually. Maybe this war will be the start of that change. We need people to beat Hitler. People. Not colours, creeds and religions.'

Their eyes locked and Sylvia fell a little deeper to see quiet vulnerability in his eyes. The man was strong, consistent, hard-working and seemingly entirely unaware of the effect that combination had on her.

She reached for his hand and, this time, his fingers curled around hers. 'Running away isn't the answer, Jesse. Should never be the answer when you're doing that rather than face the problem. So, the answer to your previous question is a definite no. I will not be leaving Bath with you, or anyone else for that matter. It's here I'm needed and where I'll stay. And, if I'm honest, it is at home you are needed more than any other place in the world right now.'

The seconds passed with every beat of her heavy heart, but Sylvia refused to fill the silence. She had said all she wanted to say. He knew where she stood and how she felt. What happened next was up to him.

He slipped his hand from hers and swiped it over his face, blew out a heavy breath. 'Dad's death changed my mum in so many ways. I just don't know what to do for her any more. Her groundless anger towards other people is just part of it. God knows, it was never there before. She used to help anyone.' Sadness and concern mixed with frustration in his dark eyes. 'Now she's just cleaning all the time. Scrubbing and polishing, brushing and sweeping. It's obsessive. She used to welcome visitors into the house day and night. Now no one is welcome. She covers the furniture with paper before we're allowed to sit on it, she's clearing our plates away before we've finished eating. Something is wrong with her. Something I can't seem to fix.' He stared into her eyes. 'And I don't know what the hell I'm going to do about it. And me and you? We're just making it worse.'

Guilt prodded and poked at her conscience, but she would not take the blame for his mother's suffering. That blame was laid firmly on the war – on Hitler, nobody else. 'Then she needs help, not you leaving her. How will that make anything better for either of you?'

'It can only be her grief,' he mused as if she hadn't spoken. 'It all started once she learned Dad was dead. I got the doctor to her months ago and they thought getting her out of Bristol would do her good so, once again, we upped sticks and moved to Bath, but...' He reached for his pint and drained it. 'It hasn't done a damn bit of good. If it wasn't for me meeting you' – he looked into her eyes, the passion there wonderful and frightening at the same time – 'then I would be thinking why the hell we bothered.'

Sylvia clasped her fingers in her lap so she couldn't act on the urge to lean across the table and kiss him. She wanted to comfort him, bolster him, love him, but, at the same time, sensed the end between them was on the horizon. She would not deepen her pain by touching him. For what could quite possibly be the last time.

'It sounds as though your mother needs patience, love and understanding from her family and everyone else in Castle Street,' she said quietly. 'You'd be completely in your rights not to believe me, but our neighbours are good people, even if they do need to learn some lessons about live and let live.' She smiled wryly, her heart lifting when a shadow of a smile curved his lips. 'Your mother will come to see that if she doesn't move away. Instead of leaving her, maybe it's more important than ever that you stay and show her how she could find friends here.'

He shook his head, his smile dissolving. 'Once again, your words are evidence of how you always see the best in everyone. Give one and all a chance, no questions asked.' He drew his gaze over her face, lingering a moment at her lips before meeting her eyes. 'But my mother doesn't deserve that from you. Not after the way she talks about you, despite me making it perfectly clear how much I care about you.' His gaze bored into hers. 'We'd be so much happier on our own.'

Her heart picked up speed, her need to touch – kiss him – growing ever stronger. He made her feel like such a better person than she was, but she couldn't entertain what he was asking of her. She wouldn't.

'I won't move away from my friends or my mother, Jesse. I'm sorry, but I've had things happen to me and I've been hurt, which has meant I've learned the hard way not to lean on a man based on emotion alone. We either stick together here and fight for what might be, or we go our separate ways.' She exhaled a shaky breath. 'The question is, do you feel strongly enough about me to fight for me?'

A muscle flexed and relaxed in his jaw as his beautiful gaze wandered over her face, lingering on her lips a second time. 'I'd slay dragons for you.'

Her heart hammered and her eyes burned with tears of relief as she reached for her water, the liquid trembling in the glass. 'Then why are you even thinking of moving away?'

His smile was slow, sexy... 'I don't know.'

'No, me neither,' she said nonchalantly, even if her breasts and core were tingling with the most God-awful awareness. 'So we're agreed. We'll see where things go from here. In Bath. In Castle Street.'

He blew out a slow, steady breath. 'I think I'm falling in love with you, Sylvia Roberts.'

Her smile froze, fear rippling through her. 'Well, that's very nice of you to say. Now, how about you get me a proper drink?'

He winked, his contemplation of moving away seemingly, if momentarily, forgotten, and he raised his hand to the waiter. Sylvia sat straight backed in her seat, scared to death that her heart once again was in the palm of a man's hand. Albeit this one wasn't running away just yet. He would eventually, of course, but for now, Jesse Howard was sticking with her, and she couldn't be happier.

30

FREDA

The air raid sirens continued to blare all around them, and Freda covered her ears as she, Sylvia and Veronica stopped to look up at the huge formation of planes that flew over the hospital towards Bristol, or maybe they were headed for the south coast, which had recently taken Hitler's interest. Once the ghastly thunder of their engines subsided, she pushed her hand through the crook of Sylvia's elbow and then Veronica's, sending up a silent prayer for whomever the bombers had in their sights. Innate sadness pressed down on her. She could only guess how many more lives would be lost today; how many more people injured in the next few hours.

The three of them walked through the hospital's arched entrance, now without its tall iron gates, and into the grounds. Last night, exploding bombs could be heard in the distant north of Bath and soon Sister Dyer was warning of the possibility of a busy shift tonight. God only knew what tomorrow would bring.

For now, though, Freda drew in a grateful breath and embraced the lull before the storm with her friends. They had bumped into one another at the end of the street and warmth spread through her as Sylvia and Veronica chatted either side of her. She had missed their company so much since Kathy Scott's interference meant their working time together had hugely lessened over the last couple of weeks. Kathy Scott. The person she had no choice but to mention to her friends before they went inside. She and Veronica had tried to persuade Sylvia to give Kathy the benefit of the doubt on several occasions, but it seemed their wise friend had been right about her from their very first day as qualified nurses.

Even tonight, she, Sylvia and Veronica were starting simultaneous evening shifts but carrying out different tasks that would keep them apart. Considering Veronica had started permanently working with Mr Martin in surgery this week, it looked as though shifts with her were on hold for the foreseeable, but Freda at least hoped that the new rota, which was given out every Thursday, would confirm her and Sylvia would see each other a little next week.

But that was by the by. Right now, she had something to tell them while they were alone and away from the prying eyes and listening ears on the ward. Regretting necessity meant spoiling the happy atmosphere between them, Freda gently tugged on their arms.

'I need to speak to you both before we go inside.' She met their curious gazes and grimaced, her annoyance from the day before once again burning inside her. 'It's about Kathy Scott.'

Sylvia groaned, her cheeks reddening and her eyes blazing with undisguised loathing. 'What about her? God, that girl! What has she been saying to you?'

Crossing her arms, Freda frowned. 'Will you calm down? I'm about to tell you, but the last thing we need is anyone getting wind of what I'm going to say, and you raising your voice doesn't help.'

Sylvia continued to glare. 'Just tell me what she said.'

Freda sighed and turned to look at Veronica, whose big green eyes were filled with apprehension. 'Don't look so worried, V. It's just Kathy being Kathy, but I thought you should both know she saw what we were up to the night we took Mrs Harlow from the hospital.'

'Damn that woman,' Sylvia said from between clenched teeth. 'I really thought she'd keep schtum.'

'You knew?' Freda looked at her in disbelief. 'And you didn't tell us?'

'There was nothing to tell!' Sylvia bristled. 'She told me she knew and proceeded to use that information as a way of throwing her weight around. She wouldn't dare tell Sister or she'll know what's coming to her. From me.'

'Well, you're right,' Freda said, battling her hurt that Sylvia hadn't told her and Veronica what Kathy was up to. 'She hasn't told Sister... yet. But she did say she'd like to come out with us now and then... and if that is not acceptable to us then maybe we shouldn't be working together. In other words, invite her out with us or we stand a good chance of losing our jobs.'

'What are we going to do?' Veronica cried. 'I have given her so many chances, have been as nice as I possibly can. Why would she do this?'

'Because she's a cow,' Sylvia said firmly. 'That's why.'

'Look...' Freda blew out a breath. 'We'll just have to ask her to come out for a drink with us sometimes, that's all. We don't even have to set anything definite in place. At least not straight away. Just mention it now and then, take it from there. If she says anything else about our jaunt with Mrs Harlow again, then...' She glanced towards the hospital entrance and her heart stopped. 'Oh.'

A familiar figure stood shadowed beneath the canopy above the hospital's main double doors, the brim of his hat obscuring his eyes, the collar of his coat pulled up. Freda's stomach knotted, a small frisson of pleasure whispering through her.

'Well, now...' Sylvia smiled. 'Who's the gentleman that has so wholly caught Miss Freda's attention I wonder.'

Now it was Freda's turn to blush. 'Don't start...' she said, battling to calm the sudden nerves that had taken flight in her stomach. 'His name is Richard Sinclair and he's a reporter at the *Chronicle*. Your guess is as good as mine why he's—'

'Miss Parkes!'

Freda snapped her gaze to Richard and he raised his hand, flashing a smile before it disappeared beneath his customary frown. She returned his wave. His perpetual – entirely masculine – broodiness only added to her pleasure at seeing him again. It was his seriousness, his commitment to his work, that made Freda like him more and more.

'Right, we'll talk more about Kathy later. You keep walking straight inside, Sylvia. Do you hear me?' she whispered. 'I will not be introducing you to Richard. Not right now.'

'Aww, you are such a spoilsport,' Sylvia whined, albeit it with a wide smile. 'Come on, V. We won't stay where we're not wanted.'

Freda stopped in front of Richard, her gaze on her friends as they walked inside, both grinning like a pair of fools.

Once the doors closed behind them, she turned. 'Hello. This is a surprise. I have to start a shift in' – she looked at her watch – 'ten minutes so I can't talk for long.'

'This won't take long and I'm sorry to come to your workplace like this, but...' He hesitated, his gaze wandering over her face. 'I wanted to strike while the iron's hot.'

'Oh?'

'I'm sure you must have heard the bombing in Bristol last night?'

'Of course. I'm afraid the planes that went over moments ago mean a second attack is imminent.'

'We've heard tonight's attack will be further south.'

'How do you know?'

'We don't know everything...' He sighed and looked at the sky. 'But we do get bits and pieces of government information come to us and that sometimes includes where they anticipate bombing is likely and when. Look...' His intense gaze bored into hers once more. 'William wants me to go to Bristol tomorrow or the next day. He wants a true update of how the land lies there, the depth of destruction, what people are doing to cope.'

'I see.'

'And I wondered,' he continued, 'if you truly meant it when you said you would find a way to come with me to Bristol. Because if you did...'

She quirked an eyebrow to disguise her immediate nervousness. 'The time is now?'

'Exactly.'

His gaze was bright with fervour and Freda's heart beat faster. She hadn't dared bring up the subject of her writing with her parents since their almighty fall out over breakfast, despite the paper's editor commissioning the last two articles she'd submitted to him. What with her mother's hatred of Freda's new career venture and Dorothy's worrying new quietness causing her concern, their mother was likely to suffer a seizure if Freda mentioned accompanying Richard to Bristol. Yet...

'I do want to come with you,' she said, exhaling a shaky breath. 'But it's going to be hard for me to lie to my mother about it. Not to mention how I can sort it out around my shifts at the hospital.'

His brow furrowed, his gaze confused. 'Why would you have to lie to your mother about it?'

Freda briefly closed her eyes, embarrassed to have to confess something that should not even come into consideration when she was twenty-two years old. 'My mother steadfastly believes that only "good girls" deserve to get on in the world.'

'Good girls?' His eyebrows shot to his hairline. 'What in God's name does that mean?'

The warmth in her cheeks grew hotter. 'Humble, unassuming girls. Pious girls. Not girls who go to Bristol alone with a man they hardly know.'

The confusion in his eyes melted into amusement. 'I see. And you feel there is no possibility of you being a bad girl from time to time?'

The question was laced with innuendo and her attraction to him rippled through her once again. She smiled, suddenly tempted to give him a playful shove like Barbara might have, but she did not possess the secretary's easy flirtation and very much doubted she ever would... no matter how much she wished that wasn't the case.

'Of course.' She smiled. 'But if I go with you to Bristol and my mother finds out' – she sighed – 'she would think me very bad indeed. My father supports my writing for the time being, but accompanying you on a lone trip would undoubtedly be a step too far for him, too.'

His eyes grew solemn once more. 'In this job, propriety more often than not takes a back seat. You have to do what you must to get the story. The real story. You have to go to the worst places, sometimes speak to the worst kinds of people. But there are other times when the job takes you to the most wonderful places and gives you the chance to speak to the most wonderful people. There is no room for hesitation or waiting for the right time. You either want to be a journalist or you don't.'

She stared into his dark blue eyes, before purposefully looking at the hospital doors. 'I should go in.'

'Freda.' He touched her arm and she forced herself to look at him. 'Please,' he said. 'Come with me to Bristol. When is your next day off?'

To do this, to go with him, was more than a work opportunity. This was her chance to fly free. To experience something she never had before; to take a leap of faith that might change her forever.

'The day after tomorrow.'

'Then say yes.' His gaze softened. 'You have everything to gain by doing this. Your parents will have to take you seriously if your report tells the people of Bath what is truly happening. That's what you want, isn't it?'

'Yes. More than anything.'

'So, you'll come?'

Her heart thundered, her every instinct telling her to trust this man to teach her, look after her. He was right. She had so much to gain, but if she thought about her family turning their backs on her, she possibly had more to lose. Yet...

She pulled back her shoulders as excitement unfurled inside her. 'Yes.'

He smiled. 'You'll come?'

'Yes, God help me. I'll come to Bristol with you, Richard.'

31

VERONICA

Veronica was about to tuck into the cheese on toast in front of her when she glanced across the room at the canteen doors and saw Freda and Sylvia approaching, laughing and talking. She smiled and waved them over.

'Ooh, that looks good,' Sylvia said, nodding at Veronica's plate as she sat opposite her.

'How has your shift been so far, V?' Freda smiled. 'Anything more from Kathy?'

Veronica finished chewing and swallowed. 'No. She's been all sweetness and light tonight. We'll wait and see what tomorrow brings. Fingers crossed, she might give us a bit of breathing space now she's said her piece.'

'Hmm, I wouldn't count on it,' Sylvia said with a scowl. 'It wouldn't surprise me if she's just got started. We'll see the lay of the land over the next few days and then decide what to do next.' A hint of concern seeped into her eyes and she looked from Veronica to Freda and back again. 'I'm so sorry if what I asked you to do for Mrs Harlow lands you in trouble. This whole thing is my fault and I want you to promise me you will tell Sister Dyer as much if it comes to it.'

Veronica put down her cutlery and reached for Sylvia's hand, squeezed her fingers. 'It won't come to that, alright?'

Freda put her hand over hers and Sylvia's. 'She's right, Sylv. One way or another, we'll make sure Kathy keeps what she knows to herself. If she wants our friendship – which is what I am beginning to suspect is the real root of all her nonsense – then we'll do what we must to make her feel included. Carole and Martha too, for that matter.'

'I agree,' said Veronica with a firm nod. 'None of us set out to exclude them, it's just...' She smiled. 'We got on from the get-go, didn't we?'

Sylvia and Freda grinned.

Veronica turned back to her cheese on toast. 'How are things going with your writing, Freda?' she asked. 'Mr Martin only said this morning that the number of casualties and fatalities has risen sharply since the end of November and with Christmas most likely to be ignored by those issuing the orders, things are only going to get more intense in the New Year...' Veronica looked at each of her friends, all thoughts of Kathy Scott overshadowed by the grim realities of war. 'He's suggested that, once I'm fully trained in theatre assistance, and working smoothly with him and Betty, we might occasionally be needed further afield than Bath or even Bristol.'

Freda's eyes widened. 'He's not suggesting you'll be asked to go to one of the airfields, is he? Or worse?'

'Don't be daft.' Sylvia laughed, but her gaze showed her worry. 'Tell her she's got the wrong end of the stick, V.'

'I can't,' Veronica said. 'Because I think it's a possibility. Not that I'd want to go, but how could any of us refuse if we were asked to go where we were needed the most? We're trained nurses.'

'Trained nurses who work in a bricks and mortar hospital!' Sylvia protested. 'Can you imagine what it's like in the field? Working in tents and God only knows what else.'

'It doesn't bear thinking about,' Freda said quietly. 'But we must think about it. We can't ever forget the men and women out there, Sylv. Not ever.' She exhaled a heavy breath. 'Which is why I've agreed to go to Bristol with Richard Sinclair from the *Bath Chronicle*.'

'The man who was outside the hospital?' Veronica asked.

'The one and only.'

'Why would you do that?' Sylvia stared at Freda in disbelief. 'You know how bloody dangerous it is in Bristol right now.'

Where Sylvia's mind had flown straight to Freda's safety with regards to the bombings, Veronica's mind flew straight to the dangers of her friend being alone with a man, a relative stranger as far as she knew.

'This war is bigger than Bath,' Freda said. 'It's bigger than England.'

Veronica's heart hitched to see such deep fear mixed with stalwart care in her friends' eyes as they stared at one another. The fact that Sylvia's usual vivaciousness and good cheer had slipped showed just how serious things were becoming up and down the country. She and her friends could no longer hope things would not get worse, each of them aware that something they could not see, but somehow sensed, was coming to Bath. Facing attack was inevitable for all. Hitler had made no secret that his intention was to rule the whole of Europe.

The silence stretched as the three of them slipped into their own thoughts, the atmosphere unusually grave.

Veronica picked up her teacup and drank.

It had been just her and her mother for the last two years, her pilot father taken in the first six months of war. Just her, her mother and the relentless ghost of her rape, along with the very real horror that Mr Riley still lived just yards from her house. She looked at Freda's and Sylvia's strained expressions. All three of them still had so much to live for. So much to hope for…

'Everything will be all right,' she said quietly. '*We'll* be all right, you'll see.'

'Well, I for one will not be volunteering to leave Bath any time soon,' Sylvia said firmly. 'I belong here. Bath is my home and always will be. The people coming here from outside the city and the people who are working their backsides off on the home front need us, too.'

'Of course they do,' Freda said, her face sombre. 'So many people need us, and we are doing the best we can for all of them.'

As she looked at her friends, Veronica's heart filled with a passion she had not felt since she was a young girl, whose innate optimism had been stolen from her in twenty violent, horrifying minutes at the tender age of seventeen.

'Which is why,' she said, 'alongside our work, we should also be doing all we can to make ourselves happy. War or no war.' Veronica purposefully held her friends' curious gazes. 'I mean it. You have both shown me that, although it's scary taking risks, doing so is the only way to discover new things and new happiness.' She looked at Sylvia. 'You've been going out with Jesse for a few weeks now despite his mother's objections.' She turned to Freda. 'And you're writing like you've always dreamed of doing. And now I finally want to see what is possible for me, too.'

Sylvia grinned, her eyes brightening. 'At last! So, what exactly do you have in mind, Nurse Campbell?'

Veronica swallowed down her fear because what she was about to say felt real and right. 'I'm going to start putting money away. Every penny I can possibly spare so, once this war is over, I can find a place of my own. A place where everything is new and fresh, and I can start again after' – her mouth dried and she cursed her weakness – 'what happened to me in my own home. I want to find somewhere new, clean and mine.'

'Oh, V.' Freda's eyes shone with tears. 'That sounds like the best plan of all.'

Sylvia frowned. 'You shouldn't let him get away with what he did to you, V. I love the idea of you moving as far away from him as possible... as long as what he deserves hits him hard, right between the legs, at some point.'

Veronica swallowed. 'I can't think about that. Moving away is all that matters to me for now.'

Freda smiled. 'Then that is what we will support you with.' She turned her gaze on Sylvia, raised her eyebrows. 'Won't we?'

Sylvia continued to stare at Veronica and she battled to hold her friend's vengeful gaze. 'Please, Sylvia. I need you to understand what feels important to me right now.'

Her friend's eyes suddenly shone with unshed tears beneath the canteen's lights before she blinked, her smile appearing. 'Of course I understand.' She laughed, the sound forced. 'And I love your plan of moving house. What's more...' She winked. 'When the time comes. I might be asking if you need a roommate.'

Freda grinned. 'Me too!'

'I would love nothing more than the three of us to live together!' Veronica cried. 'But, in the meantime, whatever might or might not happen with this war, whatever we might or might not do, or where we might or might not go, we're friends for life. Right?'

'Right!'

'Abso-bloody-lutely!'

32

SYLVIA

A few days later, Sylvia left the butcher's shop, humming a jaunty tune she'd heard on the wireless that morning, gratified she'd managed to snag such a good cut of mutton. Old Mr Austen had seen her right today, just as he had a hundred other women who came through his shop door. Sylvia could have sworn he kept a log somewhere of who'd had what, and when they were next due a treat. He was a good soul. She smiled softly, even if he was as daft as a brush to look so doe-eyed at her mother whenever she deigned to go food shopping.

But, for tonight, she and her mum would eat well. For once, Sylvia had finished her day shift on time and her mother wouldn't be leaving for the pub for a couple of hours, so maybe they could sit down and share a decent mealtime together. As per usual, Sylvia slowed her steps as she came to the point in the street where she was directly opposite Jesse's house. She frowned. The house was in darkness, the same as all the others in the street after dusk on a cold December night, but something didn't feel right. With Jesse, his mum and four younger siblings living in the house, it never felt entirely still. There always seemed to be someone coming or going, a blackout curtain twitching or a window being opened or closed. Now, there was nothing but complete and eerie stillness.

Unease wound through Sylvia and squeezed like a fist around her heart.

Had the family gone? Had he left her without a word? He wouldn't. Would he?

The thought – the certainty – came from nowhere, and tears sprang into Sylvia's eyes.

Oh, Jesse. Why would you run away? I would've made sure your mother was looked after. I would've seen her right with the other women on Castle Street. The last thing she needs is starting again somewhere else, surrounded by strangers.

Unable to face uncovering what she knew would turn out to be true, she hurried to her own front door and let herself into the house, sickness pooling in the pit of her stomach even as she forced cheerfulness in her voice. 'Only me!'

'I'm in the kitchen,' her mother shouted. 'And stop your bloody yelling!'

Her heart cracking under the pressure of knowledge and past experience, Sylvia walked into the kitchen with a wide smile, holding her string shopping bag aloft. 'I come bearing gifts,' she declared. 'I've bought home our tea. So, you stay right where you are, and I'll stick the kettle on. You can keep me company while I cook.'

Her mother squinted at her through the smoke swirling from the smouldering cigarette balanced on the edge of the ashtray beside her on the small kitchen table. 'Spending money you haven't got again, I see. Don't you know, with this war on, all the traders are charging the same for bad cuts as they would have for good 'uns?'

'Maybe some are, but not Mr Austen,' Sylvia said, trying to

maintain her smile while her mind wasn't even in the kitchen but halfway across the street. 'And certainly not when I told him the cut is going to find its way onto *your* plate.'

Her mother smiled with blatant satisfaction, instantly making her appear five years younger. 'Ah, he's a good 'un, is Mickey. I might have to let him have a little grope of my chest pillows one day soon. Keep him sweet. What do you think?' She cackled and coughed. 'That would make him forget the war for a while. If he doesn't keel over from a heart attack first, of course.'

Sylvia laughed. 'What are you reading?' she asked over her shoulder as she began unpacking the shopping. 'I can't remember the last time I saw you open a newspaper.'

'I know, but all the ladies on the street are talking about this new woman writer at the *Chronicle*, told me to have a look at some of the stuff she's been writing. Seeing as I am trying my best to have a couple of our lady neighbours give me the time of day, I thought I'd have a read.' Her mother sniffed. 'It actually ain't half bad. Whoever this woman is, she seems to know what it's like for us women doing the best we can at home.'

Sylvia grinned as she spun around and whipped the paper from the table, scanning the page until she saw Freda's name in black and white. 'So proud of you, my girl. So bloody proud!'

'Who are you talking about?' her mother scowled. 'Are you saying you know who this writer is?'

'Yep. She's my good friend, Freda Parkes.'

'How would you know anyone posh enough to write for a newspaper?' her mother asked, her eyes darkening with suspicion.

'She's not posh, and you also just said she knows what she's talking about and how it is for us, so don't start bad-mouthing her, now you know she's my friend!' Sylvia retorted. 'I've told you about Freda. I went out with her and Veronica a few nights ago, remember? She nurses with me at the hospital. She's a wonderful nurse with dreams of writing for a living.' She skimmed the article, pride for her friend growing ever bigger. 'Which is very likely to happen if she keeps writing like this.'

'Look at your face. You look half in love with the woman!' Another high-pitched cackle.

Sylvia tossed the newspaper onto the table and turned back to the sink. 'She's my friend, Mum, and I love the bones of her. Even you aren't going to sully that for me.'

'I don't need to sully anything. Did you happen to glance across the street at your lad's house on the way home?'

Sylvia's mouth dried as she stopped laying out carrots and onions and gripped the edge of the counter. The utter triumph in her mother's tone could only mean she knew what had happened at Jesse's house and was about to take great pleasure in telling her daughter.

'They've gone, haven't they?'

'Yep. They packed up and left early this morning.'

Sylvia's breaths turned harried as she fought to control her rage, her hurt... her damn stupid heartbreak. She turned around, the satisfaction in her mother's eyes adding insult to injury. 'All of them?'

'Yep. God knows how much stuff they've left behind, but the whole lot of 'em went out with as much as they could carry, climbed into a great big van that looked like it come straight from the railway yard.' She carefully eyed Sylvia as though gauging her reaction. 'Bet your lover called in a big favour to borrow a van like that.'

'Yeah, I suppose he must have.' Sylvia fought to hold her mother's gaze and not crumple to the linoleum floor. 'It's a shame they've gone. I know for a fact his mother could have done with some friendship on this street. Some support.'

'Support? Pah, you must be off your rocker if you think that mother of his needed support. The woman was a right snooty so-and-so, walking around with her nose in the air.'

'Don't go judging what you don't know, Mum. People aren't always what they seem.' Her voice cracked and, mortified, Sylvia quickly turned her back and picked up a knife from the side. 'Now, let me get on with making our tea.'

The wall clock ticked off the seconds right along with the heavy thump of Sylvia's breaking heart.

'You'd better fight back those tears, my girl,' her mother snapped. 'Women like us don't cry over men, do you hear me? You're better off without him and his whole family. He thinks himself better than you, Sylv. The whole bloody family think they're better than us.' The legs of her chair scraped sharply across the tiles as her mother stood. 'No tears. Good riddance to 'em.'

Sylvia remained stock still as her mother stormed from the kitchen and didn't allow herself to slump against the counter until she heard her mother's slippered feet stomping up the stairs. Swallowing against the lump stuck like a rock in her throat, Sylvia cursed the tears that dared to roll over her cheeks. She could've sworn she saw a glimpse of care for her on her mother's face. Maybe even a little anguish. Had she started to think Jesse might stick around, too? That he might think more of her daughter than any man had before him?

Sylvia swiped at her cheeks and stabbed her knife into a carrot. *Well, if she did, she was wrong and I'm right. I knew all along he wouldn't stay. They never do.*

'God damn it, Jesse.'

She put down the knife and strode from the kitchen and along the hallway into the small front room. Heedless to the blackout, she pulled aside the sheet at the window and stared across the street at Jesse's house.

'You're a bloody fool and I couldn't care less you've gone. This time is different,' she murmured, her voice catching. 'This time I know I'm too good for you or any man, Jesse Howard.'

Sylvia dropped the curtain and marched back into the kitchen to finish preparing the tea. Her heart might be shattering into a million pieces, but when she found the strength to put it back together again, it would remain firmly and utterly closed.

Quite possibly forever.

Jesse Howard was no more as far as she was concerned, and he never would be again.

33

FREDA

Freda stood with her back to the grassy area surrounded by frost-covered flower beds in the centre of Charlotte Square and tried not to fret how many people would see her waiting by the side of the road for a car to pick her up. A car driven by Richard Sinclair.

She shivered, telling herself it was due to the falling temperatures rather than trepidation that she would shortly be sitting in close proximity to a man she increasingly found herself thinking about. She tightened the belt on her coat, checked the clasp on her handbag, anything to deflect her nerves and ignore the fact her mouth had drained dry. The lies she had told her family about what she was doing and where she would be this evening would surely be enough to damn her to the devil for eternity, but what choice did she have?

If she hadn't before now – Freda exhaled a calming breath – she had well and truly destroyed any chance of living up to her mother's 'good girl' status. Worse, she didn't hold an ounce of remorse or regret to the fact.

A dark blue car came around the corner and slowed.

Freda's heart picked up speed as it pulled up in front of her and Richard leaned across the front seat to open the passenger door.

'Jump in,' he said with a small smile and a lift of his hat. 'I'd normally stop and open the door for you, but we're likely to get beeped at if I do that.'

She smiled and fought to bury her nerves. 'That's all right,' she said, sliding into the leather seat beside him. 'I'm as capable as the next person of opening and closing my own door.'

'Noted,' he said, his jaw slightly tightening as he pulled back into the traffic.

Freda silently admonished herself. He had been perfectly nice and she'd rebuffed what would have been a wonderfully gentlemanly gesture. They continued to drive along the main road from Bath to Bristol, turning left and right until the roads became less populated with cars and darker without streetlamps. Freda tried not to fidget as tension ebbed and flowed through her body, and she pondered her intelligence for coming on this trip with a man she hardly knew.

'So,' he said, breaking into her self-doubt. 'I assume you concocted a dastardly getaway story for your parents?'

'Oh, don't.' Freda smiled and closed her eyes against the teasing in his, her shoulders lowering. 'I'm becoming one of the best women in Bath at subterfuge, I swear.' She opened her eyes, thoroughly pleased his smile remained as he stared through the windscreen. 'I could tell my sister was more than a little suspicious about what I was up to,' she said. 'But I think she might be hiding something of her own right now and won't be too bothered with me.'

'Good, because being a master of subterfuge is no bad thing in journalism, and you'll certainly need to banish the "good girl, bad girl" thing you told me about from your conscience as soon as we get to Bristol. I need to know what you're made of and that means no room for worrying whether or not you're doing the right thing.'

Unease whispered through her. 'Whether or not I'm doing the right thing? I thought we were going to Bristol to see the devastation, talk to people, help them if we can. Why would I have to be concerned if I am doing the right thing? Surely what we are doing is absolutely right?'

He glanced at her. 'We're going to see people at their best and worst. Witness their pain and grief, anger and frustration. We will witness desperate love, desperate measures, but in spite of all that, we are there for a story.' He stared ahead, his jaw tight. 'Hopefully more than one. We must use whatever tactics we can to uncover the truth of this infernal war. The truth of people's sacrifices and how this conflict is about more than the poor men and women actually fighting, it is about those at home, too.'

'I've seen the sacrifices, both physical and in people's hearts and minds.' She stared at his turned cheek before looking through the window beside her. He wanted something more from her. What, she didn't know, but her unease only grew stronger. She faced him again. 'Are you telling me that, no matter how immoral or unfair our tactics, we have to find a way to make people talk to us? Is that it?'

'I'm afraid that's exactly it. Look...'

He blew out a breath and checked his mirror before easing the car into a small layby at the side of the road. Nerves shot through Freda, her entire body on alert as he pulled to a stop on the dark and lonely road.

'What are you doing?'

'I don't mean to be harsh, but...' he said, ignoring her question as he turned in his seat and looked deep into her eyes. 'I meant what I said to you before. If you want to be a writer, a journalist, you have to be willing to go after a story hell for leather, and right now the war *is* the story.' His gaze burned into her. 'Do you know who you are, Freda? What you want in this life?'

'I am someone who loves people,' she said with utter conviction as she purposefully held his questioning gaze. 'Someone who wants to help others. Through words as much as medically.'

'As much? Or more than? Do you want to write or be a nurse?'

She swallowed, the intensity of his gaze unsettling her. 'Can't I do both?'

'Only you can answer that. All I know is that not being entirely committed to your writing – when you are likely to face obstacles to the topics you want to write about – is only going to make the job all the harder.'

'I do know that. And, as I pursue my writing, I have no doubt my mother is likely to become one of those obstacles. Shaking off her accusations, implications, even threats towards me is not likely to happen overnight, but I'm determined to write regardless of how much upset I suspect it will cause my family. Knowing that I am going to do that to my mother is incredibly hard, when she's already lost one, possibly two, children to this war.' She stopped, hating that he might consider her weak or uncommitted when she was doing more for herself in that moment than she ever had before. She wanted him to see her as strong and brave. In everything. 'And, I have to admit, even though me becoming a nurse was a decision made by my mother, it was a good one and I am not prepared to give nursing up until the war is over. But my writing? That is entirely for me. It's who I am.'

He stared at her, his thoughts indecipherable as they flicked through his gaze, the moonlight shining into the car lighting his eyes. At last, he nodded. 'Good, because to uncover the truth of what is going on at home and abroad, we must stick our noses into everything – even government business and government decisions. That, in itself, brings bigger danger than almost anything else.'

'But we can't possibly uncover what they have planned.'

'Maybe not. But we can start powerful conversations. Stir ordinary people into action and fan the flames of their courage.' His eyes were dark with fervour. 'Do you think Churchill tells us the whole truth? Do you think Hitler is being honest with the German people? Of course they aren't. So it's our job to write what lies between the lines of curiosity or suspicion and answer the people's questions as best we can.

'Look...' He reached his hand towards hers and then seemed to think better of touching her and rested his hand on his thigh. 'You writing about women's roles in the country right now will give those same women the chance to have their voices heard.' His wonderful eyes softened with undisguised admiration. 'I think your voice is one that will come to matter in Bath, maybe beyond, once the war is over, and I'd hate to think I haven't done all I can to help you develop the skills and methods that will help you. I want to do that for you. Even if there might never be a permanent position for you at the paper.'

'Believe me, you are doing so much more than I expected to help me with my writing,' she said quietly, as something shifted in the air around them. Something that seemed to break down a little of the staid professionalism between them and bring a little more of who they were as individuals into the conversation. 'There's no need for you to do anything more, Richard. Really.'

'Good, because you will never become a successful female writer if you're a "good girl". And it's my job to show you how getting the story no matter what, or being good, is a choice, Freda. Trust me, there is no room for virtue in the pursuit of the truth.'

He abruptly faced front and pulled back onto the road, his

speed steadily increasing as they drove ever closer to Bristol. Freda stared blindly ahead, wondering what just happened and how much danger she had put herself in by being alone in a car with such a passionate man on a winter evening where the sun had already set on one of the worst bombed cities in the country.

34

SYLVIA

It was a bitterly cold night as Sylvia left the hospital and she rubbed her hands together, having decided that she'd treat herself by grabbing the bus home. And then she saw him standing a little distance away from her, his hands in his pockets as usual, his hat perched at that damn stupid angle that she found so bloody sexy.

She drew in a strengthening breath and hardened her heart. It had been three weeks since Jesse had upped and left, and it had not been easy convincing her heart to remain strong and resign herself to accepting that yet another man had left her. Worse, he had left her far too close to Christmas, meaning once again she'd been without a man whom she was dangerously close to falling in love with over the festive season. Instead, she was forced to endure two days of her mother coming home from the pub, drunk as a skunk on Christmas Eve and nursing a hangover Christmas Day.

And now she would have the picture of Jesse in this moment replaying over and over in her mind to start 1942 off in the worst possible way. Why was he here? If he was here for her, he'd had an entirely wasted journey.

She pulled her shoulders back and strode past him. 'Go away, Jesse.'

He gripped her arm and she stopped, glaring at his hand until he lifted it. Triumphant, she finally forced her gaze to his – and that was when she saw the dark bruising around his left eye and cheekbone.

Without thinking, she touched her fingers to it, her heart hammering. 'What happened?'

'My uncle.'

'Your uncle?'

'My mother's brother.'

Foreboding rippled through her as she gently touched the area, checking him over. 'Why would he—'

'The first punch was for upsetting his sister. The second when my mother told him I plan to leave her and the whole family for a girl who'd used some sort of voodoo on me to make me care for her.'

'What?'

'Oh, don't worry, Mum and her brother are both as bad as each other. When my uncle swung for me a third time, the first and only punch I threw at him left him on his backside on the kitchen floor. Conversation closed. Safe to say, I had little else to say to my mother for quite a while afterwards.'

Sylvia slowly drew her hand from his face and crossed her arms, anger simmering inside her as she forcefully buried her care – her love – for him. 'I see. Then can I ask what you were thinking by coming here and fraternising with the enemy?'

'I love you, Sylvia.'

Her heart gave a painful kick and she looked deep into his eyes, saw nothing but sincerity, yet still she turned away, the buildings lining the road and the people walking back and forth along the street blurring through her tears. Hating her weakness that she was unable to look at him, Sylvia shook her head, not trusting her voice wouldn't crack if she spoke.

'Sylvia? Won't you at least look at me?'

Slowly, she turned, frustration at the unfairness of what he was doing to her unfurling deep in her stomach. 'What do you want me to say, Jesse? You left. In the early hours of the morning like a sneak. Am I supposed to just forget that? Accept you're here now, standing in front of me, claiming you love me?'

'I'm not claiming anything. I damn well mean it.'

'And now you're cussing at me?' She lifted her eyebrows and stepped back, readying to walk around him. 'I am no longer a doormat for men, or anyone else for that matter, to treat me as they please. I won't be taken for a fool again, Jesse. Not by anyone, including you.'

'I want you to be my girl, Sylvia.' Hard, undisguised determination seeped into his eyes, holding her captive. 'Do you understand me? I've left my family in Wales in the hope they'll be as safe as they can be. I'm not going back. I want to be with you. Here, in Bath. I shouldn't have left. The pain in my mother's eyes...' He stopped, dropped his head back and stared at the sky. 'I hope she comes to understand and accept how much I love you. I hope...' He dropped his chin and met her eyes. 'I hope she gets the help she needs.'

Sylvia closed her eyes, her heart breaking for him, for his mother whose grief had manifested in ways that some wouldn't understand, but as a nurse she had seen grief in every possible form. Even Mrs Howard's.

'It's not her fault,' she said. 'And I pray she finds a semblance of happiness again, just as I do for every patient who comes onto my ward.'

'You are so bloody good, Sylvia.'

'Listen to me. I pray your mother comes to see that no one is to blame for your father's death except for the tyrant who started this damn war. And when she does, you should be with her.' Mentally wrapping a cape of self-preservation around her like armour, Sylvia steeled herself against the hurt in his eyes. 'I'm sorry, I told you I won't go through a man hurting me again, Jesse, and I meant it.'

She walked away, but his footsteps came behind her until his fingers were at the base of her spine. She stopped and fought not to turn, not to take just a small step closer into his arms. She couldn't do it. She wouldn't do it.

'We can take it slow, Sylvia,' he said, gently turning her to face him.

His beautiful gaze moved over her face, the adulation in his eyes weakening her.

Why did he have to make her feel like the most beautiful woman in the world whenever he looked at her that way?

'Jesse—'

'I can find lodgings, and the station will snap my arm off to get me back to work. I barely got to work in Wales with Mum being the way she was so the yard I was on let me go, no questions asked. Nothing has to change. Everything can be as it was before between us.' He gently cupped her cheek in his hand, his thumb moving back and forth over her skin. 'We can step out together again. Please, Sylvia. Give me one more chance. Allow me the honour of courting you. I will prove to you how much I love you. I won't hurt you.'

Tears burned behind her eyes. 'But you've already hurt me.'

He closed his eyes, opened them again. 'And I'm so sorry.'

As he stepped closer, every instinct in her body screamed at her to step back. When he tentatively, inch-by-inch, dipped his head, his gaze on her lips, she yearned to turn her head away. She didn't and when his lips brushed over hers, her heart whispered his name.

He eased back and Sylvia slowly opened her eyes, her lids heavy. 'I've worked so hard these past weeks to get you out of my heart,' she said quietly. 'I accepted you were gone, was determined to start enjoying life on my own terms, speaking up for myself at home and the hospital. If I give in to you now...' She shook her head. She wouldn't go back. She'd come too far. 'I'm sorry, Jesse. I can't.' She pressed her hand to his chest, to his heart. 'It's over between us.'

Straightening her spine, Sylvia walked away.

'I'll wait for you, Sylvia,' he shouted. 'I'll wait for you forever if I have to.'

She kept walking, didn't look back and didn't waver... even as tears clogged her throat and loss ripped a fresh cut in her heart.

35

FREDA

Freda followed Richard through the rubble and dirt that mired the streets surrounding the outskirts of Bristol's city centre. They had walked as close to the docks as they dared, mindful that there was reason enough for the Germans to bomb the area, yet, after the previous night's attack, carrying a small hope of escaping an onslaught in the same place two nights running. Every hundred yards or so, collapsed buildings and houses smouldered; bricks, debris, furniture and household appliances reaching higher than chest-level in some places.

The rumble of machinery and crackling of fire, crying and yelling coming from every direction seemed entirely common-place to the people around them, and Freda did her best to appear unaffected and stalwart in her courage when inside she quaked, her heart in her mouth to see so much devastation. Her father's warnings that Bath would not escape Hitler, that no one would, resounded in her head. She shivered and kept pace with Richard as they entered another street and then another until they reached a terrace of houses that looked entirely uninhabited, yet he continued towards them.

As they walked, Freda could be under no illusion that they were in one of Bristol's poorest areas, where people had clearly struggled to survive even before the war.

Richard turned, his gaze concerned as he seemed to hesitate, his expression uncertain. Without speaking, he held out his hand to her, his eyes never leaving hers, and Freda slid her fingers through his. With a curt nod, he led her purposefully forward. Shouts and groans, the sharp sound of slaps and ensuing screams and yelps echoed from within the damp, soot-blackened houses they passed, the cloying stench of human and animal waste drifting into her nostrils.

Battling to keep the shock and horror from her face, she concentrated on Richard's back, shamefully stealing a moment of appreciation over his strong shoulders and the locks of dark hair that curled over the collar of his wool overcoat. Freda breathed deep to settle her nerves, her resolve strengthening. It did not matter that her parents thought she was spending the evening with Veronica and her mother. What mattered was that Richard showed confidence in her that she could help Bath's women and children, maybe even England's women and children, and now the time had come that she must believe it herself.

He drew to an abrupt stop outside a door standing ajar at one of the houses. 'Are you ready for this?'

She glanced at the door. 'For what exactly?'

His intense gaze lingered on hers before he flashed a small smile. 'You're ready. Don't worry.'

Before she had a chance to object, he pushed the door fully open, leaving Freda no choice but to follow him into the dark hallway.

Children's raised, happy voices were interspersed with bursts of laughter and a woman singing 'Three Blind Mice' so beautifully that nothing had ever seemed so out of place.

Richard stopped, his head tilted as he listened, a fond smile curving his lips. 'That's Susan Beckett. The young woman I brought you specifically to Bristol to meet,' he said quietly. 'The kind of woman she is and what she's doing here will be a great starting place for your words to make a difference. Susan is unlike any woman I have ever met, but I'm sure there are thousands more like her doing the same as she is throughout the country.'

'And what is it she's doing?' Freda asked, glancing along the hallway at the open door from where Susan's singing drifted. 'And why didn't you tell me about her before we got here? I feel like I'm intruding.'

'She finds children who are wandering the streets alone and takes them in, does her best to reunite them with their parents, or else passes them to someone in authority she trusts. Which, under the circumstances, takes quite a while. She can be looking after children for weeks before she lets them go. She's one in a million, believe me.'

'So you already know her well?'

'Not well, no. But well enough that she will talk to me as and when she is in the mood, even if she doesn't entirely trust me.' He grimaced. 'Or any man from what I can gather. She's hard as nails, which I can only presume comes from the things she's seen and done before and during the war.' He blew out a breath, his brow furrowed as he glanced at the open door. 'I'm hoping she might be more candid with you. Being a woman.' He shrugged. 'But the chances are I could be entirely wrong about that, too.'

Freda nodded, drew back her shoulders. 'Well, I'm here now, so we'll see, shall we?'

They continued forward, stepping over torn newspapers, broken toys, rags and some things that were entirely unidentifiable until they entered the room at the end of the narrow hallway.

The woman Freda assumed to be Susan Beckett stood in the

centre of the room, her back turned. She swayed as she sang, an infant in her arms and a little girl with her arms encircling Susan's waist and her head tipped back as she laughed, and Susan smiled down at her. Susan's hair was as black as night and pulled high on her head in a messy bun, two thin wooden sticks stuck in the tresses to keep it in place. Dressed in a calf-length skirt and a green jumper with patched elbows, Susan clearly did her best to keep up standards, regardless of her surroundings. And it seemed she tended to the children in the same way.

The warmth Freda felt towards the other woman was immediate, but she couldn't help thinking that Susan, who looked to be around the age of twenty-two or three, seemed far too young to be so concerned with children's welfare, which only made her admire her all the more. Two young boys of maybe eight or nine scowled at Freda through narrowed eyes, their lips pinched tight as they sat side by side on a filthy, threadbare settee. Another little girl of six or seven and another, maybe two or three years younger, played with bits of brick and stone on a sheet of newspaper in front of an empty, black fireplace.

The singing suddenly stopped.

'Hey, what's the matter with you two?' Susan laughed. 'You look like you've seen the dev—' She swung around, her face immediately hardening as though ready for a fight, one hand gently guiding the little girl behind her. 'Oh, it's you.' She stared at Richard. 'What are you doing here?'

He raised his hands and stepped closer, but Susan's distrusting gaze had turned to Freda.

'Who's this?'

'We come in peace, Susan,' Richard said firmly. 'This is Freda Parkes. She just started work at the paper.'

'So, you're bringing your fancy woman to have a gawp at us now?'

'She's a colleague.'

'That's neither here nor there. We don't need anyone coming here to have a look-see like we're a circus attraction.'

Freda did her best to contain her embarrassment and hold Susan's steely gaze as the little girl walked from behind her and joined the two boys on the settee.

Susan hitched the infant higher onto her hip. 'What do you want?'

Freda opened her mouth to respond, but Richard got there first. 'There's no need to look so wary. I thought I'd earned at least a little of your trust,' he said, taking off his hat and laying it on the small table beside him. 'I've just brought Freda here to talk to you.'

'About what?'

'About what she can do to help you and the other women and children here and in Bath, hopefully further afield, if we can get people interested in what she has to say.'

Susan's cheeks mottled. 'You want to write about me in the paper? Why now? You ain't done that before now despite sticking your nose into my business time and again.'

Richard smiled, seemingly nonplussed by her attitude towards him. 'I have, but my editor wants me writing other stuff about the war. Freda here is perfectly placed to be on your side to write about what you're doing. What it is like trying to protect and look after children with bombs exploding all around you. Where you are finding food. What—'

'You can talk to me about whatever you want, Susan,' Freda interrupted, offering the other woman a small smile. 'I just want to write whatever you think will help you and other women like you. How you are helping these poor children should be known about by the public. Especially by those with the money to help.'

Susan locked her eyes on Freda and she stood a little taller, the seconds passing as they appraised one another. Freda held her ground, surprisingly unruffled by the other woman's hostility. Why wouldn't Susan be suspicious of her motives? She had never seen her before. She didn't know her from the next person. Freda might not be a mother herself, but she had met enough mothers, including her own, to know how understandably protective they could be under normal circumstances, let alone in a city that was bombed almost every night.

There was a scrape of chair legs on the bare concrete floor as Richard sat down on a chair by an upturned box that served as a table in the corner of the room.

A few more strained seconds passed before Susan came closer and offered Freda her hand. 'Pleased to meet you, but I'll hold judgement of whether or not it's a pleasure for the time being.'

Freda smiled and shook her hand before she looked at the two boys on the settee and then at the little girl who had left her seat beside them and decided to climb onto Richard's lap. Her heart stumbled to see how easily he wrapped his arms around her, but she kept her face impassive.

'Would you be willing to talk to me, Susan?' she asked, facing the young woman once more. 'I'd really love for you to tell me your experiences and struggles in the hope I can help in some way. I'm not so arrogant to think I can change things on my own or without knowing what it's like living in the very centre of Bristol during wartime, but I'd love to hear more about what you are doing to help these children.'

'Would you now?'

Freda held the other woman's disdainful gaze. 'Yes.'

'I doubt you'll learn much from listening to me and then going back to your cosy little house in Bath, do you? A city that remains intact and hasn't been hit once. Whereas there isn't a person in the whole of Bristol who doesn't remember a time, not so long ago, that we were targeted at least three or four times, every bloody night, for weeks.'

Passion and the need to write about Susan and what she was doing burned ever more fiercely despite the truth in her words. Freda wanted to hear her story, wanted to talk to the children. She wanted to help.

'I might have only had a few articles published in the paper,' she said firmly, 'but I work full-time at one of Bath's hospitals and we have been taking in Bristol's injured for months. I have spoken to a lot of people who have lost family, friends, children, their homes, their animals. It feels right that what I have been exposed to so far has led me to making myself known to Mr Sinclair and now...' She stared at Susan, praying she believed her sincerity. 'You. Who knows what the three of us can achieve for women's and children's welfare? It has to be worth trying, doesn't it?'

The silence stretched, the children eerily quiet... Richard eerily quiet.

Then Susan softly smiled until it slowly grew so wide, the sight of it was entirely infectious.

'Well then,' Susan said. 'Who am I to refuse when you put it like that, Miss Parkes?'

Freda grinned and looked around the room, a burst of inexplicable laughter bubbling inside her to see Richard smiling like she'd never seen him smile before, the boys smiling, the little girl on Richard's lap smiling and even the tot in Susan's arms.

She walked to the dilapidated settee and the boys scrambled to one end so she could sit down. Taking out her notepad and pencil from her brown leather bag, Freda looked at Susan. 'Why don't you start by telling me why and when you started taking children into your care and we'll go from there.'

Susan looked at Richard, her eyebrows raised. 'I reckon you've gone and got yourself a right little firecracker here, Mr Sinclair.' She winked. 'Wouldn't you agree?'

His eyes met Freda's and she returned his smile.

It was knowing Richard trusted her enough to introduce her to Susan, let alone write about her, that had ignited her courage and sass, and if this was how she was going to feel working with him, she would do so again and again. With or without her mother's blessing.

36

SYLVIA

Sylvia fought back her own tears as Mrs Thornton's flowed down her cheeks. The poor woman had been recuperating on the ward for just over two weeks and would soon be ready to leave the hospital. Yet, heartbreakingly, leaving was the last thing Mrs Thornton wanted to do.

'I don't want to go back there, Nurse. I can't bear to see any more devastation, any more death. When I crawled from the rubble of what was once the post office, my home bombed just a couple of weeks before, I looked and...' Mrs Thornton shook her head, her eyes pleading with Sylvia. 'I just wish I had died in the attack. I can't do it any more. The frequency of the bombing might have lessened, but the memories of the raids that went on night after night have not. The screaming, the horror and terror. It's all still there and I can't do it. I can't go back.'

Immediately thinking of what she, Freda and Veronica had done to cheer and fortify Mrs Harlow all those weeks ago, Sylvia glanced at Kathy Scott, who was feeding a patient at the adjacent bed. So far, calling Kathy over to hers or her friends' table when they spotted her in the canteen or taking some time to indulge in a bit of mindless gossip with her in the staffroom seemed to be enough to placate her – or prevent her from revealing their shared secret. Of course, how long that would be the case was anyone's guess, and taking Mrs Thornton out for a moonlight flit to cheer her up would almost certainly be a step too far...

'You don't have to,' Sylvia reassured her, squeezing Mrs Thornton's hand where it lay fisted on the bed, her heart breaking for the woman who had lost her husband and only son during a relentless overnight raid on Bristol a week before. 'Once your injuries are stable enough for you to leave the hospital, there are a number of wives and mothers we can telephone who are offering rooms to those in need. I will personally see to it that we find somewhere for you to stay, right here in Bath.' She smiled. 'How would that be?'

Mrs Thornton dabbed a handkerchief to her eyes, a tiny spark of light coming into her blue eyes. 'Wives and mothers? Women like me who have lost...'

Sylvia nodded. 'Yes. These women's whole lives have been turned upside down by devastating loss and they have no wish to go through the rest of the war alone, but also want to help. Taking in women in situations like theirs is their answer. Now, dry your eyes and I'll get you a nice cup of tea and a slice of the cake I brought in with me this morning.'

'Thank you, Nurse.' Mrs Thornton sniffed, a ghost of a smile curving her lips. 'You really are the most wonderful young lady.'

Sylvia smiled as she stood. 'I'll be right back.'

Heading for the staffroom, Sylvia's smile faded.

The cake was from Jesse.

She'd opened her front door that morning and found a boxed cake on her doorstep, a handwritten note from him tucked inside.

For you, beautiful Sylvia, to remind you how I courted you at the beginning and how much I want to court you again, love Jesse x

Her heart had betrayed her once again upon seeing the shop-bought cake that must have cost him half his weekly rations. The cake he'd given her when they'd first met had been made by his mother, which only added to the sweet gesture now that Jesse lived alone, albeit in Bath. Almost two months had gone by since Sylvia had spoken to him outside the hospital and she was sticking to her guns and not falling back into his arms, no matter how much she wanted to in her weaker moments.

She must have seen him twenty times wandering along Castle Street when he had no legitimate reason to be there, their eyes meeting across the cobbles when he stood across from her house as though letting her know he hadn't forgotten her. She'd memorised the work timetable and read the notes he'd pushed through her door, telling her over and over again that he was staying at a boarding house on Gay Street and to pop by night or day if she wanted to see him. Her heart constricted painfully. Oh, how she wanted to see him, touch him, kiss him...

But she wouldn't risk her heart again. Wouldn't risk that sooner or later something would happen with his family, and he would return to where they still lived in Wales, in a home where she would not be welcome. That was no future for either of them, and the last thing she wanted was to be the cause of Jesse being estranged from the family he loved.

'Nurse Roberts.' Sister Dyer walked into her path and eyed her over the rim of her glasses. 'A word, please.'

Pushing all thoughts of Jesse from her mind, Sylvia followed the sister's rapid steps along the busy ward to her desk.

'Take a seat, please.'

The sister gestured with a wave towards the chair in front of her desk and Sylvia sat down, wariness unfurling inside her. She could count on one hand how many times the sister had invited her to sit down during a shift. Her mind scrambled to think what she might have done wrong, what misdemeanour she had committed. Her heart picked up speed. God, had Kathy finally delivered on her threat?

'Not that you'll have had reason to notice, Nurse,' Sister Dyer said as she leaned her forearms on the desk and laced her fingers, 'but I have been keeping a close eye on you over the last month or so and I am pleased, maybe I'd go as far as to say impressed, with your ever-increasing level of care, instinct and willingness to work hard.'

Sylvia stared as shock stilled her. 'Thank you.'

'I made no secret of how little I expected of you and the other newly qualified nurses when you came onto the ward, but you have proven my presumptions wrong.' She lifted her eyebrows and almost glared at Sylvia as though blaming her for the sister's mistake. 'And so with that said, I would like to offer you a small promotion.'

'A promotion?' Sylvia smiled, her pride blooming. 'Really?'

'Yes, really.' The sister flashed a tight smile before it vanished again. 'I would like to offer you the role of Senior Ward Nurse.'

Sylvia's smile stretched to a grin and, for the first time in her life, she felt an overwhelming worthiness, of being seen as more than a woman who liked to dress up, wear lipstick and give the boys as good as she got. She felt like a nurse making a difference in what was categorically the hardest time Britain was going through since the Great War. It was beyond her comprehension that the person making her feel that way was Nurse Dyer, the woman Sylvia had convinced herself gave no credit to anyone, ever.

Her pleasure only increased as she pondered how Kathy Scott

would react to this unexpected news. Despite knowing this could cause immeasurable ructions to what was already a delicate – and somewhat dangerous – situation as far as her job was concerned, Sylvia couldn't stem her smile or the anticipation of witnessing the look on Kathy's face when she learned of Sylvia's recognition.

'As you can see,' she said, blowing out a breath, 'I am quite lost for words, Sister. Something we both know doesn't happen very often.'

'Well, I hope you can appreciate the lesson this promotion provides, Nurse.'

'Lesson?'

'I understand from one of the other nurses that your romantic life has been put on the back burner for a while now.'

Sylvia raised her eyebrows. 'One of the other nurses? Would that be Nurse Scott, by any chance, Sister?'

The sister's cheeks reddened, and she cleared her throat. 'I don't recall who told me, but I do know your enhanced performance over the last few weeks has proven once again that in order to flourish in a career, we women must all too often sacrifice a love life if we wish to maintain any semblance of worthiness and respect.'

Sylvia swallowed, desperately wanting to tell the sister she was wrong, but was she?

'So.' Sister Dyer exhaled heavily as though what she had just said affected her too. 'I assume my offer pleases you?'

Sylvia huffed a laugh and pressed her hand to her stomach, trying her hardest to rid Jesse and all he meant to her from her heart and concentrate on keeping hold of her current happiness. 'I'm flabbergasted and chuffed to bits at the same time.'

'Good.' Sister Dyer flashed another smile. 'Then your answer is yes to taking on this new role?'

'Yes,' Sylvia said with a firm nod. 'Most definitely.'

'Very good. Then I will get your new contract, along with details of the requisite salary increase, drawn up in the next day or so.' Sister Dyer stood and offered her hand across the desk. 'Congratulations, Nurse Roberts.'

Sylvia stood and shook the sister's hand. 'Thank you.'

'Right. Then off you go,' Sister Dyer said, all sternness once more. 'Back to work.'

Sylvia could not wipe the smile from her face as she walked along the ward and, when she caught Freda's eye and then Veronica's, she winked at her friends, barely able to resist running across to them to share her good news. No, she would wait until Kathy Scott was nowhere near and they could put their heads together. It would be better to have a defensive plan in place before Kathy found out... Unless, of course, the sister told her first. No, that would be unprofessional, and the one thing Sister Dyer did not do was anything remotely unprofessional.

Sylvia's smile slowly dissolved.

It seemed the sister was right about a woman's route to worthiness and respect, and Sylvia now saw that she had to tell Jesse to stop sending her notes and little gifts. There was no chance of them getting back together.

She wanted to hold on to how she felt right now forever, and if that meant no love life, so be it.

37

VERONICA

Veronica stamped her feet to keep warm as she stood alongside Kathy in the ambulance bay at the rear of the hospital, waiting for a new patient to arrive. Sister Dyer had sent them outside over three quarters of an hour ago, telling them an ambulance was due in minutes. It had yet to materialise, and the sister had been out three times so far to check that she and Kathy weren't 'wasting valuable time'.

'My God,' Kathy said, blowing on her hands. 'We're not going to be of any use whatsoever if the ambulance is much longer. My hands are frozen.'

'Mine too. I can't believe in less than a week it will be March.' Veronica pushed her hands under her armpits. 'I'm sure the ambulance will be here any minute.'

'How are you finding splitting your time between theatre and the ward?' Kathy asked, her eyes alight with interest. 'I must admit I am quite impressed how you've managed doing both. I thought it would be a bit much... even for you.'

Having got used to Kathy's backhanded compliments over the weeks they had been working together, Veronica ignored the slight and shrugged. 'Mr Martin only needs me three or four times a week, sometimes more, but not very often. It's fine. I'm glad to keep being able to treat patients on the ward.' She smiled wryly. 'The ones in theatre are usually past conversation, unfortunately.'

Kathy turned at the sound of an engine approaching the gates. 'Here we are. At last.'

They strode forward as the ambulance reversed into the bay. They waited for the driver to disembark and open the back doors, but as he came around the vehicle, Veronica's heart leaped into her throat. She hadn't seen the driver who'd propositioned her for months and everything about that journey came flooding back. She held his mocking gaze as his mouth lifted with a smug smile, recognition clear in his eyes.

'Good evening, Nurse.' Mr Allen smirked. 'Nice to see you again.'

A wave of confidence washed through her, and Veronica pulled back her shoulders. She was not the same woman she'd been then.

She gave him a curt nod. 'Good evening, yourself. Although, I'm surprised to see you still working at the hospital, quite frankly.'

'You are, are you? And why's that?'

'Because I'm mystified why you haven't been reprimanded for harassing the nurses you take to and from the rural hospitals by now, that's why,' she said, her voice all sweetness and light. 'I'd assumed your dismissal was the reason I hadn't seen you for a while.'

He threw a hurried glance at Kathy and quickly turned to the ambulance, lifted the door handles, pulled out and lowered the ramp. 'Don't know what you're talking about.'

'Oh, I think you do,' Veronica said, moving alongside him once the doors were open and leaning inside the ambulance to release the floor bolts on the stretcher inside. 'Unfortunately for you, I am not the same nurse you thought you could frighten the last time I saw you.'

Mr Allen climbed into the ambulance to release the front locks of the stretcher as Kathy climbed in beside him, her hands moving to grasp the head of the bed. 'What's going on between the two of you?' she asked.

'Your colleague isn't right in the head,' he said gruffly before he stepped away.

'Oh, I'm absolutely right in the head.' Veronica smiled. 'So right that once I'm done here, I'll be speaking to someone who can make sure you don't come near another nurse again.' She looked at Kathy. 'Ready?'

'Yep,' she said, eyeing Veronica curiously before taking the strain. 'One, two, three.'

The two of them lifted the patient onto the ramp and, once the stretcher was safely on the ground, Mr Allen quickly shut the doors and bolted them, clearly keen to get away.

'I know your name, Mr Allen,' Veronica said loudly. 'I look forward to our paths crossing in the hospital manager's office next time.'

His cheeks mottled as he glared. 'What is your problem, lady? I ain't done nothing to you or anyone else.'

Kathy left the stretcher and came closer, her gaze darting between Veronica and the driver. 'What's going on here? Are you all right, Veronica?'

'Oh, I'm fine,' Veronica said, not taking her eyes from Mr Allen. 'I'm just making it clear to our driver here that his days of harassing the nurses and working at this hospital are numbered.'

'Harassing the nurses?' Kathy pinned him with a glare. 'We stick together on the ward, mister. If I find out you've as much as talked to one of my colleagues the wrong way, God help you.'

Flinging a cuss at them, Mr Allen marched to the front of the van and started the engine, leaving Veronica and Kathy waving away exhaust fumes.

'What on earth was all that about?' Kathy asked, planting her hands on her slender hips. 'When did you have a run-in with that disgusting man?'

'Oh, ages ago.' Veronica glared after the retreating ambulance. 'But now I know he's still working here, I'm going to do all I can to change that.'

'He didn't touch you or anything, did he?'

Veronica looked into Kathy's eyes, half expecting to see morbid interest there, but only concern shone back at her.

Dropping her shoulders, Veronica glanced at the patient on the stretcher, but his eyes were closed and, as far as she could tell, he was not listening to their conversation.

'No. Nothing like that. Luckily, the patient I was travelling with was an officer and he was decent enough to cut Mr Allen's insinuations short.' The concern in Kathy's eyes turned to relief and Veronica smiled. 'I'm all right now. Honestly.'

Kathy frowned. 'Are you sure?'

Veronica nodded.

'Good, because I know you, Freda and Sylvia don't give me much of your time, but that doesn't mean I wouldn't have your backs if push came to shove.' She raised her eyebrows, a glint of the usual Kathy sparking in her gaze. 'Otherwise, I would've said something to Sister about you-know-what by now. As I haven't, you should have realised I'm not as bad as you all assume me to be.'

Before Veronica could respond, thank Kathy for her silence or even point out that she hadn't exactly confirmed she would *never* say anything to Sister Dyer, Kathy tilted her head towards the stretcher.

'Come on, we'd better get our man here on to the ward.'

'Let me just have a look at who we have,' Veronica said, lifting the information chart from the bed.

She scanned for the patient's name and then looked at him properly for the first time. Her heart inexplicably stumbled when his open eyes met hers. He was wrapped in bandages and plaster from his toes to his face, only his eyes, charred ears and mouth visible. His eyes were the most startling shade of blue she had ever seen, yet they conveyed absolutely nothing of what he was thinking or feeling. Her heart beat faster as a strange familiarity came over her, along with the insane urge to climb onto the bed beside him and rest her cheek on his plastered chest.

She blinked and forced a smile. 'Let's get you inside, shall we, Officer Matthews?' she said, her sing-song voice insincere to her own ears let alone his. 'It's not exactly the time of year to be standing around outside, is it?'

Swallowing hard, she replaced the clipboard and moved to the head of the bed. Inhaling a long breath, she and Kathy pushed the stretcher inside.

Officer Eric Matthews.

Age twenty-seven, unmarried. Pulled from the field having been caught in the blast of an exploding mine. Broken legs, arms, ribs. Head-to-feet burns...

Veronica's heart raced. What was wrong with her? Never before had she had such a strong reaction to a patient, to their injuries.

'We'll get you nice and comfortable as soon as we can, Officer Matthews,' she said. 'And I'll see about some soup, maybe a cup of tea. Yes, a cup of tea. That's what you'll be wanting, I'm sure.'

Even when Kathy was called away by Sister Dyer to help her with something else, Veronica kept up her chatter as she wheeled Officer Matthews back to the ward. Even when Sylvia and then Freda paused in their work to watch her walk by, questions and shock provoked by Officer Matthews' condition clear in their eyes, Veronica didn't stop talking. Protectiveness for her patient rose inside her and she stepped up her pace, thankful there was a spare place for his bed at the very end of the ward. Instinctively, she felt like she already knew this man, knew he would want minimum contact with other people. Maybe even her.

Not that she had any intention of adhering to that request should he ask for it.

A huge sense of purpose came over her. Every fibre of her being told her that it should be her who nursed him and, even with her work in surgery, she would ensure that happened for as many of her hours spent on the ward as she possibly could.

'Here we are,' she said, positioning his bed and clicking on the wheel locks. 'Welcome to your new home.' She smiled and came around to the side of the bed to look into his eyes. Her heart stumbled a second time. 'I'll go and get you that cup of tea. We'll muddle through, me and you, just you wait and see.'

As she moved to walk away, he grunted and Veronica halted.

She returned to the bed, gently touched the tips of his fingers just visible at the edge of his plastered arm. 'What is it, Officer Matthews?'

He intensely stared at her, his blue eyes burning with rage and frustration before they shimmered with unshed tears and he turned away, his fingers leaving hers.

Veronica briefly closed her eyes, her stomach in knots before she walked away, fighting back her own tears. Why did she feel like she knew him? How could she know him? It was impossible.

Wasn't it?

38

FREDA

Freda took a final look at herself in her full-length bedroom mirror and inhaled a long breath. She had bought a second-hand dress and had even gone as far as drawing a stocking seam along the back of her legs for this celebratory dinner that Richard had insisted upon. A meal to celebrate the success of her article about Susan Beckett's selfless mission to help the children found lost and alone in Bristol. Since the article had been published over a week before, the *Bath Chronicle* had been inundated with letters addressed to Freda from female readers eager to temporarily rehome one child or more until their parents or foster parents could be found.

Not only had the reaction been overwhelming, but it had also led to the paper's editor giving her free rein on how she wanted to carry her success forward. She had the option to further help Susan and instigate a new campaign of rehousing children right here in Bath, or write something new that would promote further awareness of just how vital the efforts of women on the home front were to the war.

Satisfied that she looked the best she could in the current

times, Freda grabbed her handbag from the bed and left the bedroom, pride mixing with anxiety that she had agreed for Richard to pick her up from her home in his motor car. Nerves knotted her stomach, and a faint sickness coated her throat, but the more vehemently she showed her mother she was making her own way from now on, the better. It might be that she would one day give up nursing altogether in favour of her writing, and who knew where that would lead. It was just as well she started laying the groundwork with her parents now.

With another fifteen minutes to pass before Richard was due to arrive, Freda walked across the landing to do something she should have done days ago. Despite asking Dorothy if everything was all right at least a dozen times over the last couple of weeks, her sister had either ignored the question or fobbed her off with a dismissive wave. She'd been just the same a few months ago, but then suddenly bounced back to being her usual annoying self.

This time that wasn't happening, and Freda was determined to get to the bottom of it. Tonight.

She knocked on Dorothy's closed bedroom door.

'Come in.'

Freda entered to find Dorothy lying on her bed staring at the ceiling, her hands on her stomach. 'Hey, Dorothy.'

'Hey.'

Her niggling concern for her sister gathered strength as Freda lowered onto the bed. 'I've been meaning to talk to you for days,' she said, rubbing Dorothy's arm. 'I know we don't always see eye to eye, but I'm worried about you. You haven't been right for a while now. I know something's wrong. Please, Dot. You can tell me anything, you know that, right?' She smiled, hoping to evoke the same from her sister. 'What else are big sisters for if not to sort out the dramas, huh?'

Dorothy continued to stare at the ceiling and Freda was just about to speak again when her sister abruptly pushed up onto her elbows. 'You look nice. Are you going somewhere?'

Tracks of dried tears on Dorothy's cheeks reflected in the lamplight and her brow was creased with furrowed lines. 'I'm... going out, yes,' Freda said, studying her. 'With a colleague from the paper.'

'A male colleague?'

'Yes.'

Freda forced a teasing glare, knowing exactly what Dorothy was insinuating. 'And he is only a colleague.'

'Do you like him?' Dorothy asked, a ghost of a smile playing on her lips.

'I do. Quite a lot actually, but I didn't come in here to talk about me.' She stared into her sister's eyes. 'What's wrong, Dot?'

Her sister got up from the bed and walked to her chest of drawers, her back to Freda as she opened the top drawer. 'What are you worried about? I'm absolutely fine.'

'Are you sure? It must be hard not knowing how Robert is faring. Have you heard from him recently?'

'No, but I'm sure he's all right.'

'How can you be? Surely, you must—'

'So, tell me about your *colleague*,' Dorothy said, spinning around, her smile far too wide to be genuine. 'Is he handsome? What's his name? Does Mother know you are going courting with a man she hasn't approved of?'

'Yes, he's handsome, his name is Richard and we are not courting so there is nothing for Mother to fret over,' Freda said firmly as she battled to hide the depth of her disquiet over Dorothy. 'So, back to you. What's happened?'

'Nothing's happened.'

'Dorothy, please. You have barely argued with me at the dinner table for days. Neither have you taken Mother's side over mine, and you are even doing your household chores without looking for compliments once you've finished. Something is definitely wrong.'

When Dorothy's eyes glinted with tears, Freda leaped from the bed to wrap her sister in her embrace. 'Oh, Dot. What is it? Tell me, please. I know we have our differences, but I love you. Believe it or not, I'm not very fond of this new you.'

Her sister sniffed against her shoulder. 'Oh, Freda. I can't tell you. I don't know how to tell you.'

'Just try.' Freda eased her back and wiped Dorothy's tears with her thumbs before cupping her sister's face in her hands. 'Please.'

There was a knock on the front door downstairs, followed by the sharp clip-clop of their mother's shoes along the hallway.

'Oh, no.' Freda groaned, dropping her hands from Dorothy's face. 'I wanted to open the door to Richard rather than Mum. I wanted to tell her a little about him before she met him.'

Dorothy gave a strained smile. 'Go on, you'd better get downstairs and do your best to douse the fire before it erupts.'

Torn between her sister and Richard, Freda glanced at the doorway and back again, her mother's voice mixing with Richard's downstairs.

She squeezed Dorothy's hands. 'We aren't finished with this, all right? Tomorrow, we'll talk. Promise me.'

Receiving an almost imperceptible nod in return, Freda sighed, whipped her bag from the bed and hurried from the room.

'Richard!' she exclaimed as she descended the stairs, steadfastly avoiding her mother's gaze. 'Sorry to keep you waiting.'

He intensely appraised her from head to toe as she continued to walk, his gaze sombre and filled with an unexpected, if flattering, appreciation.

Unsure what to think or do about his reaction to her, Freda

quickly faced her mother. 'Mum, this is Richard Sinclair. I work with him at the *Chronicle*.'

'So I've just been told.' Her mother's glare was in danger of burning holes in the wall plaster. 'Your father isn't home, Freda. I am not sure he would like you to go out to eat with a man he hasn't met.'

'I agree, Mum. If Richard and I were courting,' Freda said, reaching for her coat from the stand beside her. 'But as we are going out to discuss work, I'm sure it will be all right, just this once, for me to go out without Dad's approval. You can tell him all about my misdemeanour when he gets home.'

Richard cleared his throat and took Freda's coat from her hands, opened it. 'She'll be well looked after, Mrs Parkes,' he said as Freda pushed her arms into the sleeves, and he smoothed the material over her shoulders. 'I am nothing if not a gentleman, of that much I can assure you.'

Her mother narrowed her gaze, carefully watching his hands that had lingered just a little too long on Freda's shoulders. What was he doing? He had never shown the slightest interest in her beyond work... had he?

'Well,' her mother said stiffly. 'If you feel the need to tell me that, Mr Sinclair, it only escalates my concern.'

'Mum!' Freda's cheeks burned as she stepped away from Richard. 'Stop it. I am going out with Richard for dinner and won't be back late. I'll see you later.'

'I would like her home by ten-thirty, Mr Sinclair,' her mother said as Freda opened the front door. 'Not a minute later.'

'I'll be home when I'm home, Mum,' Freda said. 'I am twenty-two, not twelve.'

Stepping outside, her head held high, Freda approached Richard's car where it was parked at the kerb and, much to her delight, he hurried ahead of her to open the door. Thank goodness he hadn't taken her previous response to his suggestion of opening a door for her to heart. She slid onto the leather seat and stared through the windscreen as he closed the door and raced around the bonnet to the driver's side.

He started the engine, touched the brim of his hat in the direction of her front door and then pulled away.

'Well.' Richard blew out a breath. 'I think I'm your mum's new favourite person, wouldn't you say?'

Freda laughed and faced him, her heart giving a little stumble at the sight of his grin. She had never seen him smile so widely or for so long. 'Just drive faster before she finds a way to have us followed.'

'We could always ask her to join us?'

Freda grinned. 'And why on earth would we do that?'

'Because I'm going to do my best to persuade you to stay out eating, drinking and dancing for as long as possible tonight and it might be easier to do that with your mother not sitting at home waiting for you.'

The suggestion – the almost certain flirtation – in his voice caught Freda completely off-guard, but she somehow managed to maintain a façade of relaxation. Did he like her? Really like her? Did she like him... that way?

A tell-tale thrill twisted her stomach. 'There's no need to go that far. I'm sure I can calm her down soon enough whenever I get home.'

He glanced at her, his gaze lingering on hers. 'Good, because you look beautiful and I am determined that it not go to waste.'

Smiling, Freda stared through the windscreen, entirely lost for words and wondering why she wasn't demanding that he take her home after such impudence. Maybe the good girl in her was disappearing faster than she thought.

EPILOGUE
SYLVIA

One month later – April 1942

It had been another warm, clear day as Sylvia followed Freda and Veronica outside so the three of them could take a breather together before heading back inside to finish their night shift. It was no good, she couldn't wait another three hours to read the unopened letter she'd carried first in her skirt pocket at home and then her apron pocket since she started work that evening. A letter hidden in a sealed envelope bearing the familiar handwriting of a man she had tried and failed to completely erase from her heart.

It had been two months since she had heard anything from Jesse and now dread clutched hard and fast around her heart. Why was he writing to her after all this time? Once she had called a stop to his visits to Castle Street, to leaving her gifts on her doorstep and the beautifully written letters he pushed through her door every Friday, everything between them been sliced through with utter and complete finality.

Finished. Over. Done. On her say-so.

The letter trembled in her hand as Sylvia watched her friends sit on a low wall to the side of the hospital entrance, chatting and laughing. It wouldn't be long before they called her over, asked her what was wrong. Sylvia tipped her head back to look at the night sky.

It neared eleven o'clock, and stars spangled the sky between the sparse clouds, the moon a bright, white crescent. It looked like a beautiful piece of art, and a feather-light sensation rippled along her spine and she knew, in that moment, Jesse looked at the same sky, the same moon.

Where was he?

'Sylv?'

She started and turned, her smile slipping into place. 'I'll be two minutes,' she said in answer to Freda's call, both her and Veronica looking at her. 'I just want to open this letter that came for me this morning.'

'A letter?' Veronica smiled. 'I did wonder why you brought a torch out here.'

'Be quick,' Freda hissed, glancing at the hospital doors. 'If Sister sees you, she'll have your guts for garters.'

'Oh, stop your fretting,' Sylvia said, trying to keep up her usual devil-may-care attitude when it came to what she should or shouldn't do. 'I won't be long.'

Freda nodded and turned back to Veronica.

As soon as she was sure her friends were more interested in their conversation than her, Sylvia drew in a long breath and quickly ripped open the letter.

Dear Sylvia,

I pray to God I'm doing the right thing by writing to you, but I still love you – fear I always will – so I wanted to feel close to you, even if I am likely to be stationed thousands of miles away come Monday.

Sylvia's eyes leaped to the top of the letter. It was dated a week before. She swallowed and stared blindly ahead, her heart pulsing in her ears.

Stationed thousands of miles away...

Tears rose and she fought to keep them at bay, but still they broke over her lashes and trailed over her cheeks. He'd done it. He'd signed up. Was this his way of escaping? Of going after the life he had told her he wanted to make on his own terms? A life that once-upon-a-time had included her being with him.

'Sylvia? What is it?'

She snapped her gaze to her friends. Veronica was on her feet, Freda slowly rising too. She lifted her hand, gesturing for them to stay where they were, and shook her head.

Pressing her hand to her mouth, she continued reading.

When you told me in no uncertain terms that you didn't want to be bothered by me any more, I knew you would never love me as I love you, and I respect that. I really do, but it was all I needed to hear to make me do something about moving away and serving my country at the same time. I have been in Cornwall for the last eight weeks and have now finished my naval training. God only knows where they'll send us, but I'd love to hear from you now and then if you have time to write.

Send anything you are willing to share with me to the address on this letter and they'll do their best to get it to me.

I love you, Sylvia. Always.

Jesse x

An audible sob caught in her throat and Freda and Veronica rushed forward before she had time to hold them back, their arms coming around her, holding her up as her knees weakened and her already broken heart split wider open still.

Oh, Jesse. I love you, too.

Every bit of love she had for him and had battled so hard to deny came rushing to the surface, biting and hurting her heart more than ever before.

'He's gone,' she sniffed. 'Jesse did it. He's joined up.'

Her friends' arms tightened around her until her tears were spent and they slowly eased back, Veronica brushing the tears from her cheeks.

'He'll be fine,' Freda said, her fingers shaking as she tucked Sylvia's fallen hair behind her ears, her own eyes glinting with tears. 'You've always said how big and strong he is. He'll be as right as rain, you'll see.'

Before she could protest, the screech of the air raid sirens split through the air, followed by the familiar rumbling of approaching aircraft in the distance.

All three of them looked at the sky as Sylvia suppressed the urge to scream and swear at the German planes as they approached, most likely on a mission to further terrorise Bristol. How much more the poor city could take was anyone's guess. Yet, if they carried on showing the tenacity and strength they had up until now, there was no doubt in her mind they would get through this war.

God willing, we all will... Please, God, look after Jesse. Please.

'I just can't believe he's out there somewhere doing God knows what,' Sylvia whispered, looking at the sky.

'Freda's right,' Veronica said, sliding her arm around Sylvia's waist. 'Jesse will be all right and, when he comes back for a visit, you'll finally introduce him to us. Right? We can all go to the pub for a drink. How does that sound?'

Fresh tears pricked Sylvia's eyes as shame pressed down on her that she had never found the courage to tell her friends Jesse was black and therefore never orchestrated a way for them to meet him. Now they might never know one of the best men to grace God's earth…

'It just seems such a sudden decision.' She swallowed and swiped her fingers under her eyes. 'And I can't help worrying it was more about me and him than him and the war.'

'Hey,' Freda said, her brow furrowed. 'You don't know that.'

The rumbling of planes came closer.

'Here we go again.' Sylvia sighed. 'Bristol could be in for a big one tonight. When are the buggers going to give them some bloody space to get their heads back together? It makes me so damn mad.'

Her friends slid their hands into hers and squeezed tight as they lapsed into silence.

After a few moments, Freda blew out a breath. 'I cannot believe how much has happened in the hospital, in the whole world since we came here as fully-fledged nurses.'

'Me neither,' Veronica said. 'There was a time I thought you wouldn't even be here by now.'

Freda sighed. 'As long as I can still manage to write a fort-nightly article for the paper, the editor has promised to keep me on the books until the end of the war. Maybe I'll give up nursing then but not before. At one time, I thought I'd be able to give it up regardless, but I can't. Not when this war is still waging on.'

Sylvia forced a smile. 'Hmm, that and the fact you are begin-ning to look at Richard Sinclair a little differently and not entirely sure what to do about it, of course.'

'Not at all,' said Freda, feigning insult. 'Richard and I are colleagues, nothing more.'

'Hmm, maybe. How's your Officer Matthews, V?' Sylvia asked, more concerned than ever about her friend and her deep care for the soldier to whom she had become far too attached. 'Is he talking yet?'

'A little.' Veronica inhaled a shaky breath. 'But the gauze and bandages on his face make it hard, not to mention painful. His bones are healing well. Although Mr Martin thinks he may have a permanent limp because of the depth of damage to his right leg. But the burns... they're the worry.'

'And not just because of how scarred he might be. Injuries like that are equally affecting to the mind as they are the body.' Freda exhaled heavily. 'Come on. We'd better get in. Sister will be on the lookout for us before we know it.'

As Freda and Veronica walked on ahead, Sylvia held back, her gaze on the sky once more as a strange foreboding crawled over her shoulders and lay there like a lead weight. Something felt close. Too close. She scanned the sky looking for God only knew what and tried to shake off the horrible feeling knotting the pit of her stomach. Drawing in a deep breath, she followed her friends into the hospital and walked onto the ward, her foreboding growing stronger.

She nodded at Kathy Scott, who was becoming easier to tolerate the longer they worked together. Sylvia was tentatively beginning to hope any risk of her putting her and her friends' jobs on the line was over. Of course, because of that fear, Kathy had a way to go as far as Sylvia's fondness of her was concerned, but Veronica seemed to grow more and more friendly with her as the weeks passed, so that was reason enough to give the woman a chance to prove herself.

Boom!

The explosion came from nowhere.

Sylvia's yell was stolen from her lungs as she was thrown across a patient's bed, glass and medical equipment flying in every direction, the screaming and yelling ear-splitting as terrifying blast after terrifying blast rained down on the hospital.

'My God...'

She lifted her head and struggled off the bed to plant her feet on the floor that seemed to vibrate. Disorientated and shaking, Sylvia squinted against the thick grey dust obliterating her view of everything and everyone.

'Damn you, Hitler,' she muttered. 'You've finally come for Bath.'

ACKNOWLEDGEMENTS

There are so many people I want to thank for helping me write this book. From WWII survivor, Ken Hall, to the amazing archivists at Wiltshire & Swindon History Centre, the amazing producers, writers and directors of all the many, many documen-taries I watch and the fellow authors of the many books I read!

I also want to pass on my huge thanks to my new editor and all-round fabulous lady, Isobel Akenhead, for all her guidance and support throughout the entire process of bringing *The Home Front Nurses* to life.

Finally, to my beloved family, thank you for putting up with so much from me, day after day, as I do the job I love!

ABOUT THE AUTHOR

Rachel Brimble is the bestselling author of over thirty works of historical romance and saga fiction. The first book in her series, The Home Front Nurses, is set in Bath.

Sign up to Rachel Brimble's mailing list for news, competitions and updates on future books.

Visit Rachel's website: www.rachelbrimble.com

Follow Rachel on social media here:

facebook.com/rachelbrimbleauthor

x.com/RachelBrimble

instagram.com/rachelbrimbleauthor

bookbub.com/profile/rachel-brimble

tiktok.com/@rachelbrimble

Sixpence Stories

Introducing Sixpence Stories!

Discover page-turning historical novels from your favourite authors, meet new friends and be transported back in time.

Join our book club Facebook group

https://bit.ly/SixpenceGroup

Sign up to our newsletter

https://bit.ly/SixpenceNews

Boldw⊕d

Boldwood Books is an award-winning fiction publishing company seeking out the best stories from around the world.

Find out more at www.boldwoodbooks.com

Join our reader community for brilliant books, competitions and offers!

Follow us
@BoldwoodBooks
@TheBoldBookClub

Sign up to our weekly deals newsletter

https://bit.ly/BoldwoodBNewsletter

Printed in Great Britain
by Amazon

48931329R10149